'You are nothing but a barbarian and you have no honour…'

'Be careful, lady. I have only so much patience, and you walk a fine line. If I wished I could punish you.'

Harriet was silenced. She knew that she had risked punishment several times already. She had made the slave master fear her, but curses and insults would not sway this man. There was something harsh and commanding about him, something that made chills run down her spine—and yet when she looked into his eyes she almost believed that she could see compassion in their depths.

No, she must not allow herself to weaken. There was nothing soft or decent about this man. Kasim was a savage, a barbarian, and she despised him.

Anne Herries lives in Cambridgeshire, where she is fond of watching wildlife, and spoils the birds and squirrels that are frequent visitors to her garden. Anne loves to write about the beauty of nature, and sometimes puts a little into her books, although they are mostly about love and romance. She writes for her own enjoyment, and to give pleasure to her readers. She is a winner of the Romantic Novelists' Association Romance Prize. She invites readers to contact her on her website: www.lindasole.co.uk

Previous novels by the same author:

MARRYING CAPTAIN JACK
THE UNKNOWN HEIR
THE HOMELESS HEIRESS
THE RAKE'S REBELLIOUS LADY
A COUNTRY MISS IN HANOVER SQUARE*
AN INNOCENT DEBUTANTE IN HANOVER SQUARE*
THE MISTRESS OF HANOVER SQUARE*
FORBIDDEN LADY†
THE LORD'S FORCED BRIDE†
THE PIRATE'S WILLING CAPTIVE†
HER DARK AND DANGEROUS LORD†

A Season in Town trilogy
†*The Melford Dynasty*

and in the Regency series
The Steepwood Scandal:

LORD RAVENSDEN'S MARRIAGE
COUNTERFEIT EARL

and in *The Hellfire Mysteries*:

AN IMPROPER COMPANION
A WEALTHY WIDOW
A WORTHY GENTLEMAN

BOUGHT FOR THE HAREM

Anne Herries

MILLS & BOON

First published in Great Britain 2011
by Mills & Boon, an imprint of Harlequin (UK) Limited,
Eton House, 18-24 Paradise Road, Richmond, Surrey TW9 1SR

© Anne Herries 2010

ISBN: 978 0 263 88795 2

Harlequin (UK) policy is to use papers that are natural, renewable and recyclable products and made from wood grown in sustainable forests. The logging and manufacturing process conform to the legal environmental regulations of the country of origin.

Printed and bound in Spain
by Blackprint CPI, Barcelona

BOUGHT
FOR THE HAREM

Prologue

'You know that you are as a son to me, Kasim?'

'Yes, my lord.' Kasim, councillor and adopted son of Caliph Kahlid bin Ossaman, inclined his head in assent. 'I am honoured by your confidence in me.'

'This is an assignment I would trust to no other, Kasim. Prince Hassan is very precious to me. He will soon be of the age to marry and I must find the right wife for him. He already has many beautiful women in his harem, but none of them are what is needed. Hassan will take my place when I die…' The Caliph waved his hand as Kasim would have protested. 'It is as Allah wills, my son. All men must die to take their place in Paradise. I shall not shrink from death when my time comes—but I would have my son secure. He needs a woman of both exceptional beauty and intelligence, but also spirit. She will produce his heir.

His mother was such a woman and this is what I want for my son.'

Kasim looked at him thoughtfully. 'Is there no one within the ranks of your fellow lords with a daughter that would fill your requirements? She at least would be a Muslim and trained in all the things she should know to fit her for her duties as the prince's chief wife.'

The Caliph was silent for a moment. His eyes held a cold glitter as he looked at Kasim and his mouth formed a thin hard line. 'If I chose a wife from one important family I should make an enemy of another. You know the jealousy of the tribal chiefs, Kasim. We constantly have to suppress uprisings and small rebellions amongst the chieftains of the north. My own wife came from the country that gave you birth and I wish for an English wife for my son.'

'You wish me to buy a woman from the slave markets of Algiers?' Kasim repeated the request to make certain he had heard correctly.

'Yes, that is my wish. Choose wisely, my son. The price is immaterial. I want a jewel beyond price for Prince Hassan.'

For a moment, Kasim hesitated, then, 'It shall be as you command.'

He bowed to his royal master and took five steps backward, before turning to leave the presence chamber. He was frowning as he made his way towards his own apartments in the palace. The Caliph treated him with respect and even affection. Kasim was a tall, handsome man with dark hair and deep blue eyes; he owed his position here to a man he knew to be ruthless and yet compassionate, wise and yet sometimes ruled by his ruthless nature. Kahlid was a just ruler of his province, which he held in subservience to the Sultan, but he gave no quarter to his enemies. To raise your hand against him and fail was to die. Kasim had recently returned from an expedition to crush a rebellious tribe to the north of the Caliph's territory. He had done so efficiently and with as little wanton bloodshed as possible, but he knew that the prisoners the Janissaries had brought back would receive harsh punishment. There was nothing he could do to change that fact, and any interference would be frowned on. It was a part of the life he had chosen here and he must accept it.

However, he would not be around to see the punishments for he must leave as soon as he could to provision his ship. A request from the Caliph was an order. Kasim must find a bride for the young prince—and an English girl of exceptional beauty and intelligence.

It would not be easy to find the right woman. Kasim knew that he might need to spend many months searching for such a woman—if indeed it could be done.

Kasim understood the thinking behind his ruler's request. To favour the daughter of one tribal chieftain would certainly cause jealousy and unrest. Yet something about this mission did not sit well with him. If it were possible he would have refused, but he had no choice—unless he wished to leave the palace and seek a new life.

He had risen high in the service of the Caliph and was already in possession of a considerable fortune. Kasim was aware of a restless need inside himself, a desire for something he could not name. A wry smile touched his mouth. He had left England under a shadow many years before. Fortune or Fate had brought him here after a period of hardship and suffering, and he would be a fool to question the life he had found as an honoured member of the Caliph's household.

Chapter One

'What is happening to us? Where are they taking us now?'

Lady Harriet Sefton-Jones looked at the young woman who clutched her arm so desperately, feeling a deep shaft of sympathy. Corsairs had captured their ship some weeks earlier and they had been kept in the hold for days, shivering and terrified. When the ship docked they were taken to a house somewhere in the busy port of Algiers. The men captured with them that terrible night were shackled with chains about their ankles, but at least she and her cousin, Marguerite, had been spared that fate. Once at the house she and her cousin had been cared for by an old woman, taken to bathe and given the apparel they were wearing now. The clothes were clean, but felt strange; they consisted of long narrow pantaloons that clung to the ankle and dark tunics that covered them from head to toe.

'I am not sure, dearest,' Harriet said in a low voice. They had been forbidden to talk by the man who accompanied them. 'I think the corsair captain sold us to Ali Bin Ahmed, at least that is what I gathered from Miriam—but I do not know where we are going now.'

'I couldn't understand a word she said,' Marguerite said tearfully. 'If only we had stayed with the ship, Harriet. Father and Captain Richardson put us into the rowing boat with others in the hope of saving us, but…' A shiver took her and she could not continue. 'Do you think they were killed?'

Harriet did not answer immediately. Her uncle, Sir Harold Henley, and the brave young captain had last been seen fighting the horde of pirates who had boarded the ship during the night. The vessel had been becalmed for lack of wind and the lookout must have neglected his duty for they had been woken by Marguerite's father and told they were being boarded by pirates. He had hurried the ladies from their cabin and sent them up on deck, where they were put into the boats with other passengers and crew. They had hoped to reach the shore while the corsairs were fighting for the ship, but the fierce pirates had come after the boat, perhaps because of the women.

Marguerite was beautiful and would be prized in the slave markets, which was in all probability where they were headed now. Harriet was older than her cousin, attractive in her own way with dark hair and soft eyes. She had studied languages with her father before his death just over a year previously and could speak French and Spanish fluently. She could also read in Arabic and Greek, and it was because she could recognise a smattering of various other languages that she had managed to communicate with the elderly woman who'd helped hold them captive, Miriam.

As yet Harriet had not told her cousin what she feared, because she had hoped she might be allowed to ransom both Marguerite and herself. She had tried to tell Miriam that she was willing to pay, but the woman just shook her head. Although she was apprehensive herself, Harriet had no intention of giving up. Sooner or later she was bound to come in contact with someone who would listen to her and not pretend they did not understand, as the corsair captain had when she pleaded with him and received a blow for her pains. The bruise on her cheek still hurt her, but it had not daunted her spirit.

She reached for her cousin's hand. 'Whatever happens, we must not be separated,' she said. 'Just do as I do and hold on to me even if they threaten us.'

'Oh, Harriet…' Marguerite's eyes filled with tears. 'If you had not accompanied Father and me to Spain, I should have been alone and I just could not bear it.'

'I will not let them part us,' Harriet vowed, holding tightly to the younger woman. 'I promise that as long as I live I will do my best to protect you.'

'I am so afraid…'

Harriet comforted her as best she could, knowing that amongst people who seemed ruthless and capable of any violence anything could happen. She saw the high metal fencing that surrounded the building to which they were being taken, her worst fears confirmed.

They were about to be sold in the slave market, as if they were beasts or chattels—and anyone could buy them.

Kasim wandered round the busy marketplace. It teamed with people of many nationalities; voices, harsh and shrill, assaulted his ears with perhaps a dozen different languages and dialects. He had visited the market every day for nearly two months looking for the special woman that the Caliph had requested him to find, but as yet he had seen none that would please his exacting master. There were many beautiful women to be found in the auctions that were held most days, but only one had been English in the past few weeks. She was already bearing a child and was neither as beautiful nor as clever as the Caliph required.

'Will your highness attend the auction of Ali bin Ahmed this day, honourable lord?'

Kasim looked down into the impish face of the young slave boy, who was tugging at his sleeve. The lad was thin, dressed in filthy rags and smelled none too sweet, yet his heart was touched by something in the boy's eyes. His life as Ali bin Ahmed's whipping boy could not be easy.

'Did your master send you to me, Yuri?'

'Yes, gracious lord, master of the Caliph's household and exalted one. Ali bin Ahmed told me he has heard that you are looking for a special woman.'

'There is no need to call me by such titles,' Kasim said with a wry twist of his lips. There was something about the lad that touched a chord in his memory, but he could not place it. No doubt it would come to him in time. 'I am merely Kasim, servant to the Caliph. Tell me, does your master have a special woman in his compound?'

'There is a woman of great beauty but she weeps all the time and clings to the other woman who I've named the hellcat,' Yuri told him with a grimace. 'I do not think they would interest you, lord.'

Kasim hid his smile for the lad amused him. His spirit and courage was remarkable and his eyes told of a wicked humour. 'Tell me what is this woman like—the one of great beauty?'

'She has hair like sunbeams, fine and silky, and it falls to the small of her back. Her eyes are blue as a summer sky and her mouth is pink and soft…but she clings to the hellcat and will not be parted from her. Even though my master threatened them with the whip, the hellcat would not let go of her. She faced him down and he grunted and left them together.'

'Indeed?' Now the smile tugged at the corner's of Kasim's mouth. 'I am surprised that Ali has not had them separated before this.'

'The hellcat told Ali that his privates would dry up and fall off if he dared to separate them and she said it in our own tongue, though she and the beautiful one are both from the land called England. My master is scared of her, lord. I think he believes that she has put a curse on him.'

'Is she a witch then?' Kasim was intrigued. What kind of an English woman could curse the slave master in his own language? Certainly none that he had ever known in another life—a life he had no wish to remember. 'You may tell your master that I shall attend his auction this afternoon.'

'Yes, honourable lord…' Yuri was about to run off when Kasim caught his arm. The lad looked up at him inquiringly, but made no attempt to pull away.

'How old are you, boy? Ten…eleven?'

'I do not know, my lord. No one has ever told me.'

'Where did you come from?'

Yuri looked puzzled. 'I was always here, lord. My mother was the slave of a merchant who purchased her from the corsairs. When she was sold to a new master, she tried to escape and no one saw her again. My master's wife took me in and cared for me and I grew up in his household. That is all I know for no one speaks of her.' A slightly wistful expression came to his eyes, as if he wished he might have known his mother.

'Are you happy in Ali's service?'

'My master does not beat me unless he is angry. If I see that things do not go well, I hide until he is in a better temper.'

Kasim nodded. The boy's life was no worse than

a thousand others in this place; however, over the last few weeks he had developed a soft spot for the young lad and he would mention the possibility of buying him when he visited the auction later. The boy could serve him until he was older and then choose his own destiny. He would not be the first slave Kasim had set free.

His thoughts turned to the women the slave master had in his compound. If the blonde woman was truly English and as beautiful as Yuri claimed, his search might be at an end, though the other woman must somehow be persuaded to part with her friend…

'What will become of us?' Marguerite asked, as they were herded into a pen with other prisoners. 'Will they ransom us, as you asked?'

Harriet reached for her hand. Marguerite had lived in a permanent state of terror since the day they were captured. The first few hours had truly been terrifying, but since then they had not been harshly treated and Harriet believed that if they behaved sensibly they would not be harmed. She suspected they were too valuable, though once they were sold it might be different. However, she refused to give into fear. She had tried to speak to the slave master when they arrived at the market, but though she sensed that he understood her, he merely shook his head and refused to answer her questions. Harriet had tried in vain to get news of her uncle and maid, who had become separated from them, also her uncle's servant and Captain Richardson. She had told Ali bin Ahmed that her family would ransom them for money, but he glared at her and made a negative sound.

She spoke to one of the other prisoners in the compound. The woman told Harriet that she was French, taken captive some days earlier from another ship. There had been no sign of Marguerite's father, Captain Richardson or Harriet's maid. She could only hope that the others were still alive and safe.

'I shall be worth little for I shall be sold as a body slave,' the woman, who was called Francine, told Harriet. 'But your friend will be bought by a rich man for his harem, and you may be, too, for you are both young and unmarried.'

'Surely they will allow us to be ransomed?' Harriet said, her heart sinking. 'My brother is wealthy and he will pay for our release.'

'Sometimes a ransom may be arranged,' Francine agreed. 'Some slave masters are wary of such an agreement. It is far easier to sell captives in the slave market than to trade with the foreign devils, as they call us.'

'Perhaps the buyer will listen,' Harriet said, but saw only pity in the older woman's eyes. 'Surely there must be someone who can help us?'

'If your brother uses his influence with the French ambassador, it might be possible to trace and rescue you, but by that time…it may be best if you are never found. If you still live, you will be a shame upon your family's name, but you may choose to end your life before—' The woman broke off, clearly too distressed to continue. She did not need to: Harriet was well aware of her meaning. Both she and Marguerite might be taken to a harem and used to pleasure whoever bought them.

Marguerite had asked her what the Frenchwoman had said to her, but Harriet shook her head. She had allowed Marguerite to believe they would be ransomed, but since they had been transferred to the compound behind the slave market it was difficult to keep her cousin's spirits up.

'I do not know what will happen,' she told Marguerite now. 'We must stay together for as long as possible. If we refuse to be parted, they may have to sell us together; while we are together there is hope for us both.'

'Oh, Harriet,' Marguerite sobbed and clung to her. 'If you had not come with me I should have been lost for ever. I would have died in the sea rather than let these beasts take me.'

'You must not give way to despair, my love,' Harriet said. 'If I can find a way to have us both ransomed, I shall. I have a fortune and I will use it to see us both safely home again.'

'What of Papa and…Captain Richardson?' Marguerite asked. 'Do you think they were killed on the ship? I have wondered if it would have been better to have stayed with them. If he is dead…' She choked back her grief. 'I would truly rather be dead than live as the concubine of one of those terrible men.' She shuddered. 'They frighten me, Harriet. I do not like their voices or their smell…'

'The corsairs are brutes and there is an unpleasant

smell about them, but I believe it will be very different in the har…household of a wealthy man. I understand that the Turks and Saracens can be highly educated men and that they like to bathe frequently. They are more likely to smell of perfume than sweat.'

'Harriet!' Marguerite stared at her in horror. 'How can you say they are intelligent when they treat women as slaves? It is wicked and inhuman! I would rather die than be forced to… I should die of shame.'

'Yes, I know that we should be ruined as far as the chance of a good marriage is concerned, but there are other pleasures in life. Besides, if a man of honour buys us, he may allow us to be ransomed in time.'

Marguerite gave her an accusing look. 'You are saying that just to comfort me. You know it won't happen, don't you?'

Harriet cast down her gaze. She had begun to think that the hope of being ransomed was fading fast, but, seeing the fear and distress in her cousin's eyes, knew she must not give up.

'I can only promise to try, Marguerite. As yet I have found no one who will listen—'

Harriet broke off as she saw that something was happening. The slave master was choosing men and women and they were being taken from the compound. She grabbed hold of Marguerite, her heart beating wildly.

'I think we are being taken to the auction. Hang on to me, Marguerite, and don't let go whatever they say to us.'

Marguerite nodded, her face ashen. She took hold of Harriet's arm, determined that she would not let go even if they were threatened, as they had already been several times.

'Let go of her,' the slave master commanded. 'I want the fair one, not you.'

'We go together.' Harriet faced him down. In a tone of utter loathing she muttered an insult that he would understand, which she had once found in a rather *risqué* book in her father's library. The stories had been about Arabia, but told as amorous adventures, and something she ought never to have touched, let alone read. Yet it had opened her eyes and perhaps she was more prepared for what was happening, because she had read of things most women might not have heard of and would think horrifying.

The slave master's face was a picture of surprise and shock, yet a gleam of appreciation showed in his eyes and Harriet realised that he had a reluctant admiration for her vocabulary.

'Go on, then, but you are to be sold separately.'

'Quickly,' Harriet hissed as they followed the other slaves through a dark tunnel. 'Help me tie your wrist to mine. If they want to separate us they will have to cut us, apart.'

'Oh, Harry…' Marguerite trembled, her eyes dark with fear. 'What will happen to us? Supposing someone horrible buys us?'

'I shall protect you,' Harriet said, though she could not help wondering who would protect *her*. Her own fear was like a hard knot inside her chest and she wished herself safe at home with her dogs and horses, but she lifted her head proudly, refusing to show her feelings. If only she had never agreed to accompany her uncle to Spain, she might have been out riding now with the wind in her hair. Yet that was selfish. Marguerite could not have survived her ordeal alone. 'Whatever happens to us, I shall try to keep you from harm.'

Kasim watched the procession of slaves brought on to the block to be sold one by one. There were some strong men by the look of it, some of whom would make excellent Janissaries. However, he was not here to purchase male slaves, only a bride for the Caliph's son. A few women had been brought out, but none of them would be looked on with favour even for the Caliph's harem. He frowned, wondering if he had been lured here on a false pretence; then, as he heard a small disturbance and two women were pushed on to the auction block together, he sat forward with renewed interest.

Kasim saw instantly that one of the women was exceptionally beautiful. Her hair was long and fell down her back in silken waves just as Yuri had described. She looked pale and frightened, which was not surprising in the circumstances. Having experienced what it was like to be captured by Corsairs as a young man, Kasim could understand the fear. He looked at the beauty's companion and frowned. She was older, attractive, but not beautiful by any means. Her hair was a rich dark brown with a hint of red, her face pale, but she did not seem as frightened as the beauty. She held herself proudly, her hand holding on to her companion tightly. A grim smile touched his lips as he saw the two women had tied themselves together. Yuri had named the older of the two the hellcat and perhaps it was an apt name.

There was an argument going on. Several men were interested in buying the beauty, it seemed, but they were not prepared to take both women. One of the slave owner's servants tried to pull the older woman away, but she spoke to him fiercely and he dropped back, clearly stunned by what she had to say. Kasim was not close enough to hear what was said, but he had seen enough. He got to his feet and called out. 'I bid one thousand gold pieces for the two women.'

For a moment hushed silence fell, then a voice in the crowd called out that he would pay twelve hundred for the women. Kasim waited to see if there were any more offers, then raised his arm.

'I will pay fifteen hundred gold pieces.'

A hushed silence fell on the crowd as they waited to see what would happen next.

'Sixteen hundred.'

'Two thousand,' Kasim said. This time there was no rival bid. It was a huge sum to pay for a slave, because no one counted the second woman. It seemed she refused to be parted from her companion, but she would learn to obey her master once she was taken to the harem, most likely as a body slave.

'Sold to Kasim, master of the Caliph's

personal household,' the slave owner said swiftly. He genuflected with reverence towards the man who had bid such a fabulous price. 'May Allah bless your union and make you many sons, honourable lord.'

'I will take them with me now.'

Kasim left his seat and walked down the steps leading to the block, then mounted it, moving closer to look his purchase over. Close to, the beauty was even more lovely than he had imagined. All she needed was some more becoming clothes. Kahlid would be pleased with what he had found. He frowned as he looked at her companion. The older woman met his gaze unflinchingly, her eyes intelligent and inquiring; they reminded him of a smoky haze in an English sky and he felt a little jolt low in his stomach. Suddenly, he was remembering his home and his childhood, when he had run free in the fields about his home. He banished the thought instantly. That life had gone for ever.

'You are both English?' he asked in their own tongue. 'You have nothing to fear, ladies. I am Kasim, controller of the Caliph's household and you are in my care. You have suffered a terrible ordeal, but from now on you will be cared for and pampered as ladies of the Caliph's household.'

'You speak English.' The beauty looked at him in relief. 'Please, will you ransom us? The price you paid will be repaid and you will be well rewarded for your trouble—won't he, Harriet?'

'My brother is Viscount Sefton-Jones of London, England,' the older one said. 'My cousin speaks truly, sir. We should be so grateful if you would ransom us to our families. I promise you would not lose by it for I have my own fortune. I would make certain your price was met.'

Kasim's gaze narrowed as he looked at the one the beauty had named Harriet. He saw that she realised they had been bought for a fabulous price, though her companion seemed less aware of it.

'Forgive me, ladies,' Kasim said without a flicker of emotion in his face. Her voice had made a strong appeal and for a moment he was tempted to listen to her plea, but he crushed the weakness swiftly. To find another woman who was both English and beautiful might take many months, if it were even possible. 'I am merely the Caliph's servant. The money I must now pay to Ali bin Ahmed belongs to my royal master. I am not at liberty to ransom you, but my master may listen to your request for he is a just man. Come, there is nothing to fear. If you behave with dignity you will not be harmed.'

The beauty looked at him, then turned to her companion, tears trickling down her cheeks. 'Don't let him take us, Harry. Please, don't let him take us.'

'He will not listen to us any more than the others.' The older woman looked at Kasim with scorn. 'We must do as he says for the moment, Marguerite. Try not to be frightened, my love. Perhaps the Caliph will be a reasonable man and show some compassion.'

Kasim inclined his head. There was something about her that commanded respect, and he wondered what she had said to the slave master. Few women managed to keep such men in check, but he thought he understood why the man had been in awe of her. As a youth he had met women like her, women who could command with a look or a softly spoken word. Her scorn made him feel a little uncomfortable for he knew that he did have a choice. He could turn his back on the life he had made for himself in the Caliph's palace, and yet he was not truly free, for he had given his word when he was released from the slave quarters and made a trusted member of the household. He was free to come and go as he pleased, but it was a matter of honour to remain loyal to the man who had given him so much. His royal master treated him as another son, giving him honours, position and money. He was not going to break his word to the Caliph for a woman he did not know. Even so, he was vaguely uneasy as he steered the women away from the slave market towards the harbour where his ship awaited them.

He tried not to remember that he had once come from the same world as these two young women. Had it not been for an unfortunate quarrel with his father, he might still be living in England, leading the life of an idle wastrel with nothing to fill his days but gambling and fighting over the women he shared with his so-called friends.

It was one of those friends who had been the cause of Kasim's downfall, and his subsequent lies that had led to the quarrel. Kasim had left England as a privateer looking for riches and adventure, but he had been shipwrecked and taken on board a corsair ship more dead than alive. He knew all about being sold and beaten, but fortune had led him to the Caliph's palace, and his own bravery in saving the Caliph's son from an assassin had made him what he was today.

Kahlid bin Ossaman had treated him with respect and fairness from that day to this. He would be failing in his duty if he did what the beauty asked, but he could not quite rid himself of a niggling feeling of guilt as he escorted the women to the harbour.

His ship was waiting to take them to Constantinople—or Istanbul as it was known throughout the Ottoman Empire. Once the women were safely locked in his cabin he would return and pay the slave master—and he would purchase the young boy Yuri for himself if it were permitted. He would do his duty and forget his personal doubts.

He had been given a commission, which he had fulfilled to the best of his ability. If the Caliph's son did not find the beauty desirable the Caliph might indeed listen to the women's pleas to be ransomed. He eased his conscience by reflecting that if they had been bought by the tribal chief who had tried to bid against him, their fate would be much worse than it was at present. The older one would have been beaten and, if she continued to resist, might have died a cruel death; the beauty might have preferred death to her likely fate at that devil's hands. They were fortunate that he had been at the auction that day, though as yet they might not realise how close to disaster they had come.

* * *

Harriet looked about her as they were escorted through the port. It was teaming with people, dogs, donkeys and carts. All kinds of merchandise was being sold or loaded on to ships, and there was much confusion. She considered whether or not it would be possible to break away from the man who had bought them and disappear into the crowds. If he should be distracted for a moment, she might take the chance—surely anything would be better than simply allowing this man to make them slaves?

'Do not even think of escape.' A hand of iron gripped Harriet's wrist. She jumped, feeling as if something seared her skin, and lifted her eyes to his. The look he gave her was angry, terrifying, because she felt he read her mind. 'You are the Caliph's property. He may have little use for you, lady, but I should pursue you both and take her back. You, I might leave to your fate. Think carefully what that means—you would not last long if I were not here to guard you in this place.'

'What do you mean?' She felt chilled as she saw the warning in his eyes.

'There are men here who would think nothing of abusing you. They would fight over you like a pack of dogs, snarling and quarrelling to decide who had you next. You would be used until your spirit was broken and you died of some foul disease if you did not starve to death. Is that what you want—for yourself or your companion?'

'No...' Harriet shivered—there was something

about him that reminded her of a dream that had frightened her the night before she left England. In the dream she looked into the face of a man and been very afraid, but she had not been able to recall the rest of the dream when she woke. 'I want both of us to be free. We are English gentlewomen from good families. How could you think it right to buy us as if we were beasts of burden? You had no right to offer all that money. It was ridiculous.'

'I was making a statement. I hoped none would bid against me. You were fortunate that my purse is deep.'

'Fortunate?' Harriet glared at him. 'I do not consider myself fortunate to be sold as a slave.'

'Had I not been there you would still have been sold, probably separately—and to a man who would have slit your throat if you defied him.'

'No…' Harriet felt chilled. 'Can you not see that it is wrong to make a free woman a slave?'

'I am not prepared to debate these things with you.' His expression was forbidding. 'You are not in England now. You must adapt to a different culture.'

'Why? You can buy another woman for your harem. Why will you not let us be ransomed? I promise I will pay twice what you paid.'

'It is not possible. I was commissioned to buy an English woman of beauty and intelligence. The fair one is a rare beauty. I am not at liberty to free you.'

'No one would know.'

'I should know. It is a matter of honour with me.'

'What honour is there in making slaves of two women?'

A little pulse flicked in his throat, as if she had touched a nerve deep within him. 'You will have comfort and a measure of freedom in the palace if you behave. Do not ask for more. You belong to the Caliph and I shall never let you escape. Yet in the harem you will be treated kindly enough if you behave in a sensible manner.'

Harriet raised her head proudly. 'You could have let us be ransomed. If you had compassion or decency, you would sell us to our families and make a profit for yourself. You are nothing but a barbarian and have no honour—'

'Be careful, lady. I have only so much patience, and you walk a fine line. If I wished, I could punish you.'

Harriet was silenced. She knew that she had risked punishment several times already. She had made the slave master fear her, but curses and insults would not sway this man. There was something harsh and commanding about him, something that made chills run down her spine—and yet when she looked into his eyes she almost believed that she could see compassion in their depths.

No, she must not allow herself to weaken. There was nothing soft or decent about this man. He was a savage, a barbarian, and she despised him and all his kind.

* * *

The cabin in which they had been housed was not uncomfortable. Harriet thought it might belong to the master of the ship. She was not sure, but by the way they had been greeted when they came on board ship she believed that the man with the blue eyes might own the vessel.

The suspicion made her feel angry and frustrated. Why could he not have taken them to England? If he was his own master, he could have set her and Marguerite free on payment of a generous ransom. She would willingly have repaid him what he had spent and more from her own fortune, though it would have meant she had none left for travelling.

A shiver went through her. After what had happened, she would never want to leave her home again. She wished that neither she nor Harriet had left the shores of England.

'Harry…' Hearing a wail of despair, Harriet turned to look at her cousin. Marguerite was vomiting, her gown stained with brownish liquid. 'I feel so ill. My stomach hurts…'

'Sit down, dearest. Is it the same as you felt when we had the storm?'

'No, it is worse. I think the food they gave us in that terrible place was bad.'

'Lie down on the bed and I will get help.'

Harriet went to the door of the cabin. She had expected that it might be locked, but found it opened at her touch. She went out into the narrow passage and looked to left and right, hoping that she might see someone.

'Help…please help…'

'There is no use in calling for help. No one will help you to escape.'

Harriet glared at the man with the blue eyes, raising her head proudly. 'I am not foolish enough to imagine I could escape from a ship. Had I wanted to try I should have done so while we were in port. My cousin is ill.'

He stared at her, considering. 'What ails her?'

'She has been sick and she has pain in her stomach. I think the food we were given at the slave master's compound was bad. I ate nothing but a piece of bread, but Marguerite was hungry and ate some meat.'

'What kind of meat?'

'I do not know. She said it tasted horrible.'

'It was probably too well spiced. You would not have been given bad food. Your companion is too valuable to risk giving her bad meat.'

'She is my cousin and I love her. Can you give her something to ease her?'

'I may have something in my belongings that will ease her. Look in the sea chest in your cabin and you will find a small blue bottle. Three drops of the liquid inside mixed with water should ease her sickness, and the pain will go.'

'You seem very sure?'

'The remedy was given to me when I experienced similar sickness many years ago. I have kept it with me in case it was needed, though I have become accustomed to spiced food, as you will in time.'

'I do not intend that we should stay in your country for long enough to become accustomed to anything. When I see your master I shall demand our freedom.'

For a moment a smile flickered in his eyes, as if he laughed despite himself, but then it vanished and his expression became hard once more. 'I doubt that you will be noticed by the Caliph, lady—but even if you were, you would do well not to make any demands. Otherwise, you would soon find yourself in a place you would not wish to be.'

Harriet gave him a haughty look, turned and went back into the cabin. She opened the sea chest, found the small blue bottle and tasted one drop on her mouth. It was bitter, making her pull a face, but she knew it could not be poison, for the man with the blue eyes would not be so careless with the Caliph's money.

Making up the medicine as she had been told, Harriet gave the cup to her cousin. Marguerite made a face as she swallowed it, but soon after she seemed easier and in a little while she had fallen asleep.

She was worn out with weeping. Looking at her with compassion, Harriet understood that her cousin was terrified of the future and with good cause. Her beauty would ensure that she would find favour in the eyes of the man for whom she had been bought. Harriet might spend her days as a servant if she were fortunate, but Marguerite would become a concubine.

Sinking to her knees, Harriet bent her head in prayer.

'Please keep her safe,' she whispered. 'I can bear whatever happens to me…but please keep my cousin safe.'

Kasim was frowning as he went back on deck. The hellcat was living up to her name and he did not doubt that she would cause trouble in the harem. He felt a pang of conscience for he knew that it was within his power to set them both free. He could have found another woman for the Caliph's son—or simply returned to the palace and reported his failure to find the right woman.

For a few moments he toyed with the idea of sailing for England, but then the bitter memories crowded in and he knew that he could never return to the life that had been his. He was settled in the palace and his life was not unpleasant. He would be a fool to throw away all that he had worked for, for the sake of a woman he did not know.

'My lord Kasim…' a voice called to him and he pushed the women from his mind.

Climbing to the bridge, he turned his mind to the voyage ahead. There were reasons why he needed to return to the palace. He must put away his vague feelings of guilt and concentrate on his duty.

Chapter Two

Harriet was bending over her cousin, bathing her forehead with cool water when the cabin door opened behind her. She swung round, feeling a little shock when she saw the man who had purchased them.

'What do you want?' she asked sharply, her heart racing. He had told her they were purchased for the Caliph, but the sight of him made her nervous—supposing he had decided to keep Marguerite for himself?

'I came to see how your cousin was faring,' he said and frowned as he sensed her apprehension. 'You have nothing to fear from me, mistress.'

'She is still unwell. Her skin is hot and she is sweating.'

'Did you give her the medicine?'

'Yes. It eased her for a while, but then she was sick again.'

He walked to the bed and placed a hand on Marguerite's forehead. 'She is warm. Perhaps you should sponge her down with cool water. I have heard it helps with a fever. She may have taken a fever rather than eaten something unpleasant. I imagine you were kept in a hold before you reached Algiers?'

'Yes. It smelled foul and the air was dreadful. Your people have much to answer for, sir!'

'The corsairs are not my people,' Kasim replied, his eyes dark with thought. 'You are not the only ones who have suffered at their hands. You will find life very different where you are going, for you will have the best of everything.'

'We shall not be free.'

'Were you truly free at home, Lady Harriet? If so, you are a remarkable woman. Most English ladies I knew were constrained by the rules of society and their families.'

'You have been to England?' Her eyes narrowed. His skin had a deep tan, but there was something about his features that made her wonder. 'Are you English? Why are you here?'

'You ask too many questions,' he replied as Marguerite moaned. 'I will mix another preparation for you—and then I shall leave you so that you can bathe her.'

'Thank you.' Harriet bent over her cousin, smoothing a damp cloth over her brow. She put an arm under Marguerite's head as he returned with the cup, lifting her. 'Drink this, dearest. It may ease you.'

Marguerite swallowed and lay back against the pillows, her eyes closed.

'It will be a day or two before we reach port,' Kasim said. 'On board this ship you are free to come on deck if you wish. If you jumped overboard my men would fetch you back. I would ask you not to waste their time by trying to escape.'

'Marguerite cannot swim,' Harriet replied. 'I would have tried to swim for the shore when the pirates took us, but she would have been left behind. I cannot desert her.'

For a moment his eyes met hers and she saw an odd expression in their depths. 'You may not always be able to protect her. She is a grown woman and one day must choose for herself.'

'She was going to Spain to meet a man who had asked for her hand in marriage, but she begged me to go with her. I think she was afraid that she might be compelled to marry against her will, but her father loves her. He would have let her choose—but she was anxious and I thought I might travel, see something of the world.'

'Perhaps you have seen more than you would have wished. This is the world as it is, whether you and I like it or not,' Kasim said, walked to the door and went out.

Harriet bent over her cousin once more. She pulled back the covers, bathing her limbs one by one, then, turning her on to her stomach, she lifted the tunic and bathed Marguerite's back. She pushed back the loose sleeves of the kaftan and bathed her arms, then her face and neck. After that it seemed that Marguerite was easier.

Harriet watched her for a while, then went to look out of the porthole. The sky was dark, lit only by a few stars. She sighed and felt the sting of tears, but brushed them away impatiently as she went to lie down beside her cousin. Marguerite was sleeping and she was tired...so very tired.

You are mine. You shall always belong to me. There is no escape for you other than death. I have claimed you and you shall be mine.

Harriet woke shivering and damp with sweat. She had never experienced quite such a terrible dream before and it left her feeling very much afraid, and aware of a sense of terrible loss.

For a moment she lay in the darkness, wondering where she was, then everything came flooding back and she realised that she was on a ship being taken to the Caliph's palace somewhere in the Ottoman Empire.

No wonder her dream had been so terrifying, because it was all happening, just as she had dreamed that night before they left England. This time she could recall that she had been a prisoner of the man who had said those terrifying words—and that man was the one who had bought them from the slave market. What had he called himself—Kasim? Yes, that was his name. He was a high official in the Caliph's household and he had bought them for the harem.

The lantern had gone out while she slept and she had no means of lighting it again. Leaving the bed, she went round to the other side, bending over Marguerite to touch her forehead. Thankfully, she was cooler and seemed to be sleeping well.

Taking the lantern from its hook near the door, Harriet opened the cabin door and went out. She could see a faint light near the steps that led up to the deck and walked towards it, intending to see if there was sufficient candle left in the lantern to re-kindle it.

'What are you doing? There will be a watchman on deck if you were thinking of escape.'

Harriet swung round. A shiver went through her as she saw that he was wearing a long loose white kaftan, his feet bare. Now he looked exactly as he had in her dream!

'I told you that I would never leave Marguerite. The lantern went out as I slept. I was going to try to light it.'

'Let me see…' He took the lantern and opened the glass panel, then frowned. 'It has burned down. Take this one instead and I will replace this.' He handed her the lantern that had been hanging near the steps. 'How is your cousin now? Has the medicine worked for her?'

'Yes, I believe it has. She is sleeping peacefully.' Harriet's moment of fear had passed. In her dream he had been fierce and passionate, but standing close to her like this in what resembled a nightgown to her English eyes, he seemed no more frightening than her brother. 'You were thoughtful to come and enquire, sir. I thank you for your kindness.'

'It would be foolish to lose my investment, would it not?'

His words were like a slap in the face. For a moment Harriet had felt a closeness, almost a kinship with him. She looked into his face and, seeing that he was determined to go ahead with his plans for her and Marguerite, her heart sank.

She suspected that he had once been English and a gentleman, but it seemed he had forgotten his past and owed allegiance only to the Caliph. She had been foolish to imagine that he might change his mind and take them back to England.

Kasim frowned as he returned to his own cabin. He was not sure what had woken him earlier, but he thought he must have been dreaming of something he had long ago driven from his mind. Waking with a start, he had thought immediately of the two English women and gone in search of them. For a moment as he saw the dark-haired woman he had thought she was trying to escape and for some reason his stomach spasmed with sudden fear. Surely she would not throw her life away by jumping overboard? In the dark she could be lost. He felt a curious ache inside for a moment, but it faded swiftly as she explained about the lantern.

Usually, Kasim slept well, but this night he had been unable to rest. He tried to tell himself that it had nothing to do with the women he had purchased.

They were not the only ones to experience the distress of being bought and sold as slaves. Here in this part of the world it was an accepted custom and worked to advantage in many cases. It was true that some masters were cruel and treated their slaves worse than beasts of burden, but others were no worse than the men who owned great estates in England and Europe. The workers might not be called slaves, but were often treated no better. Justice was often summary and brutal. Men languished and died in the Queen's dungeons, and many were put to the torture of hot irons and the rack.

In the Caliph's household the slaves were treated fairly and some might earn their freedom in time; indeed, many men and women sold themselves into slavery rather than die of starvation on the streets. Kasim himself had learned how fair the system could be. He was now a wealthy man in his own right, most of his fortune earned from trading and importing goods from other lands. He trusted his captain to obey his orders, and thus far his trust had been repaid. Perhaps one day he might leave the Northern Territories and push the boundaries of his empire, but for the moment he was content to live at the palace and give his loyalty to the Caliph. He owed everything to the man who called him his son—and indeed, he loved Kahlid as a benevolent friend. His son, Prince Hassan was his brother in all but blood.

Kasim thrust thoughts of giving in to Lady Harriet's demands to return her to her family away. To go against the wishes of his friend and master would be to betray all the promises he had given…the trust that had built up between them would be destroyed. He would be a fool to throw away all he had worked for these several years.

Yet even as he changed into the clothes he found more comfortable than the dress of an English gentleman, lacing the leggings beneath his white tunic and tying the red sash about his waist, he could not quite banish the pleading look he had seen in those eyes…

'How are you this morning, dearest?' Harriet asked when her cousin woke and stared up at her from the tumbled sheets. 'I think the second medicine that he gave you helped the sickness. You seemed to sleep peacefully after you drank it.'

'I thought it was all a nightmare, but it is real, isn't it?' Marguerite pushed herself up against the pillows. 'We are slaves, aren't we? He said we belong to the Caliph…' She gave a little sob of despair. 'What are we going to do, Harry?'

'We must bear it as best we can,' Harriet told her. She saw tears well in Marguerite's eyes and moved towards the bed, reaching for her hand. 'Perhaps it will not be as bad as we fear, love. Kasim said the Caliph was a better man than the one who tried to buy us. He said we were lucky he was there…'

'Lucky to be slaves?' Marguerite brushed a hand over her eyes. 'I would rather be dead.'

'You should think carefully, dearest,' Harriet said. 'Would you rather be dead, truly? If we live, we may be rescued one day—I may manage to find someone who will let us be ransomed. If we die, that is the finish. We shall never see our homes or the people we love.'

Marguerite looked at her in silence. 'I think…' She shook her head. 'You will think me foolish—but I believe I was falling in love with Captain Richardson and he with me.'

'I do not think you foolish. He is young and handsome and he clearly liked you. Had you been given time to get to know him you might have loved him, Marguerite.'

'Do you think he is still alive? Would the pirates have killed him—and my father? I do not think they would have surrendered easily.'

'No, I am perfectly certain they would not, for they were trying to give us time to get away. It is a pity that the pirates saw what was happening and sent men after us.' Harriet shivered. 'Had we reached the shore, Don Sebastien Gonzales would have helped us I am certain.'

'I wish he had never asked for me,' Marguerite said suddenly angry. 'If Papa had not been flattered by the proposal, we should still be in England.'

'Yes, though I was thinking of travelling…'

'I should never have left my home if I had guessed what could happen.'

Harriet sat on the bed beside her, reaching for her hand. 'There is no point in wishing that we had not left home, dearest. We are here and must make the best of it.'

'I do not know how you can be so cheerful.'

'Weeping will not help. I am going on deck for some fresh air. Why don't you wash your face and join me? There are some clean clothes for you to put on. Captain Kasim has been thoughtful enough to send water and these garments, also some fruit. The grapes are delicious.'

'I want my own clothes…' Marguerite pulled a face.

'Some of these are quite pretty,' Harriet said. 'I chose white again, because I thought you might like the pink. If you do not wish to come, I shall go on deck for a little air.'

'Are we not prisoners, then?'

'We are free to go on deck. There is no escape, Marguerite. Even if you jumped into the sea they would come after you. Be sensible and wait until we are at the palace. I shall ask to speak to the Caliph and perhaps he will listen.'

Harriet left her cousin to decide whether she would get up or stay in bed. She climbed the small iron ladder to the deck above and hesitated as she stood looking about her. She had seen very little of the corsairs' ship, because it had been dark when they were taken on board and she saw little shut away in the hold. This ship was very like an English ship, though most of the crew were Arab or perhaps Turkish. They glanced her way, but turned back to their work as the captain spoke to them in a language she did not understand.

He came to her then, looking at her oddly. 'You

should have used the veil to cover your hair, my lady. It makes the men curious when they see you without a covering.'

'Forgive me. I did not realise.' Harriet's cheeks were pink—she had known what the fine shawl was for, but had deliberately ignored it. 'I was just admiring the ship—is it yours?'

'What makes you think it is mine?'

'Because it is unlike the corsairs' vessel. I thought perhaps it was an English ship and I thought you might…'

Kasim did not smile as his eyes met hers. 'Even if it were my ship I could not change course and take you home, Lady Harriet.'

'May I ask why you owe such loyalty to the Caliph?'

'He has been like a second father to me and his son is a younger brother.'

'I see…'

'Clearly you do not,' he said. 'But we shall not argue. Will it content you if I promise to tell the Caliph of your request to be ransomed?'

'Would you do that for us?'

'For you, yes,' Kasim said. 'I fear it would not be possible to do the same for your cousin.'

'Then I cannot leave her.'

For a moment hope had flared bright in her, but it was dashed as she saw this was his final word on the matter.

'Then you have made your choice. Please feel free to enjoy the air on deck whenever you wish.'

He tipped his head to her and walked away to speak to his crew. Harriet bit her lip, watching from a distance as he gave orders the men jumped to obey. He was clearly in his element, a powerful man.

Why must he be so stubborn? Why could he not accept her offer of a ransom and set them both free? He had offered to ask the Caliph if she could be ransomed, she supposed because she was not beautiful enough to attract the Caliph's attention—but Marguerite would have been left behind.

Harriet would not leave her. If they wanted to part them, she would hold on until they tore them apart.

Marguerite was better the next morning, but nothing could raise her spirits. However, she had ceased to weep at last. They had been treated well, given food and wine to drink and water to wash, also more clean clothes from which she had picked something to suit her colouring.

Since Harriet's brief visit to the deck, they had seen little of the man who had bought them, though he had sent a young boy to ask if they were comfortable and had all they needed. She had recognised him as the slave master's boy and asked if he too had been purchased for the Caliph.

'The lord Kasim bought me for his own servant,' Yuri told her with a grin. 'I could have had my freedom had I wished, but where would I go? I shall be happy enough to serve my lord. He is an honest man and there are not many as generous as the lord Kasim.'

Harriet wondered why the lord Kasim did not come to the cabin himself, for it was surely his. He must be sleeping somewhere else for the time being. She had discovered things in the sea chest that must belong to him, and could not help wondering if he had deliberately been avoiding their company. Was he afraid she would ask again if he would ransom them?

Late in the afternoon on the second day, they reached what she believed must be the port of Istanbul. The buildings were strange and beautiful and Harriet stood entranced when she went up on deck to look.

'It is a magnificent sight, is it not?'

Harriet turned to look at the man who had spoken. Unbidden, a smile came to her lips; her fear had somehow fled and she felt that she was on the verge of a great adventure.

'I should have thought so had I come here as a visitor.'

'Very few English ladies have come here as visitors, I imagine,' he said. 'I have heard of one or two bold spirits who adopted the life of their own free will. One woman in particular converted to the Muslim religion and was allowed to live here without being married or being a slave. I think she visited the court of the Sultan and talked to him of many things.'

'She must have been an intrepid explorer. I should have enjoyed her life, I think.'

'Indeed?'

'My father and I travelled in Europe before he was taken ill some years ago. I always intended to see Constantinople one day…'

'I am sorry it should be in this way, Lady Harriet.'

'Are you?' She arched her brows at him. 'I am not impressed by words, sir. Actions would have spoken louder in your case.'

'You asked too much. Please go below now. You will be sent for when we are ready to go ashore.'

'Do you imagine I might dive into the sea? I see no point when I should be brought out and made to look foolish. I have told you before that I will not leave my cousin—until she is restored to her family. I shall not give up, sir. You and your master may do as you will, but I shall protect my cousin with my last breath.'

'She is more fortunate than she knows.'

Kasim inclined his head to her, but not before she had seen a flash of doubt in those blue eyes. She was seething inside as she went below to wait for the order, but she said nothing to Marguerite. Her cousin was pale and wan, but she had stopped crying. Harriet thought that she must have accepted there was nothing to be done, at least for the moment.

Somehow, she must manage to speak to the Caliph. She must make him understand that it was wrong to enslave women who had been accustomed to freedom.

* * *

Kasim watched as Harriet went below. He was surprised at the feeling of unease he was experiencing. According to the culture in which he lived he had done nothing wrong in buying the women. He had, in fact, saved them from a far worse fate. Yet the look in Harriet's eyes was accusing and made him feel vaguely guilty. He had tried to stay away from her as much as possible during the voyage, because although he had made his decision, when she was near he was aware of mixed emotions. Had she agreed to accept his terms he would have spoken to Kahlid and was almost certain a ransom could have been arranged for her—but the beauty was exactly what Hassan needed for his first wife.

However, when they were went ashore a little later, he dismissed his doubts as he made all the arrangements for their journey. The women were taken up in litters with silken curtains to hide them from the public gaze, each carried by four strong men.

'You will travel in privacy,' he told Harriet. 'The *casacche* you are wearing will protect you from prying eyes, but you must keep your face covered at all times.'

'My cousin is weary. Must we travel on at once? Could we not rest here for a while?'

'You will be able to rest once we reach the Caliph's palace. If we stayed here your cousin might be noticed—and you would discover that there are worse fates than the one you fear. Even the Caliph must bow if the Sultan requests a woman be sent to him. You would have no place in his harem, while your cousin would become a houri to a man much older than herself—at least this way you will be together for a while longer.'

She threw him a look of dislike and he knew that the thin thread of trust that had begun to form between them had snapped. It was obvious that she had continued to hope he would relent and take them home. She was angry with him. He thought perhaps she hated him.

Kasim set his expression in grim lines. He did not like the way this English woman affected his sense of honour, reaching a part of him he had thought long dead. He was no longer an English gentleman and could never return to the life he had once known even if he wished. His life was here, but more than once he had been tempted to give way to her and do as she asked, but that would be weakness. He had given his word to the man who had been almost a second father to him and he would not break it for a woman he hardly knew—even if she was a rather special woman with the power to keep him awake at night.

Harriet bit her bottom lip. She had known that escape would be difficult even if it were feasible, but he was giving them no chances, making threats to deter them from trying. Yet even had they managed it, Harriet knew there was nowhere to go. They would be searched for and found, and then they might be punished—and looking about her at the men that passed by on the docks, she realised that she felt safer with their captor than if she were alone. Perhaps if there had been no Marguerite and it was his harem she was headed for she might not have minded so very much.

No, she would not allow herself to have such thoughts. He was a barbarian, a man without morals or honour. She would be foolish if she let herself like him, though he had been concerned for Marguerite when she was ill.

'It would be foolish to lose my investment, would it not?'

Bitterness welled up inside her. He was only concerned that the woman he had paid so much money for should not die.

Yet something told her that wasn't true. He had been concerned and he had offered to ask if Harriet could be ransomed. It would be stupid to make an enemy of him, because he might be the only one that could help them…if he would. Harriet could not help thinking that he might still have some of his old values left. Perhaps deep inside him there was a little voice that told him it was wrong to enslave others.

Harriet threw a speaking glance at him before climbing into her litter, but he was not looking her way.

Because it was impossible for them both to go in the same litter, she and Marguerite had been forced to part. Harriet was anxious lest it was a cunning way to separate them and she risked looking out of the curtains about her litter several times to make sure that her cousin was still with them.

It was mid-day when they stopped for refreshments. The sun was high and its heat felt fierce to Harriet as she and Marguerite took shelter under an olive tree. They were offered fruit, bread, cheese and water; all but the water was refused by Marguerite who still looked unwell, but Harriet ate hungrily, enjoying her meal.

They had paused at a stream where several palm trees were growing. After she had satisfied her hunger, Harriet got up and wandered to look at the trees curiously. She knew what they were for—she had seen drawings—but they were the first she had seen growing and she was interested in all that was new and different.

'The fruit is not ripe,' Kasim said as he came to join her. 'I would not advise picking the dates. They would not taste like those you were offered.'

'They were very good,' she replied, 'as was all the fruit and the cheese—though different from the cheese I am accustomed to at home.'

'We eat cheese made from the milk of a sheep. It is different, as many of our foods are here, but you will become accustomed to them.'

'Yes, I suppose we shall.' Harriet frowned at him. 'My cousin still feels unwell. Would it not be possible to rest somewhere for a few days before we go to the palace?'

'You seek to delay the inevitable,' Kasim told her,

his mouth set hard. 'Word has been sent to the palace of our arrival. It is too late to draw back now. However, my offer to you still stands.'

'You know my answer.'

'And you know mine. You do not understand, Lady Harriet. I have given my word and I cannot break it even if I regretted…'

Harriet's heart jerked as he hesitated, because something told her that he was having second thoughts. Perhaps she could persuade him to see things her way even yet.

'I know you are not without honour, sir.' She touched his arm, a look of appeal in her eyes. 'I was wrong to abuse you, but I was distressed by what had happened to us. I believe you when you say we might have fared much worse, but can you not understand what the loss of freedom would mean to my cousin? There is someone she cares for.'

'She was not married?' Kasim asked. 'Perhaps if there was some form of betrothal…' His words were lost as they heard the sound of shouting. Harriet saw that his men were gesturing to the horizon and, as she looked in the direction they pointed out, she saw a group of horsemen riding towards them fast. 'Put your *casacche* on at once—and tell your cousin to do the same. I am not sure who our visitors are.'

Harriet rushed to tell her cousin and they both hastily donned the heavy outer garments they had taken off as they ate because of the excessive heat. Kasim told them to go back inside their litters and they obeyed him. The noise of horses' hooves and the cloud of dust had grown bigger as the group of riders drew nearer.

'It will be all right,' Harriet said, catching her cousin's hand moments before they parted. 'Kasim will protect us.'

She knew her cousin was terrified that they were to be attacked. Kasim and his men had all drawn their swords, as if they too feared an attack. As she sat in the litter with the curtains drawn, Harriet tried to control her own fear. Kasim would not let anyone take them. He would protect his investment—yet she believed that, moments before he saw the riders, he had been thinking of giving in to her pleas.

Suddenly, she heard a burst of cheering and risked a glance through the curtains. She saw at once that the mood had changed and Kasim's men were greeting the newcomers with smiles and laughter.

One of the men seemed to be a leader for the others genuflected to him. He was younger than Kasim and handsome in a wild, fierce way. He looked towards the litters, as if he wished to discover who was inside, but Kasim placed a hand on his arm and said something to him. For a moment his expression was mutinous, but then he nodded and for a few minutes the two men talked eagerly together, obviously great friends.

Then Kasim came towards the litter where Harriet sat. She withdrew inside, holding it open just a little so that she could see him.

'Who is it?'

'Prince Hassan came with some of the Janissaries

to escort us to the palace. There have been hill tribes-men seen in the area and he knew I had only a few men with me. It is a great honour to have the prince as our escort, Lady Harriet. He was concerned for our safety, but his father would not be pleased if he knew—he does not like the prince to risk his own life.'

'You seemed pleased to see him?'

'The prince is like a brother to me,' Kasim told her. 'He is young and handsome and soon now he will take a bride.'

'Oh…' Harriet was at a loss to know what to say. She had hoped that she could persuade Kasim to let them rest for a day or so before they reached the palace, but now that the prince had come to escort them himself it was impossible. 'Thank you for explaining.'

'You should not concern yourself overly for your cousin, Lady Harriet. The future may bring more happiness for you both than you imagine.'

Harriet made no reply. She sat back in her litter as the order to move off was given. How could either Marguerite or she be happy as prisoners of the Caliph's harem?

Chapter Three

The journey took much of the day, but they did not stop again for more than a few minutes so that the bearers could change places with other men. Once a hand appeared through the curtains and she was offered fruit and water, but the awkward, swaying motion of the litter made her feel disinclined to eat or drink on the move. She thought of the few moments at the stream and wondered what might have happened had the prince not arrived with his men. Would Kasim have made a concession? Sighing, she put the faint hope from her mind. Now that the prince was a part of their escort there was no prospect of a delay. Perhaps even Kasim could no longer control their destiny.

Harriet had begun to think that the journey would go on for ever, but towards dusk she heard the sound of trumpets, and, glancing out, saw a cluster of buildings, which she imagined must be the Caliph's palace. At first glance it was very strange to her English eyes, but then she began to see how well it fitted its situation as a fort with a backdrop of forbidding hills.

As soon as they were inside the palace walls, the litters were deposited on the ground. Marguerite immediately jumped out and ran to join Harriet as she too emerged. She took Marguerite's hand and they clung together, trying to take in the strangeness of their surroundings and yet glad to have arrived at their journey's end. It was a relief to stand on her own two feet again, Harriet thought, and looked about her, wondering how soon she would be able to speak to someone in command and persuade him to ransom them both.

'It is pink…' Marguerite whispered to Harriet. 'The walls are pink. It looks like something out of a fairytale.'

'Yes, I suppose it does with those domes and the pink walls.' Harriet smiled at her, attempting to give her courage, even though her own pulses were racing. 'We must think of this as an adventure. Perhaps it will not be too terrible, dearest. At least we are both alive and still together.'

'Yes…' Marguerite attempted a wan smile. 'Who is that man with Kasim? He came with the riders we thought might attack us.'

'He is Prince Hassan, the Caliph's son.'

'Oh…he looks fierce.'

'Yes, but quite handsome.'

'He frightens me.' Marguerite shrank against Harriet as Kasim came up to them.

'Ladies…' he bowed before them '…welcome to the Caliph's palace. If you will follow me, I shall show you to your apartments.'

'Where are you taking us?' Harriet said looking at him suspiciously. Her heart was thudding wildly. 'We shall be together?'

'For the moment, yes,' Kasim replied. 'Later… that is for the Caliph to decide. His word is law and we must all obey him.'

'Why?' Harriet gave him a challenging look. Her eyes met his furiously. 'Are you not a free man?'

'I am free, but I have given my bond. I serve a man for whom I have admiration and respect. It is a matter of honour with me not to betray his trust.'

'But we do not have either respect or admiration for him,' Harriet replied. 'We are Englishwomen and we bow our heads to no one but the Queen.' It was not quite true, but it made her point and she saw a gleam of what might have humour in his eyes.

'You must learn to curb your pride, lady. You are now a member of the Caliph's household. By his law he may do anything he wishes with you—either of you. I would advise you to speak softly for…both your sakes.'

Marguerite pressed closer to Harriet's side. Knowing that her cousin was anxious, Harriet did not push him further. They were truly slaves now, though Kasim had not treated them as prisoners on the journey. She sensed that things were different now and knew they might already have been beaten had this man been other than he was. So far they had been treated with respect. She must simply hope that the Caliph was of a similar temper and that she would get her chance to plead for their freedom.

They had both been given soft slippers, which made no sound on the polished marble floors. Inside the palace the walls were of many hues—many of them were tiled and quite beautiful. She could hear water and they passed several little courts with indoor fountains, which gave the palace a cool feeling. It was a blessed relief from the heat of the sun in the palace forecourt. Kasim led the way as they crossed through a paved courtyard and some beautiful shaded gardens into another part of the palace. Here, there were screens with pierced fretwork and the rooms seemed more private. When their guide stopped outside an impressive door studded with what looked like silver and semi-precious stones, Harriet caught her breath. She had seen something like this in one of her father's books and understood what lay beyond. She glanced at Kasim as the door answered to his knock and a very large fat man with a shaved head answered it.

'Is this place what I think it is?' she asked Kasim as the man beckoned them inside.

'I leave you here for I am not permitted beyond this door. Only the eunuchs and members of the royal family may pass here.'

'You have brought us to the harem?' Harriet threw an accusing look at him.

'You will be safe here, ladies. I may see you again or I may not. It is for the Caliph to decide.'

'Please…' Harriet caught hold of his robes. Her hand brushed against his and she felt him flinch and withdraw. She guessed that he was finding it difficult to remain completely aloof, as he ought now that his work was done. His eyes widened, darkened, as though he had only this moment realised something. 'I beg you, speak to the Caliph, tell him that we wish to be ransomed and will pay his price. It must be for both of us…please. I ask you as an English lady to an English gentleman.'

Kasim inclined his head. He hesitated, then took her hand and prised it from his robes, holding it for one moment before releasing it, almost as if he wished to comfort her. 'You must go with Sulian now. Do as you are told and you will be treated fairly, but be warned. There are punishments for disobedience that you would not like. I should not wish to see you treated ill, lady.'

'Help us…' Harriet said as Marguerite's arm was taken and she was drawn inside the door. 'Please, sir. I do not think you belong here any more than we do. For pity's sake, help us.'

'Go with Sulian,' Kasim said, but a little nerve flicked in his cheek and she saw indecision in his eyes—eyes that were much too blue to belong to an Arab. She could not be wrong. He was English born. He must surely have a conscience. 'I have done my duty to my master. Forgive me, it is out of my hands now.'

Her heart sank at the words and anger replaced the fear. 'You should be ashamed to serve a man who keeps others as slaves. You know what it is to be free. How can you accept favours from a man who is little more than a savage?'

'Hush, woman!' Kasim's mouth was hard as he looked at her. 'I think you have not been treated ill. The Caliph is a man of culture and wisdom—and he intends her great honour.'

'But she is so young and she should be free to live as she pleases,' Harriet pleaded, though she knew it was too late for Marguerite had already been led away. 'Please help us…'

'Please go now. I can do no more for you.'

Harriet saw that it was useless to plead. The eunuch was waiting, his face expressionless. She felt a wave of pity for him. He had lost so much more than his freedom; he was no longer a true man, for only through his mutilation could he be trusted to guard the ladies of the harem.

The door closed behind them with a clanging sound, which made Harriet shiver. Until this moment she had hoped against hope that their captor might relent and ransom them to their families. She had felt that somewhere inside the man with the blue eyes there was an inner core of compassion, but he had not relented. Now they were shut away in the Caliph's harem, from which she doubted it would be possible to escape.

Marguerite looked at her uneasily. She reached out and took her hand, squeezing it as they followed

the fat eunuch along a passage. There were doors to
either side, which she realised led to private apartments, but he did not stop until he came to a large
open room, which had fountains and benches made
of stone and marble. There were flowers growing in
pots and tubs and through an open door at the far
end of the room, Harriet could see what looked like a
beautiful garden. The eunuch was talking to a woman
of perhaps forty years. Her eyes flicked towards them
and she nodded several times. Finally, as the eunuch
bowed to her and turned away, she lifted her hand,
beckoning to them.

Harriet held tightly to Marguerite's hand and they
walked towards the woman. Her skin was olive-
toned, eyes bright like a hawk's, and she stared at
them curiously for a moment before stretching out to
remove the veil Marguerite had been given to cover
her head. When she saw how beautiful Marguerite's
hair was she nodded and clapped her hands.

'The lord Kasim has done well,' she said in French.
'The young one will do well for the Caliph's son.'

'What did she say?' Marguerite asked and looked
at Harriet in alarm.

'She says that you are very beautiful,' Harriet
replied. At that moment she was pleased that her
cousin had not attended her lessons in French. 'May
we know your name, please, *madame*?'

The woman's eyes went to her. 'You understand
me? That is good. Some of the women do not and it
makes life more difficult for them. Does the young
one not understand?'

'My cousin speaks only a few words of French, *madame*. If you speak slowly she may understand a little.'

'Then I shall speak with you, wise one. You have the look of a wise woman. My name is Mellina and I am in charge of the Caliph's harem. If you cause no trouble your life here will be pleasant, but if you are surly or disobedient the eunuch has whips that can punish without marking the skin. Our master has his favourites and seldom sends for the other women. Your purpose here will be to wait on the favourites, but your companion will not long be here if things go well.'

'I hope that neither of us will stay here long. It is our wish to be ransomed. We have families who would pay a rich reward for our return.'

Mellina laughed mockingly. 'No one has ever been ransomed in the time I have been here.'

'No one? How long have you lived here?'

'I was very young and beautiful when I first came to the palace. I pleased the Caliph's son and he took me as one of his favourites. He is now the Caliph and he has grown sons of his own.'

Harriet felt chilled. 'Did you have no one to rescue you?'

'My father gave me to the Caliph as a gift in return for favours.' Mellina shrugged. 'My life here has been comfortable and for many years I was the favourite. Now I am in charge of the harem. I keep order here and the women respect me. Sometimes my lord sends for me just to talk. He still has some fondness for me, though others have taken my place in his bed.'

'Does that not hurt you?' Harriet asked.

'It is our way. I knew my fate when I was but a child. You come from a different culture and it will be harder for you to settle to the life here, but it is useless to resist.'

'What is she saying to you?' Marguerite asked, pulling at Harriet's arm. 'I am hungry. Ask her if we can have food and water. I ate nothing earlier and now I am hungry.'

'*Madame*, we have travelled a long way since leaving the ship. Marguerite could not eat because she was ill. I think she is a little better and needs something to eat and drink.'

'Ah, yes, the little one is hungry.' Mellina nodded and smiled. 'Marguerite is a pretty name. I believe the Caliph's son will be pleased with the gift his father has purchased for him.'

Harriet held back the violent protest that trembled on her tongue. How could she speak so casually of Marguerite's life? It was not right that the Caliph could just give her to his son. She recalled that Marguerite had found the prince intimidating and her resolve hardened. She would do all she could to prevent her cousin being given to the prince. However, for the moment they had no choice but to do as they were told. Mellina seemed inclined to be friendly and it would be foolish to antagonise her.

'Is there somewhere we can rest and eat?'

'Come, I shall show you to your rooms. Clothes

will be provided for you and you may wish to bathe to wash away the stains of travel.' Mellina's nose wrinkled. 'You still have the smell of the slave market on you. I shall give you perfumes and oils. You will feel much better when you have bathed and eaten.'

'Yes, I am sure we shall.'

Harriet took Marguerite's arm. They followed the woman to a more secluded area where there was a bathing pool with small cubicles set round it. Two beautiful young women were washing themselves, attended by older women, who used perfumed oils and soaps to cleanse their skin and hair. In the cubicles women were lying on couches having their backs massaged with sweet oils; it was a scene of peace and contentment. They looked at the newcomers curiously. One of them rose from the water. She was completely naked and her skin was a pale gold, her waist tiny, her hips slender, though her breasts were full and round, the nipples dark as though she had borne a child. Her dark hair was wet and curled down to the small of her back. She seemed not to notice or care that she had shocked the newcomers by her nudity.

'Who are you?' she asked in French. Her eyes went over Harriet dismissively and then came to rest on Marguerite. She frowned, her mouth thinning in disapproval as one of the attendants placed a filmy wrap about her body. 'What is your name?'

'I am Harriet and my cousin's name is Marguerite,' Harriet replied, trying to ignore that it was still possible to see every part of the woman's body. 'May we know your name, *madame*?'

'I am Fortunata, the Caliph's favourite.' Her dark eyes flashed with what Harriet sensed was jealousy. She was clearly protective of her domain. 'Where did you come from and why are you here?'

'We sailed from England and were on our way to meet my cousin's fiancé,' Harriet replied. 'Our ship was attacked by corsairs and we were captured and taken to the slave market. It is my hope that the Caliph will allow us to be ransomed.' Harriet's mind worked quickly. It was possible that the Caliph's favourite might be persuaded to help them. 'If I could speak with the Caliph, or send a message to him, he might listen to our request.'

'The young one is destined for the Caliph's son,' Mellina interrupted. 'You have no need to fear either of them, for no one will want the other one.'

'For the prince?' Fortunata nodded and some of the malice faded from her eyes. 'You both smell. I have finished here now, but my attendants will help you to bathe.'

'You are very kind,' Harriet replied. 'Perhaps we could be allowed to bathe in private?'

Fortunata stared at her and then laughed. 'I dare say you would prefer to hide your skinny bones, but the young one has nothing to hide.'

'What is she saying?' Marguerite asked and looked at Harriet in dismay. 'They don't expect us to bathe here in front of everyone?'

Harriet turned to Mellina. 'Is there anywhere else we could wash more privately?'

Mellina's eyes narrowed. For a moment she looked annoyed, then inclined her head. 'You may use Katrina's bathing pool. She is with the Caliph's young children and will not mind. Come, it is this way…'

Harriet took Marguerite's arm and steered her away from the bathing pool. She could feel Fortunata's eyes boring into her back and feared they might have made an enemy of her. The Caliph's favourite had clearly feared a rival when she first saw Marguerite, but the older woman's words had reassured her. Harriet, of course, was no rival to any of them, but she knew that her cousin might be the target of some unkind looks if the other women were jealous of her.

Mellina took them into a secluded courtyard garden. Here there was a small pool surrounded by pillars. A marble bench was placed beside it and the smell of flowers was almost overpowering.

Mellina clapped her hands and women appeared with towels, soaps and perfume jars. It was clear that their intention was to help the two newcomers to bathe. Harriet spoke to them in the language she realised was the universal one in the harem.

'Please leave us to manage for ourselves.' Her request met with blank stares until Mellina issued a similar order and they disappeared into an alcove leading from the pool. Harriet looked at her cousin. 'They think we smell and I dare say we do. I do not think we shall be fed until we have bathed—so we may as well get on with it.'

'But there are no bathing gowns,' Marguerite objected. 'You will not bathe as…that woman did… without clothes?'

'You may keep on your tunic if you wish,' Harriet told her. 'However, I think I shall take mine off, because it does smell and I am tired of being hot and sticky. Please turn your back until I am in the water and I shall do the same.'

'Very well.'

As soon as Marguerite turned her back, Harriet stripped off her clothes and slid into the water. It had been slightly warmed by the hot sun and felt deliciously cool but not cold against her skin. She began to soap herself, her back towards Marguerite until she heard a little splash. Turning, she smiled at her cousin.

'Is this not pleasant? I know my father used to swim in the lake at home. I often envied him, but this is even nicer for the water at home was usually freezing.'

'It is pleasant…' Marguerite took some soap and began to rub it into her body and her hair. She dipped underneath the water to rinse it and came up gasping for air. When she rose again she was smiling. 'This is fun.'

Harriet nodded, then splashed her. Marguerite looked startled for a moment and then splashed her back. They both laughed, feeling happier as some of the tension slipped away.

* * *

When they had finished washing, they walked up the steps leading to the bench. Harriet allowed her cousin to go first, deliberately turning her back until Marguerite called that she was decent. Harriet followed and wrapped herself about. She was wondering what to do next when Mellina reappeared with some women bearing what looked like clothes of such fine soft material that it was possible to see through it.

'You may choose which you prefer,' Mellina said and spread the clothes out on the bench and the grass. 'You will need the pants and the bodice for wear in the harem. If you are allowed outside the harem as a special treat for pleasing the Caliph, you will be given more suitable clothes to wear.'

Harriet gasped as she saw what she was expected to wear. Marguerite was looking quite interested and seemed to be inspecting them with a view to choosing her favourite colours.

'Is there nothing else for me?' Harriet asked. 'You are wearing an overdress. May I not have something of the kind?'

Harriet looked down at the overgown that covered the trunk of Mellina's body and was far more modest than the garments she had brought for them to see.

'Only the older women wear these,' Mellina told her. 'Surely you do not wish to cover yourself? You have quite a good figure, better than I would have thought from the clothes you were wearing before—but if you wish for a tunic like mine you may have one.'

'I should feel more comfortable,' Harriet said. She saw that Marguerite had chosen her pants and a filmy shirt with a little embroidered jacket that finished in gilt tassels just above her waist. She was trying to work out how to put them on when a young girl came running out to help her. She was giggling and Marguerite laughed as she saw what she had been doing wrong.

Harriet smiled as she saw that her cousin seemed to have lost her terror. For the moment Marguerite was content enough, because most of the harem ladies seemed friendly. As yet she had no idea that she was destined as a gift for the Caliph's son, and Harriet wanted to keep it that way for as long as possible.

Surely there must be some way of reaching the Caliph? If only she could speak with him, she might be able to persuade him to ransom them to their families.

Would she see Kasim again? She had thought that just for a moment he had regretted bringing them here, that he had at last been tempted to help them. Yet why had he done so when she had begged him to help them? He had seemed sympathetic at the last, but he must be as ruthless and barbaric as his Caliph or he would never have brought them here to a life of slavery.

Kasim was deep in thought as he walked away from the harem. He did not know why it should be, but he was deeply troubled by what he had done. The look in Lady Harriet's eyes as her cousin was led away had cut him to the heart. Had he been able he might have called her back and taken them both to their homes in England, but he had known once Prince Hassan arrived with his men that the time for such action was over.

He had tried to smother his feelings of guilt that he had not done so from the first, telling himself that he had saved the women from a terrible fate by buying them for the Caliph's harem. Kahlid was no longer young and he hardly ever bothered to send for one of his houris. He had a favourite wife with whom he spent much of his time. It was likely that Lady Harriet would be allowed to find her own niche and never be troubled by the Caliph's attentions. Many women were only too happy to live in the harem, especially those who had little hope of marriage in their own lands.

Kasim judged Harriet to be in her mid-to-late twenties. She was attractive, but not beautiful. Since she claimed to have a fortune of her own, she must have decided against marriage at some point. He wondered why and wished that he had taken the opportunity to ask her so many things.

He had tried to stay away from her on the ship. It was clear to him now that he had been hiding from the feelings she aroused in him, and his conscience had begun to bother him more than he cared to admit. Kasim could probably arrange a ransom for Harriet, but she had made it clear she would not leave without her cousin. Once the Caliph saw how lovely

Marguerite was, he was bound to claim her for his son's bride.

Hassan had not yet been told of his father's wishes as far as he was concerned. He had come to meet Kasim, because he was curious about his mission and wondered what had kept him away from the palace for so many weeks. Hassan had wanted to see the women once he knew that Kasim had brought some new additions for the harem, but when told he must wait until his father permitted it, he had curbed his impatience.

'My father usually allows me to pick from the new women,' he said confidently. 'Tell me, Kasim—are they beautiful?'

'One is—one is a hellcat,' Kasim said, though he hardly understood his motives for labelling Harriet with the title Yuri had given her.

What was he going to do about the two English women he had purchased in Algiers? Kasim frowned as he realised that their fates were no longer in his hands. He had delivered them to the harem and there it should end…unfortunately, the look in Harriet's eyes would haunt him both waking and sleeping.

There was little he could do for her cousin, but perhaps Harriet's fate could be resolved with a little persuasion. For the moment he must visit the Caliph for he was sure to be eager for news.

'You have done well, Kasim.' Caliph Kahlid bin Ossaman walked away from the small window that overlooked his chief wife's private gardens. It was screened from the eyes of others in the presence chamber, but gave him a clear view of the bathing pool. He had enjoyed watching the two women playing in the water. It was obvious that they were both modest, for they thought themselves unobserved, which was impossible in the harem. There were spyholes everywhere so that he might watch the women without them being aware of it. The women charged with discipline, and sometimes the eunuchs also watched them, though this last was forbidden and could be punished. The English women did not know of the spyholes yet and had played innocently together. 'I believe my son will like his gift. I shall have her prepared for him in a day or so when she has rested and become accustomed to her surroundings. If he is happy with what he sees, she will become his first wife.'

'She has been very ill,' Kasim said, wondering why he was embroidering the truth to a man he both liked and admired. 'It might be as well to give her longer to settle so that she recovers her looks. Besides, she ought to be taught the faith if she is to be Hassan's wife.'

'Yes, what you say is true,' Kahlid said and inclined his head. 'I was thinking of sending Hassan to the Sultan's court for a week or two. I believe I shall do so. The young woman will settle in after a while—but it is not necessary for her to learn everything at once. Hassan will teach her and if she is all that he requires, she may convert to the faith then.'

'But she would not be his wife under the law unless she consented.'

'You are a better servant of Allah than I,' Kahlid said. 'I shall consult with the mullah and hear what he has to say. I believe it may be enough for her to give lip service at first.'

Kasim saw that the beauty's fate was sealed. She would be his son's wife or his houri and it might be better if the ceremony went ahead, even if it were not a true marriage in accordance with the law. He knew that Kahlid sometimes took the law into his own hands, bending it to suit his wishes, and to argue would only anger him.

'The older woman… I bought her because you spoke of needing a teacher for the children. The lady Katrina is sometimes unwell now that she is with child herself, and it might ease her if she did not have so many duties in the nursery.'

'This woman is thinner than I like in a houri,' Kahlid said, 'though attractive in her way; her hair is an interesting shade. Is she intelligent? Would she be able to teach my children to speak English?'

'Yes, my lord. I am certain she would be more than capable. I believe she speaks French as well as a few words of Arabic.'

'She has studied extensively?' Kahlid looked thoughtful as Kasim nodded. 'Very well. For the moment I shall leave her in your hands, Kasim. She is not beautiful enough to interest me, but she may serve as a teacher. She will be of the harem and yet not of the harem. You may send for her tomorrow and take her to the children. You will observe her, and you may order her life as you see fit for the moment. I may watch from behind the screens. If she does well, she shall take Katrina's place as the children's teacher, at least until my wife gives me another son.'

'It shall be as you wish, my lord.'

Kahlid's eyes were on him. 'It is in my mind that you deserve a gift. You have served me well. You could have taken the gold I gave you and sailed away. Many would have done so. Why did you return? Why do you stay with us, Kasim? You embraced the faith, I know, but you find some of our customs difficult to accept, do you not?'

'Every culture has its own customs and laws, my lord. In the country of my birth there is much that I find unacceptable.'

'You do not think of returning? I gave you a test, Kasim, for I wanted to see what you would do.'

'Supposing I had deserted you?'

'I should have been saddened, but it would have been the will of Allah. He brought you back to me and now I am even more certain that my purpose is right.'

'I gave my word. If I ever leave without making a promise to return, then you will know that I do not intend it.' Kasim frowned. 'Yet I do not understand your meaning, my lord—what purpose may I serve?'

'The time has not yet come. By bringing the right woman for Hassan, the first part of my plan is set—but there is more. I believe I see my way clearly but it must be done carefully. The future of my family depends upon whether I can trust my instincts.'

'You speak in riddles, my lord.'

'All will be revealed in time.'

Kahlid inclined his head, his eyes half-covered by heavy lids. 'You ask nothing of me in return for services rendered?'

Kasim hesitated, then shook his head. If he asked, Harriet might be given to him as a wife or a houri, but the beauty would not be set free. To take one from the other might distress them both. In time they would become accustomed to their new life and then he would ask if the older woman could be given to him. He would send her back to England to her family as she had requested, and then perhaps her eyes would cease to haunt him, as they had since she was taken into the harem. He might do it now, but she was safe enough for the moment and she would hate him for separating her from her cousin.

'For the moment I require nothing but the honour of serving you, my lord. One day I may make a request concerning the older English woman, but for now I ask nothing.'

'Ah, yes, I believe I understand.' Kahlid inclined his head, a smile on his lips. 'Your compassion does you credit, my son. They should be together for a little time. You are wise, Kasim, and that is why I value your service. I should be sorry if you were to leave me, though you are free to go if you wish.'

'I know that I have your blessing.' Kasim inclined

his head. 'I must speak with the Janissaries. I am told that a report reached us this morning that there are still some rebels in the foothills.'

'Yes, I know. It was for this reason that Hassan insisted on riding to meet you, which displeased me. He is young and hot-headed, and must be disciplined. I shall not tell him of my plans for his marriage just yet. I am worried by these bandits, for their attacks have grown ever more daring and some of the outer villages are suffering. For the moment they are biding their time, but I believe it might be as well to send out a party to chase them back where they came from before they start to attack the villages again.'

'I shall send a party to investigate, if you wish it, my lord.'

'You have my permission to send a scouting party.' Kahlid inclined his head and went back behind the screen. Looking out, he was disappointed to see that the women had gone. He clapped his hands and a servant appeared. 'I wish Fortunata brought to me this night. Tell the women to make her ready…'

Chapter Four

Harriet looked around the gardens, watching as the women strolled in the sunshine or sought the shade if they felt the need. All of them were dressed in jewel-like colours, their pants fine and far too revealing. She was glad of the over-tunic that Mellina had given her. It was a dark blue in colour and suited to an older woman, but Harriet felt more comfortable. To her surprise Marguerite had adapted to the new clothes easily, though she had blushed when one of the eunuchs had come to the harem to fetch Fortunata. However, amongst the women she seemed to have lost her embarrassment. She had found one or two who could speak a few words of English and was sitting with them now and laughing as they fed the pet monkey that someone had given them. Harriet was surprised at how quickly her cousin had settled.

It was not the same for her. She had found it

difficult to sleep on the silken couch in the small cubicle she shared with Marguerite, but her cousin had slept soundly for the first time since they were captured. How long would it be before Marguerite realised what was going to happen to her? Her present calmness would soon disappear once she was told that she was to be a gift for the Caliph's son, but for the moment she seemed to be enjoying herself. The dancing and music had entertained her the previous evening and one of the women had offered to show her how to dance. Marguerite might settle to this life in time if there was no alternative, but Harriet was already restless. Without books and horses, and the long walks she had been used to taking, she knew she would be bored within days. Somehow she had to find a way of obtaining an audience with the Caliph. She needed to be free! Her mind and body rebelled from the enforced idleness. It would be better if she were given some work to do.

'*Mademoiselle…*' Harriet turned her head as Mellina approached her. 'Come, the eunuch waits for you. The lord Kasim summons you.'

'Kasim?' For some unaccountable reason Harriet's heart jerked and then began to beat very fast. Had her pleas reached him at the last? Was she to be taken to the Caliph? She stood up eagerly. 'Yes, of course I shall come. May I just tell my cousin that I am leaving?'

'Marguerite is happy. She is making friends. There is no time to waste.'

Harriet would have argued, but she had already

learned that in the harem, the easiest way was to agree whenever possible. A glance at Marguerite confirmed that she was too busy playing with the harem pets to notice that Harriet had left. Perhaps it was best to say nothing for it might arouse false hopes in her cousin's breast.

Following Mellina, Harriet's heart was beating so fast that she felt breathless. Where was she being taken and why did Kasim want to speak with her? When he had left them outside the harem door he had intimated that he might not see them again.

Her anguish was soon ended—Kasim was waiting for her at the other side of the harem door. He was dressed as always in white with long red boots and today a red sash about his waist. His head was covered with a white turban, covering the hair that she knew usually curled in his nape. His eyes went over her and she fancied that he approved of what she was wearing. No doubt he thought it a suitable dress for a woman of her age. She was beyond the age of marriage and knew it well enough, which in a place like this was a measure of protection.

'You wanted to see me, sir?' Her eyes were proud, her manner haughty. 'I do not know how to address you properly—I have heard you called the lord Kasim?' She gave him a puzzled look. 'I thought the women of the harem were forbidden to you?'

'You may call me Kasim if you wish,' he replied. 'An exception has been made in your case, my lady. For the moment I am to have the care of you. I have come to take you to the schoolroom in the nursery wing. The Caliph's chief wife normally teaches his children, but she is with child herself and sometimes unwell. She needs to rest and the Caliph needs someone to take her place. I told him that you had studied extensively and he requested that I take charge of you and bring you to the schoolroom.' His blue eyes seemed to pierce her mind. 'Do you think you are capable of such a task, lady?'

'If I am to call you Kasim, then you must call me Harriet. I am not sure whether I shall please the Caliph, for I do not know what he expects for his children.'

'You read French as well as speak it?'

'Yes, of course. I can also read Arabic quite well, but I have only a small vocabulary.'

'From what the slave master's boy told me, your knowledge of Arabic is somewhat strange for a woman of your breeding, lady.'

'I read what might be called an erotic book that I discovered in my father's library. I know it was quite improper of me to read the book, but…the language came in useful…' An impish smile lit her eyes, transforming her looks. Where before she had looked plain, she suddenly became utterly charming, almost beautiful. 'Had I not known what I did, I do not think we should have been auctioned together.'

'I am certain you would not.' Kasim blinked, taken back by the change in her—he had seen little but anger and disgust from her before this. 'I have wondered—what exactly did you say to the slave master?'

'I told him he was the son of a donkey and a she-devil and that if he broke us apart I would put a spell on him that would…cause his private parts to dry up and fall off and that he would die in agony.'

'Not quite as politely as that, I imagine. I know the words you must have used—and, I believe, the book of tales they came from. I read it many years ago myself.'

Harriet saw the amusement in his eyes. For a moment she glimpsed a different man and she felt a rush of emotion. He did have a softer side! If only she could reach him.

'I am willing to teach your master's children, and to help in any way I can—if I can earn freedom for myself and Marguerite.'

'You must not try to bargain, lady. Sometimes, if Kahlid is pleased, he will grant a boon, but he will not listen to your request concerning your cousin, and it would anger him if you insisted on making it. You must wait until he grants you permission to speak.'

Harriet's heart leaped. 'Then I shall see him?'

'Perhaps. I have been instructed to watch how you manage with the children and report to him, but he may take it into his head to watch you.' Kasim frowned. 'I must warn you that you will not know he is there unless he chooses to make himself known.'

'You mean he will hide behind the screens and spy on us?' Harriet frowned. 'I have realised that we are never alone in the harem. People are always watching us, spying on us. It is despicable. Why may

I not speak to him and put my case? Why must we be treated with suspicion and spied on?'

'There have been attempts to escape in the past. I must warn you that it is useless. You could not leave the gardens because the walls are too high for you to scale and there are spikes the other side. If you jumped down you might impale yourself and die horribly. The only way out is through the main door and that is guarded day and night by the eunuchs.'

'Those poor creatures...' Harriet's eyes flashed at him. 'Are you ashamed? You know better! You come from a civilised country. Surely you cannot condone what goes on in this evil place?'

'There are some that would dispute your claim that England is civilised, Lady Harriet. Have you not seen the heads impaled on spikes near the Tower? Have you not heard of the way prisoners are tortured inside its walls? The Caliph is no worse, and can often be compassionate. I do not consider the palace or its inmates evil. There are men who treat others worse, men who consider themselves English gentlemen.' Kasim's mouth set in a grim line, dark memories in his mind. A man he had once called friend had been far more of a savage than the master he served. 'I think you have been used to a privileged life, lady. You do not know how others suffer. Yes, my master can be cruel, but he can also be generous—and I believe he is just. He lives by his own culture and creed and who is to say that it is wrong? I have seen slaves better treated here than many a poor man on the streets of London. It is not so long ago in England that men were burned for their faith—so where is the difference?'

Harriet saw the unyielding expression and knew that it was useless to continue. She had thought for a moment that there was some softness and decency in him, but it had vanished and the stern mask was in place once more. She was conscious of an over-whelming disappointment. Now and then she had believed she was reaching the man she suspected lay behind the impenetrable mask.

Who was the real Kasim and would she like him if she knew him? Her mind told her that he was a barbarian and cruel like the pirates who had captured her, but her heart was trying to tell her something very different. When he looked at her she felt drawn to him in a way she could not yet understand.

'I do not say that our way is beyond criticism, for there is injustice everywhere, in England as much as any country—but a man should be free to make his own life—and so should a woman.'

'So, were you free to make your own life at home?'

'Yes…to a large extent.' Harriet flushed as his eyes quizzed her. 'I knew there were certain things I could not do, a line over which I must not stray. But my father was indulgent and my brother lives in town and leaves the estate to me…' Her voice caught for she was overtaken by a wave of grief for all that she had lost. 'I was happy…so happy…'

'Why did you leave England?' Kasim frowned.

'I believe you said something about your cousin's betrothal.'

'Marguerite was to meet a man who wished to marry her. She and my uncle asked me to accompany her to Spain. Our ship was becalmed…' Her eyes stung with tears. 'I do not know if my uncle and the servants survived. Marguerite and I were put into a rowing boat; they thought we might get to shore, but the corsairs swam after us.' She gazed up into his face. 'Would it be possible to find out if they are captives? Is there someone you could ask?'

'I do not know. I might ask someone, but it is unlikely that I could tell you for certain. If they were killed, there is no way of knowing their fate.'

'I know you are right, but it breaks my heart to think of my poor aunt left alone at home. She did not want her daughter to leave her and would not set foot on a ship herself. Now she may never see her husband or daughter again.'

'You should all have stayed at home,' Kasim said, sounding harsh. Yet as she looked at him, she saw compassion in his face. 'This man should have come to you. I am sorry for what happened to you…' He hesitated, then, 'Something similar happened to me. I was not as fortunate as you at first for I served as a galley slave before I came here to work in the gardens. That was the day Allah favoured me.'

Harriet stared at him in surprise, waiting for him to continue, but instead he knocked at the door they had reached without her realising it. A eunuch opened it and they were ushered inside. Harriet was taken by surprise—although the room was open to a beautiful garden as were many rooms in the harem, it was set out with small tables and benches, much as the room she and her brother had studied in with their tutor.

The older children were sitting on silken couches while the younger ones squatted cross-legged on the floor. A woman wearing a tunic similar to Harriet's, but richer and of a deep turquoise blue, was sitting in a chair with curved legs and arms. She had a book on her lap and behind her there was a beautifully drawn map of the known world, decorated with drawings of mythical creatures and inscribed with words, which, on closer inspection, Harriet realised were English.

The woman turned to face them as they entered and her smile seemed to light up the room. She was so beautiful that Harriet caught her breath. However, as she looked at the Caliph's chief wife, she realised that she must be thirty or more years of age, which was an advanced age for childbearing.

'Kasim, you have come to see the children,' she said in French and held out her hand to him. He bowed to her, but did not touch her hand. 'And your companion is the lady my husband spoke of, I believe?'

'This is the lady Katrina,' Kasim said, looking at Harriet. 'She is Kahlid's chief and most beloved wife. Lady, this is the lady Harriet.'

'Forgive me if I do not stand to greet you,' Katrina said and smiled at Harriet. 'I have been feeling a little unwell of late and this is why Kahlid has decided that I need help with the children.'

Harriet approached, feeling instantly that she was with a kindred spirit, someone she could truly like and make friends with here.

'Please do not attempt it, my lady,' she said. 'There is not the least need. I am very happy to have been chosen for this privilege.'

'Kahlid told me I would like you. I think Kasim chose wisely when he brought you to us.'

'I cannot say that I was happy to be brought to the palace,' Harriet said honestly. 'However, I am glad to be of service to you and I hope to be able to teach the children something.'

'The Caliph wishes his children to speak English,' Katrina told her. 'They speak their own language and also French, for it is the universal language of the harem. However, my husband believes that it is a changing world and he knows that your sea captains and adventurers are beginning to dominate the seas, because their ships are lighter and faster than the Spanish ships and much better than our own. Kahlid's first wife was an English lady and he learned the language from her.'

'Forgive me, I thought you were the Caliph's chief wife?'

Katrina laughed softly. 'I have been honoured by that position for two years. Before that Anna was his chief wife. She was also his first wife and mother of Prince Hassan. When she died he was devastated for months. I believe he is happier now, though he misses Anna's counsel. He trusted her and talked with her often of affairs of state.'

'I see…' Harriet hesitated, then, 'You seem very happy?'

'I love my husband and I am happy to be his chief wife.'

Harriet was silent. She could not doubt the honesty of Katrina's words, but the culture was so alien to her that she could not understand why a woman like the Caliph's chief wife would find happiness in her life. How could she be happy to be a prisoner, little better than one of the slaves who served the palace?

'For today you will listen and learn how we go on,' Katrina told her. 'Our lessons are simple—today we are discussing the countries of the world. The Caliph believes that it is important for his children to know that there are other people with other beliefs.'

Harriet nodded. Kasim had brought a chair for her; similar in style to the one Katrina was using, she found it comfortable. She sat down as Katrina went back to her lesson, noticing that Kasim had taken a stool at the back of the room.

'Today we are learning about Spain,' Katrina said. 'Who can tell me the date when the Moors were driven out and—?'

A chorus of voices called out the answer before she could finish her question. Looking at the eager faces of the boys and girls and the way they hung on Katrina's every word gave Harriet a warm feeling inside. In England it had been thought something unusual when she was taught with her brother, but it seemed that the Caliph wanted both his sons and his daughters to learn the same lessons.

Harriet wondered how a man with such liberal ideas of education could keep men and women in slavery. It did not make sense to her and she found herself studying their faces and noticing the different tones of their skin and the slant to their cheekbones, realising that, as in the harem, the children were a mixture of races. Yet sitting here together in this peaceful room they seemed in perfect harmony with each other.

'Perhaps the lady Harriet would like to tell us about England?' Katrina said suddenly.

Harriet realised that she had been dreaming. Warmed by the sun behind her, she had been quite content to watch and listen. As all the children's eyes moved to her, she felt her cheeks grow pink.

'England is my home,' she told the expectant children. 'I live in a large old house with gardens, lawns and a lake. When the weather is fine I like to ride on my horse or walk to the lake. Sometimes I take food to the swans who come to the lake, especially in winter.'

'What is a swan?' one of the boys asked.

'A swan is a very large bird with a long neck and white feathers. My father called it the king of birds, because it is very proud and fierce and can be dangerous when someone invades its territory.'

'The swan is like my father the Caliph,' the boy said in French and grinned at her cheekily. 'He is a king and he is very fierce when the hill tribesmen make trouble in the villages.'

'Yes, perhaps he might be called a swan, but the

lion is considered the king of beasts in England,' Harriet said and laughed softly. 'The kings and queens of England sometimes have a lion on their pennants.'

'What is a pennant?' a little girl asked.

'Do not be silly, Fatima,' the boy said swiftly. 'A pennant is a flag—like the ones the Janissaries carry on their spears into battle.'

'English knights have them, too,' Harriet told him. 'It is a matter of honour that the pennant must not be lost.'

'Was your father a knight?' the boy asked. 'Was your house a palace like this?'

'My father was an English viscount,' Harriet said with a smile. 'Our house is very different to this, smaller and built of grey stone. Your pink walls are pretty. When I first saw the palace I thought it had come from a fairy tale. It almost looked good enough to eat.'

Harriet heard a muffled laugh. She looked at Kasim, but did not think he had laughed. Her eyes were drawn to a fretted arch at the far end of the room. Was someone behind it, listening to what they said?

'I loved my home even though it is not as pretty as yours and one day I hope to return to see all my friends and family. My family misses me very much and would happily pay a lot of money to see me returned to them.'

A hushed silence followed her words, and then Katrina clapped her hands. 'That is enough for this morning, children. You may return to your quarters. Tomorrow we shall begin your English lessons.'

Katrina rose to her feet as the children walked from the room, talking and giggling together. Her dark eyes rested on Harriet's face for a moment.

'I must advise you not to speak of being ransomed to the children, Harriet. Such things only confuse them, for they were born here and do not understand that not everyone is happy to be brought here. If you wish to please the Caliph, you must be respectful.'

Harriet looked at her with a flash of rebellion. 'How can I respect a man who orders his servants to bring women here as slaves?'

'Have you been treated ill?' Katrina asked. 'Has anyone beaten you or refused you food and drink?'

'No…but I wish to be free. My cousin wishes to go home to her family and so do I.' Tears stung her eyes. 'Forgive me…' Seeing that Katrina had turned pale, she went to her, putting an arm about her waist. 'Are you faint? I did not mean to upset you.'

'I am not upset. This faintness comes and goes. I shall be better in a moment.'

'Have you nothing to help you when you feel faint? My nurse swore by hartshorn or a pomander filled with cloves and herbs. Something you inhale to help you clear your head.'

'Do not worry, I shall recover in a moment.'

'I should take you back to the harem, lady.'

Harriet looked at Kasim. 'May I not help the lady Katrina to her apartments? I am afraid she might faint and hurt herself.'

'You are very thoughtful.' Katrina smiled at her. 'Leave her with me, Kasim. I will see that she is returned safely to the harem by the end of the day. I should like it very much if we could talk and get to know each other better.'

'As you wish, my lady.' Kasim inclined his head to Harriet. 'I shall come for you tomorrow morning.'

'Thank you,' Harriet replied, giving him a grateful look because he could have insisted that she return to the harem immediately. 'I shall be ready.'

'We shall go to my private apartments,' Katrina told her. 'Please give me your arm, because I do not wish to fall. It is important to me that I give the Caliph a son.'

Harriet offered her arm, feeling the weight of the older woman as she leaned on her. 'Is this your first child?'

'I had a son, but last year he died of a fever,' Katrina said and her eyes filled with tears. 'My husband was griefstricken, for he adored Ossie. I want to have another son—not to replace the child I lost, but another boy who will bring joy to our hearts.'

Harriet nodded, looking around her with interest as they entered a part of the palace she had not seen before. Katrina led her towards a door similar to the one leading into the harem. It opened as they approached and they went inside to a room that surpassed anything Harriet had yet seen. At first glance it seemed to be all pink, but then she saw that though the floors and walls were pink, the ceiling was a pale blue painted with what looked like white clouds to resemble the sky, and the couches were white and covered with silken cushions. Everywhere she looked there were beautiful things. The little fountain in the centre of the room was made of what looked like pink alabaster, the water making a tinkling sound as it cascaded into a pool in which white water lilies grew. There were statues of white marble and tables made of dark wood inlaid with intricate patterns of what looked like semi-precious stones.

'What a lovely room!' Harriet exclaimed. 'It feels very peaceful here.'

Katrina smiled and sighed as she sat on one of the couches, lying back against the cushions. 'It is one of the privileges of my position. My private gardens lead into the harem and you may go back that way this evening. It is pleasant that you can visit me often that way if you wish.'

'I shall if it is your wish and I am permitted. I believe Mellina took us to your gardens to bathe when we arrived,' Harriet told her. 'I did not know that it was private. It was very beautiful and so peaceful. There are so many women in the harem and I have been used to sitting alone with a book or walking in the country.'

'You like to read? It is a favourite pastime of mine,' Katrina told her. 'There are many books in the palace. If you wish to tell me what you enjoy, I will arrange for books to be brought to you.'

'How kind you are,' Harriet said. 'I hope that we shall become friends…while I stay here.'

'I am certain we shall be friends,' Katrina said.

'You must visit me whenever you wish, but please do not make yourself sad by thinking of leaving. It is impossible.'

'I cannot promise that I shall not think about returning home, but I shall not distress you or the children by speaking of it again. It is the Caliph to whom I must make my pleas.' Harriet looked at her pleadingly. 'I think more of my cousin than myself. She has been so frightened. Marguerite is so young and innocent. She is apprehensive of what may happen to her.'

'It is the same for most wives when they are given to their husbands,' Katrina replied. 'But love comes in mysterious ways.'

Harriet inclined her head. She would not argue her point. If she were forced to live within the harem, she could see a way of life for herself, but she would do anything she needed to do to save Marguerite from an unwelcome future as the prince's concubine.

'Where have you been all day?' Marguerite pounced on her when she returned to the harem late that afternoon. 'I thought you might have been sent to another place and I was afraid I should never see you again.'

'I should not have let them take me without telling you, but you seemed content when Kasim came for me and Mellina said I should not disturb you.'

'I missed you,' Marguerite replied, looking tearful. 'Mellina made me bathe with the others and then they rubbed perfumed oils into my back and my arms. It was pleasant, but I felt embarrassed; they would not turn their heads as I entered the water. Fortunata stared at me and I think she hates me.'

'That is because she sees you as a rival. She believes that the Caliph may choose you, but I do not think that is his intention.'

'How can you know?'

'I believe you may be intended as a gift for his eldest son—Prince Hassan.'

'No!' Marguerite drew back in horror. 'Surely they would not give me to him?' Her eyes were wide with horror. 'Some of the others told me the Caliph is kind and generous. I thought he might be like my father, but the prince…' She shuddered. 'They say he thinks more of fighting than of love. I want to go home, Harry. I want to be with my mother and father.' Tears began to trickle down her face. 'I cannot help thinking of my father and Captain Richardson…'

'Perhaps they are still alive,' Harriet said. 'If they escaped, they may even now be trying to discover where we are.'

'If only we could be ransomed,' Marguerite said and wiped away her tears. 'I thought I needed time to know my heart, but if Captain Richardson were here now I should marry him. I love him, Harry. How can I think of giving myself to another man?'

'Do not give up hope,' Harriet said and embraced her. 'I think the Caliph was listening behind the screen when I was with Katrina and the children this morning. I mentioned the possibility of a ransom.

He must have heard me, though I was forbidden to say it again.'

'Is that where you went—to the apartments of the Caliph's chief wife? Is she very beautiful?'

'She has a beautiful smile and she is with child,' Harriet said. 'I liked her and I enjoyed talking to the children, which is to be my position in the household until Katrina is brought to bed—but I shall never give up trying to obtain our freedom.'

'But if I am given to the prince…' Marguerite swallowed hard. 'I should never be able to marry. I should be shamed and beyond redemption.'

'You must not think like that!' Harriet said fiercely. 'They can force us to obey them, cousin; they can command our bodies, but they cannot break our spirit. While we resist in our hearts we remain free.'

'I can bear it as long as I have you,' Marguerite said. 'But if they part us I think I shall die.'

Harriet put her arms about her, for there was no comfort she could offer. At present they were lodged in the Caliph's harem, but if Marguerite were given to the prince they would seldom meet.

Harriet had begun to settle to the life almost at once. She found her apartments charming, as were the gardens, and the sunshine was pleasant. She thought that in certain circumstances she could be happy in such a place.

However, despite the favoured treatment she was being given, she must remember that she belonged to the Caliph and not Kasim. Her heart caught because she knew where her thoughts were leading her and it would be foolish to allow herself to like him too much.

'You will need this today, my lady.' Harriet looked at the enveloping garment that Mellina had brought for her that morning. 'It covers you from head to toe.'

'I was told to wear one of these when we journeyed to the palace,' Harriet said looking curious. 'Is it not called a *casacche*? And why do I need such a garment this morning?'

'Kasim will tell you. I was merely instructed that you were going out of the palace.'

'Going out of the palace?' Harriet's heart missed a beat. 'Am I being sent away?' Had she been sold or given to someone as a gift? Her heart thudded and she felt a deep ache at the prospect of being parted not only from her cousin, but also from Kasim. If she were not to see him again, she would miss him. She looked for her cousin, but could not see her in the courtyard. 'Where is Marguerite?'

'She has been taken to bathe,' Mellina said. 'I cannot answer your questions for I do not know the answers. Come! You must not keep the lady Katrina waiting.'

'Please tell my cousin that I love her.'

Harriet felt sick as she followed the older woman. Was she being passed on to another master? Yet if the lady Katrina were waiting for her surely she was not being sent away? She clung to the slender hope, but could not understand why they were to leave the palace so soon after arriving.

Kasim was waiting outside the harem door. He too was dressed for a journey of some sort; his turban and robes were white and the leggings he always wore were criss-crossed with dark bands. On his feet he had boots of fine red leather and a sash of gold around his waist over which he wore a leather belt and a sword.

'Where are we going?' Harriet asked, her heart pounding. 'Am I being sent away? Have I done something wrong?'

'Exactly the opposite,' Kasim replied and smiled. 'You are to be indulged and honoured by being allowed to accompany the lady Katrina to the bazaar in the village to purchase trinkets and silks.'

'I am being taken to the bazaar?' Harriet's head was whirling. She was being allowed outside the palace with the Caliph's chief wife—a privilege that was not given to many slaves. 'Why should I be trusted in this way? Are you not afraid that I might try to run away?'

'And leave your cousin here alone?' Kasim's brows rose. His eyes seemed to delve into her soul, stripping it bare. 'Your devotion to Marguerite has been noted. Besides, the lady Katrina particularly asked for your company and at the moment the Caliph can refuse her nothing.' His gaze was steely as he looked at her. 'I do not think you would wish to make trouble for your cousin or the lady Katrina. You would not wish them punished in your stead?'

'No, I should not,' Harriet replied, a flash of temper in her eyes. He thought himself so clever! 'You are quite sure of me, aren't you? Have I been watched and judged worthy of trust? Or do you think you hold the upper hand?'

'If your cousin were free, you would take your chances,' Kasim replied. 'Though I think you would not betray the lady Katrina's trust.'

'No, I could not; she has made my life here bearable,' Harriet answered. 'She has given me books and needlework, and the pleasure of her company. I consider her a friend.'

'I am glad to hear this from your lips.'

'Do you accompany us to the bazaar?'

'I and two of the Jannisaries, men I trust beyond all others,' Kasim replied. 'You may purchase things for yourself and your cousin. I have a purse large enough for your needs.'

'I need very little,' Harriet replied. 'I have been given clothes, food and books. I should like to ride a horse and walk with my dogs, as I did at home, but until I am free to do those things again I am content.'

Kasim frowned at her, his eyes flashing blue fire. He reached out, taking hold of her wrist. Harriet felt a tingling sensation run up her arm and she shivered. Why did his nearness have this strange effect on her? For a moment she was breathless, tense. His eyes narrowed, as if her reaction surprised him.

'You do not fear me? I have no wish to harm you, Harriet, but I must warn you that it does you no good to cling to the past. Your life is here and you should accept your fate.'

'Kismet?' Harriet frowned. 'You believe that all life is mapped out for us when we are born and we cannot escape our fate?'

'It is the belief I have adopted with my faith as a Muslim.'

'You have become one of them?'

'It is simpler to accept,' Kasim replied, but his eyes slid away and she guessed that he paid lip service to the creed by which he must live. She doubted that he truly believed in anything but himself, for he lived by his own rules, his own code of honour. 'Here is the lady Katrina and her bodyguards. Come, lady, we must not keep her waiting.'

'You must buy something for yourself and for your cousin,' Katrina said as they paused to examine some beautiful gold bangles that one of the traders was offering them. 'I have bought silks and perfumes, but I have many bangles like these. Will you let me give you one for yourself and one for your cousin?' Katrina smiled. 'Soon she will have many others, but for the—'

She broke off as loud voices startled them all. Turning to look, Harriet saw that some fighting was going on just ahead of them. Men were shouting and a woman screamed.

'Guard the women!' Kasim ordered and went off to investigate what was happening.

The bodyguards moved closer to Katrina and Harriet suddenly found herself alone and unobserved. If she had wanted to take the chance to escape she might have run from the bazaar, but her loyalty to Marguerite held her by invisible chains. She was watching the altercation and unaware that someone was behind her until a voice spoke to her in English.

'Do not turn around, Lady Harriet,' the deep voice spoke softly from close behind her. 'Show no emotion or excitement or we may be noticed.'

'What…?' She tensed, her skin prickling, but had the good sense not to turn her head. 'Who are you?'

'I come from your uncle, Sir Harold Henley. He is alive and so is Captain Richardson. They are searching for you and your cousin. They came to us for help and we have been making enquiries. We were told where you had been taken and by whom. Your friends wanted you to know that we are trying to rescue you. Is Marguerite well? Have either of you been harmed?'

'No, we are unharmed,' Harriet said. 'How did you know me? How did you know where we were coming today?' She was afraid to trust this unknown messenger, afraid it was some kind of a trap.

'We have our spies within the palace,' the soft voice told her. 'Our organisation is secret and well established; we work constantly to rescue people who have been stolen and sold into slavery. I was told you would be here this morning and kept a watch for you, then I heard you speak and knew you must be the lady I sought. Be of good heart, Lady Harriet. You will receive a message soon and then you will be free. Do not look round or make a sign. If I were noticed, our plans might fail and someone would die a terrible death.'

Harriet controlled her burning desire to glance round. She dug her nails into her palms to stop herself showing any emotion as she saw Kasim returning to them. Her heart was beating wildly. How was it possible that someone inside the palace had knowledge of what was happening? Could she trust the messenger? Was it an elaborate plan to test her loyalty? And had Kasim noticed the man talking to her?

'You were not molested?' Kasim asked, looking at her in concern. 'I saw an Arab standing close to you just now. He was speaking to you. For a moment I thought he planned to snatch you. You were in some danger, for women like you are worth a good price.'

Harriet's heart hammered in her breast. If it was a ruse Kasim did not know of it! She swallowed hard, improvising hastily.

'He was a merchant asking me to see some more gold bangles,' Harriet lied, but would not look at him. If he looked into her eyes, he would see her guilt and somehow she hated lying to him. She was trembling inside, her palms wet and sticky. 'What was the trouble about?'

'Just some disagreement between the merchants,'

Kasim replied and there was suspicion in his voice. 'If you have all you wish, I think we should return to the palace.'

'Not yet,' Katrina said, turning in time to hear him. 'I wanted to buy a present for Harriet and her cousin.'

Harriet was unable to refuse her generosity. Besides, her mind was a long way from gold bracelets or luxurious silks. Perhaps very soon now she and Marguerite would be free.

She jumped as she felt Kasim's hand on her arm, looking up at him in surprise. His touch seemed to heat her flesh and his eyes burned with a deep cold fire. She felt a spasm in her stomach, a spiral of fear curling through her. He knew something. At least he suspected that something had happened, even if he was not sure exactly what had taken place while he was distracted by the disturbance.

A disturbance, she guessed, that had been created especially so that she could be given her uncle's message. Somehow she managed to thank Katrina for her beautiful gifts and to behave as naturally as possible. However, she was aware of Kasim watching her as they left the bazaar and the men bearing their litters were summoned. As he came to help her inside, he gave her a meaningful look, which sent a trickle of fear down her spine.

'Tell me,' he said, 'why have you never married? Were you not offered marriage in your country?'

'It was your country, too,' she said, lifting her head proudly. 'I met no one I wished to marry and my father would not press me. He enjoyed having my company too much.'

'I thought perhaps you were too wilful and proud.'

'I am proud and, yes, perhaps I am wilful—but I should not be so unless I were given cause.'

'Please curb your pride. You have been indulged and favoured, lady. Please do not give me cause to regret my generosity. If you cause trouble, I may not be able to save you from punishment.'

What did he mean? Harriet had thought it was Katrina's idea to bring her on this trip. Had Kasim arranged it for her pleasure? Why did she feel so strangely torn between wanting to assure him that she would not let him down and her desire to be free?

Chapter Five

How long would it be before she received a message telling her about the rescue that was planned for them? As the days passed with no further news, Harriet had begun to wonder if she had dreamed the whole thing. They had been in the harem for more than two weeks now and the memory of the trip to the bazaar had faded. If it were not for the bangle she had been given by the lady Katrina, she might have thought it was all her imagination. Had she mistaken the message she had been given that day? Why had nothing more happened?

Nothing untoward had happened after their return to the palace, though several days had passed. Kasim had returned her to the harem in silence, speaking not one word to her. He continued to fetch her each morning and to conduct her to the lady Katrina's apartments after school.

On the third day after the visit to the bazaar, he had taken her to another part of the palace when the morning's work was done.

'Are we not going to the lady Katrina's apartments?'

'Not just yet,' he told her. 'I want to show you something. I hope it will please you.'

She looked at him enquiringly, but he gave her no hint, then they came to what seemed to be a large courtyard. She was surprised to see that a part of it led to stables, but the other part was connected through a garden to a rather magnificent building. Hearing the calls of the birds, she guessed that he had brought her to the aviary where the hawks were kept.

'Hawks? You keep birds of prey—are they yours or the Caliph's?'

'These are mine,' he told her and smiled. 'I thought that might please you. Shall we go inside?'

Harriet followed him inside. She was amazed to see the birds had their own little palace with tiled floors and little gardens with trees that they could use as perches, pools and feeding areas. Some of the birds were tethered to their perches, but others flew free. She was startled as one flew close to her and landed on Kasim's arm. He stroked its head and it made a soft sound in its throat, welcoming him.

'Have you missed me, my lady?' he asked. 'I have brought you a visitor. She is English, but you will understand her, will you not?'

'You talk to her as if she were your lover,' Harriet said and knew an insensible pang of jealousy.

Kasim chuckled. 'Do you not think the relationship between a hawk and its keeper is a little like love? Did you not have the same feeling for your horses and hawks?'

'The hawks were my father's. He did not keep them in such splendour. I have never seen a bird of prey so tame.' Harriet smiled and put out her hand to touch the bird's head, but it turned on her and aimed a blow at her hand, breaking the skin with its cruel beak. 'Oh...'

'Forgive my little princess,' Kasim said. He held his arm up and sent the bird back to its perch, taking her hand and looking at it in silence, then he bent his head and licked the wound. 'I think it will mend and licking it is the best way to treat it. Katrina should have something for it if you are concerned.'

'I am not...' Harriet removed her hand. Her insides were churning. His eyes seemed to burn into her, making her shudder inwardly. For a moment she felt he would take her in his arms and kiss her, but then he seemed to remember who she was and drew back. 'Katrina will think I am not coming.'

'Yes, I should take you to her. I am sorry the bird attacked you. She is not usually so rude to visitors.'

'I think she was jealous,' Harriet said. 'She is a female, is she not?'

Kasim nodded, his gaze searing her. 'Tell me, Harriet—if I were your master, would you be jealous of another female?'

'No!' She moved out of reach, her pulses racing. 'Perhaps if you were my betrothed I might…but I could never love a master. Love must be free to be true.'

'Yes, I believe you are right,' Kasim said. 'Come, we must go.'

Harriet went to him, letting him lead her back through the palace. Her thoughts were in turmoil. She must not allow herself to be seduced by his intent looks or the small privileges he offered her. If the man in the bazaar had spoken truly, both she and Marguerite would soon be free.

Kasim had lapsed into silence. Perhaps she had offended him again. Glancing at his stern profile, she felt a sense of loss. If only she had met him in England—if he would give up this life and take her and Marguerite home—then perhaps she could give into the prompting of her heart, which was to trust him.

'The lady Katrina is feeling unwell this morning. She begs that you will visit her in her apartments before you see the children. For that reason I came earlier than usual.' Kasim looked at her as she left the harem. 'I trust you were not indisposed by my request?'

'I was surprised when Mellina told me you were waiting, but I am always up early. That is what I find most frustrating about this life. I have been used to taking exercise early in the mornings.' He made no answer and she turned to look at him. 'Are you angry with me? Have I offended you?'

'Only you know the answer to that question, my lady.' Kasim's eyes still crackled with ice. 'Should I be angry? The man I saw talking to you at the bazaar was no market trader. If you wish to tell me the truth, I may trust your word again, but until then I cannot trust you. I had hoped to extend more privileges to you, Harriet. I had considered asking the Caliph for leave to take you riding, especially as you've told me it was one of your favourite pastimes in England.'

'Yes, it was one of my chief pleasures at home.'

'If I was certain I could trust you, I should take you on a hunting trip I am planning soon. Would you enjoy that? I like to hunt with my hawks, as both the Caliph and Hassan do. I thought you might find it a pleasant way to pass the time.'

'Why do you tell me if you have no intention of taking me?' Harriet was angry, because the prospect of being allowed to ride with him was so tempting that it made her ache with loss. She suddenly wondered what life would be like if Kasim were her master rather than the Caliph. He had asked her why she had never married and she had answered truly. Why had he asked? For a moment her heart raced. If she were Kasim's wife... The picture was sweet and it made her realise that she was being seduced into the soft easy living of the harem. Why should she have to please anyone to gain the favour of being taken riding? It was her right to come and go as she pleased! 'I dare say it would be pleasant enough.'

'Do not sulk, Harriet.' He smiled at her oddly. 'You know that life can never be the same as it was. Why do you fight it? Why do you fight me when things could be so much pleasanter if you let me show you why I live as I do?'

Harriet refused to smile at him. He was responsible for her imprisonment. She would not be seduced away from her chance to escape—even though life as his houri would not be so terrible.

'I am sorry that you feel I have let you down in some way. You should know that I would never desert my cousin or do anything to distress the lady Katrina.'

'You may not have your cousin's companionship for much longer,' Kasim replied in a sharper tone than he normally used to her. 'Prince Hassan was called to the capital to do some service for the Sultan just after we returned from Algiers. He has sent word that he will return soon, perhaps this afternoon.'

Harriet's eyes widened; her mouth was dry and her stomach tightened with anxiety. 'What does that mean?'

Kasim frowned. 'Your cousin has had time to accustom herself to the ways of the harem. The prince will see her for the first time this evening; if he is pleased, she will be given to him.'

'No! He has no right,' Harriet protested, anger rising in her. 'She loves someone else—how can she ever feel anything for a man who forces her to surrender her honour? She will hate him—and I shall hate you, because you brought us here. Besides, she is still unwell.'

'The Caliph has been told that she is well and settling in with the other women.'

'Mellina does not understand her as I do. My cousin smiles but her heart is breaking. I shall never forgive you for what you did when you brought us here.'

Something tightened in Kasim's face. For a moment Harriet thought she saw a flash of pain in his eyes, but it was gone in an instant and the barrier was brought back down.

'It is the reason you were both brought here,' he said coldly, all emotion under tight control. 'I have no power to change things even if I would.' And that was not quite the truth, for he could remove her from the Caliph's harem in an instant, but had allowed her to stay with her cousin until the last moment.

'You could have helped us,' Harriet said bitterly. 'You had a choice. You could have taken us to a safe place. My uncle and brother would have paid for us to be ransomed.'

'I thought you were not sure what had happened to your uncle?' Kasim's eyes were intent on her face. He reached out, his fingers clasping her wrist in a ring of steel. 'Do not let yourself believe in a rescue. It has never happened and it will not, believe me. Escape is impossible. Anyone who tried would be caught and punished. I could do nothing to save you.'

'Once again, I ask to be ransomed. I would repay

the price you paid from my own fortune if I were given the chance.'

'I forbid you to speak of this matter again. You will not be ransomed and you will not escape. Put this foolishness from your mind. I do not want to see you punished. You would not like to experience the punishments that might come your way.' Kasim hesitated, then reached out, his fingers touching her cheek lightly. A flame shot through Harriet, making her tingle right down to her toes. She moved away, reacting against what her heart and mind were telling her. He was the enemy! Every now and then she saw a different man, a man she could like very well, perhaps even love—but always he returned to the stern man who had brought them here. 'Resign yourselves to what has happened and you will discover that happiness is to be found here. Believe me, this can be a good life if you accept it, Harriet.'

Harriet lowered her eyes. Had she given herself away? Would he suspect that something was going on? Would he take steps to make certain she was confined within the harem? She must escape, if only for Marguerite's sake.

'I am glad to see you home, my son.' Kahlid embraced his eldest son. 'So the Sultan was pleased with you? You performed your duties with credit?'

'Yes, Father.' Prince Hassan smiled to see the pride in his father's eyes. 'He would have kept me with him, but I told him that my duty lay with you. I must learn all you have to teach me so that one day I shall be as wise a ruler as you.'

'I am glad to have you back, Hassan.' The Caliph looked pleased with his son's answer. Some sons were impatient to take their father's place, but Hassan felt a true affection for him and sought only his approval. 'I have a surprise for you, my son. Before you left I promised that I would find a wife for you—and I think we have found a woman who is truly worthy of you.'

'A wife?' Hassan's eyes lit with interest. He had had his own harem for some two years or more, but a wife was different. 'Is she English, like my mother?' he asked. 'I would have a woman as wise and loving as my mother was to you, Father.'

'She is very young, but she learns our ways easily. I have had reports of her and they are mostly good. She is certainly English and of good family, as your mother was—but come and see for yourself. She is in the gardens with my women.'

Hassan followed his father to the window that looked out over the harem gardens. No other man was ever allowed this privilege, but his father was generous. Hassan had often been allowed to choose when new women were brought to the palace. His father had many women in his harem, though he sent for only a few, preferring to spend his evenings with his chief wife when she was well.

'Which one is she?' Hassan asked as he saw several women playing and laughing in the gardens. His father came to stand by his side, watching for a moment and smiling as he watched some women splashing each other with water from the fountain.

'The one wearing pale blue. She has long blonde hair and her eyes are blue, I think, though I have not been close enough to see if they are more blue than green.'

Hassan watched as the woman splashed water at the monkey, who had come to investigate. She screamed with laughter and looked up towards their window as the monkey scrambled up a vine. Because of the pierced screen over the window she could not see that she was being watched and for a moment Hassan had a clear view of her lovely face.

'She is lovely. Young and without artifice. I think she will make me a fine wife, Father. You are certain she is English?'

'Yes. I gave Kasim orders to find a beautiful and intelligent English woman and he brought this one for you. There is another who helps to care for the children. She is clever, but not as beautiful. I think this is the right bride for you, my son.'

'Yes, she is.' Hassan looked pleased. 'How soon can the marriage be arranged? Must she be taught the faith before we marry?'

'I think it is too soon. She is not yet accustomed to all our ways. I believe the marriage should be quite soon…perhaps tomorrow? This evening I have a meeting with one of the hill tribesmen, but tomorrow evening will be your wedding and the following day a celebration.'

'Tomorrow evening I shall be married.' Hassan

nodded his agreement. 'I need to find a gift for her, Father. Tomorrow I shall go to the merchants and see what I can find that will please her.'

'There are many items of value in my treasure chests. You may choose something from there if you wish.'

'Perhaps a jewel,' Hassan agreed. 'But I was thinking of something different. She seems to like playing with the monkey. I must get her a pet of her own for she is innocent and I would not have her sad to leave your harem and her friends.'

'The other woman is her friend,' Kahlid said. 'She is not beautiful, but you might think of taking her into your harem as a companion for your wife. However, I would suggest that you wait a while. Let your bride become accustomed to marriage before you bring them together again. Women need to be tamed, my son, but you must use a velvet glove, not a whip. Especially with English women, who are naturally stubborn and wilful. Your mother resisted me for a long time, but in the end I won her.'

'I shall be patient,' Hassan told him and smiled. 'I would have my wife love me as much as my mother loved you.'

The day had passed swiftly; Harriet had spent the afternoon reading poetry to Katrina. Her friend had been too lazy and unwell to read herself and she had not wanted to part from Harriet when it was time for her to leave.

'I do not see why you have to go back there every

night,' she said and sighed. 'You could have an apartment near me and then we could talk for as long as we wished.'

'That would be pleasant,' Harriet agreed. 'Yet my cousin will be happy to see me when I return.'

'Your cousin…' Katrina pouted, obviously not pleased with her answer. 'You will not see her very often soon for she will be in another part of the palace. Prince Hassan is home now and she will be sent to his harem.'

Harriet held her tongue. She longed to deny Katrina's words, but did not wish to distress her.

However, her mind dwelled on what her friend had said as she made her way back to the harem through the gardens that evening. She had known that it would happen one day, but after the visit to the bazaar she had hoped they might escape before it happened.

'Lady Harriet…' Harriet froze as she heard the voice speak softly to her in English. 'Do not turn. No one must know I am here or I am dead.'

'What do you want?' Harriet asked, her voice barely above a whisper. 'How did you come here? It is forbidden.'

'Ask no questions. When you are both safe all will be revealed. You must bring Mistress Marguerite here tomorrow evening just as dusk falls. Beyond the fountain and the bed of oleanders is a small gate used by the gardeners. It will be unlocked for two hours after dusk. After that it will be locked again so that the escape route is disguised. If you are prevented tomorrow, I shall get another message to you.'

'What is outside the gate?'

'Someone who knows the secret ways will be waiting for you. Go now or you will be noticed.'

'Thank you. We shall be there.'

Harriet resisted the temptation to turn her head. Whoever had come here to deliver the message was a very brave man. If he were discovered, he would almost certainly be punished and put to death. The Caliph's harem was forbidden to all but the eunuchs and the Caliph himself.

Could the messenger be a eunuch himself? Harriet wondered about it as she entered the coolness of the harem. The communal courtyard, which led from Katrina's gardens to the more private rooms, was deserted, as it usually was at this hour. Very soon now the gates that connected to this garden would be locked. There would be only a small window of time when they could make their escape. Harriet was on fire to tell Marguerite that she had to wait only one more day and then she would be free, but wisely she kept her excitement inside. To confide the secret too soon might be risky. She would wait until the last moment and then whisper it to her cousin when they were in the garden. It was the one place where they could find a secluded spot where they could not be heard.

'You have been gone the whole day,' Marguerite complained as Harriet entered the sleeping quarters they shared. Her tone was accusing, almost resentful. 'I get so bored when you are not here, Harry. I wish I could come with you.'

'Perhaps you will soon.'

'What do you mean?'

'I shall ask if you may join me in the school-room—if you would like that?'

'Oh…' Marguerite shook her head. 'You are teaching them English, aren't you? I have been trying to improve my French, but it is too difficult.'

'What do you amuse yourself with all day?'

'I play with the monkey, dance and bathe…' Marguerite yawned. 'I long to walk and ride as we used to, Harry—don't you?'

'Yes, I do, but do not despair, my love. Whatever happens we must not give up hope.'

Harriet wished that she could tell her the thrilling news, but someone might even now be watching and listening.

Harriet was on edge the next day. Kasim hardly spoke when he took her from the harem to the children's quarters, though when he left her he gave her an odd look that she could not interpret—almost as if he were asking her to forgive him for something. No, that must be her imagination! He was proud and arrogant and without compassion. She had been wrong to let herself begin to enjoy his company. Harriet shut out the thoughts that told her she was lying to herself, that she had begun to look forward to the time they spent together each day. She would not miss his company. Once she was home with her dogs and her horses she would be perfectly happy. Memories of dark lonely nights that had seemed long after her father's death were dismissed ruthlessly. She refused to admit even to herself that she found life here more pleasant than she could ever have expected.

Teaching the children was something that Harriet normally enjoyed, but that morning she could not concentrate. She knew that she would find it impossible to spend the afternoon with Katrina; after they had eaten a meal of figs, peaches and some soft cheese mixed with honey and dates, she asked Katrina if she might leave her earlier than usual.

'Yes, I must let you go,' Katrina said and her eyes gleamed. 'It is the last night you will need to leave me, because I have arranged for you to have adjoining apartments. Go then, Harriet. You will wish to spend a few hours with your cousin before she leaves for the prince's harem.'

Harriet stared at her in dismay. 'What do you mean?'

'I could not tell you,' Katrina said. 'This evening Marguerite will be taken to the prince and then you will only see her on special days when the harems are allowed to mix for a celebration.'

'Marguerite is to be...' Harriet felt the horror wash over her. All the plans made for their escape would come to nothing if Marguerite were to be moved before that evening. 'Thank you for telling me. I must go to her at once.'

'Forgive me...' Katrina called after her, but Harriet did not answer.

She was angry, her mind working furiously—even angrier with Kasim than her friend, because he had known what was happening and he had held it from her. Small wonder, then, that he had looked guilty! How could he let it happen without telling her? It was typical of the way these people behaved. They had no right to treat their slaves as if they had no feelings. Marguerite would have been told what was happening by now and she would be distraught.

Hurrying into the harem courtyard, Harriet asked Fortunata where Marguerite was and received a mocking smile in reply.

'She has been given to the prince. I remain the Caliph's favourite.' A malicious smile hovered about the woman's lips.

'She has gone already?'

'She is being bathed and prepared now. You may join her if you wish.'

Harriet hurried to the bathing pool. Marguerite was surrounded by several of the women. Her hair was being brushed and it was clear that she had been bathed, her hands and feet were being rubbed with perfumed oils and a beautiful costume of red silk with gold beads was waiting for her.

'Harry!' Marguerite jumped to her feet, pushing the other women away. She was clearly distressed, her eyes filled with tears. 'I am going to be given to the prince this evening!'

'Yes, I know. I have come to spend some time with you.' She put her arms about Marguerite, feeling her tremble.

'Help me…please help me. I don't know what to do. I want to die.'

'Hush, my love,' Harriet whispered against her ear. 'I shall help you, but you must do as I say. Say nothing, but follow my lead.'

Marguerite drew back and looked at her. Harriet arched her brows and she smiled wanly. 'I shall,' she mouthed back, but the words could not be heard by anyone else. It was a way of talking to each other they had devised so that they would not be overheard.

Harriet took her hand. She squeezed it and turned to Mellina, who was watching them. 'My cousin is nervous. I shall stay with her and help you dress and anoint her with the oils—and she will become calmer. In return you will allow us to spend a little time in private to say our farewells.' She felt Marguerite's start of surprise, but squeezed her hand again. Marguerite squeezed back, but did not speak.

'We must paint her hands and feet,' Mellina said as Marguerite sat down on the stool again.

'Oh, I like that,' Harriet exclaimed as the women began to paint little scrolls on Marguerite's feet and hands. 'May I have mine done too, please?'

Mellina hesitated and then smiled. 'It may be your only chance,' she said. 'For it is only for special occasions. Yes, Sevine may do yours.'

Harriet sat on a stool next to Marguerite and held out her hands and then her feet, exclaiming with delight as Sevine produced the same patterns for her as for her cousin. The other women were giggling amongst themselves and whispering, but Harriet kept a smile on her face. Each time the women used an oil or a perfume on Marguerite, she asked for some too. It was almost time for the evening meal when Marguerite was finally wrapped in an enveloping garment that covered her from head to toe, her face hidden by a veil.

'She is finished,' Mellina said. 'You may go to your room and wait for the summons. I shall make sure that you are not disturbed until the time has come for her to leave.'

'Come, Marguerite.'

Harriet took her hand. She held fast to her cousin, walking at a normal pace towards their sleeping quarters, though her heart was beating rapidly and she wanted to run. Time was so short! Once inside the little room, she closed the door and moved a table made of hardwood inlaid with ivory in front of it and then went to what looked like a piece of carved wood on the wall and hung a piece of clothing over it. Marguerite opened her mouth to speak, but Harriet shook her head. Putting a finger to her lips, she wrote something on a slate she had brought from the schoolroom.

Change clothes with me as quickly as you can!

Marguerite stared at her and then began to undress. Harriet did the same. She dressed in Marguerite's clothes and then wrote hastily on the slate.

Behind the fountain in Katrina's garden is a bed of oleanders. There is a gate. Tonight it will be open between dusk and the evening bell. Someone will be waiting. You must go quickly. Do not speak to anyone. If they ask something, you must just walk

*towards Katrina's apartments and then go back to
the gate. Do you understand?*

Marguerite nodded. *What about you?* she wrote,
then took Harriet's arm, looking into her face. 'How
can I escape without you?' she mouthed.

'You must go or it will be too late. The prince will
not want me,' Harriet whispered. 'Tell your father
that I shall wait for another message.'

'You were contacted by my father?' Marguerite's
voice rose. She clapped her hand over her mouth.
'Sorry…' she whispered. 'When?'

'Yesterday, but I was afraid we should be heard.
You must go now, Marguerite. Keep your head down
and your face covered as you leave here. The courtyard will be empty, for everyone will be at supper.'

'But you…' Marguerite was tearful, unwilling to
leave her. 'Why can you not come too?'

'They will come to fetch you at any minute. If
you were not here, they would search for you. As
you leave here, cover your hair and face and pretend
that you are weeping. Go as quickly as you can. They
will think that I have gone to Katrina for comfort.'

Marguerite flung her arms about her, clinging to
her. 'My best of friends, I am afraid for you. They
will punish you.'

'Katrina loves me as a sister. I shall not be treated
harshly. Go quickly or it will be too late!'

Marguerite hugged her once more and then they
pulled the table back. She covered her face with her
hands and, beginning to sob, ran from the room
towards the communal courtyard.

Harriet cleaned the slate and then sat down to wait. Her mouth was dry and her hands were trembling. She prayed that Marguerite would not be questioned.

Let her escape. Please let her escape, she prayed silently. I can bear whatever they do to me, but please let her escape.

Chapter Six

Harriet stood up as the door opened some twenty minutes or so later. She was enveloped from head to toe in a silky red wrap that hid everything but her feet, her hands and wrists bejewelled with the rings and bracelets that Marguerite had been wearing when she was brought here. Her head was covered with the same heavy silk and there was a thick veil over her face.

Her eyes! She had forgotten that they had different coloured eyes! Harriet tensed with fright. Mellina would know at once and they would set up a search for Marguerite. It had all been for nothing and they might both be punished.

As the two eunuchs entered her room, Harriet's heart did a somersault of fear. They were big powerful men—but in an instant she realised that she had never seen either of them before. They would not know her. She realised that they must have been sent in case she fought against being taken to the prince. Harriet gave a little sob of fear. It was what Marguerite would have done and yet it was not all pretence. She bent her head, making no resistance as they took an arm each and propelled her from the room.

None of the women were about as they left her room and walked down the passage leading to the main harem door. They must have imagined Marguerite would scream and cry at being torn from her and forced to become the prince's plaything; perhaps in sympathy they had kept out of her way.

If Harriet had been in her place, she would have felt much the same. She was nervous now, her heart beating so fast that she could scarcely breathe, but she did not fear that she was about to be ravished. When the prince saw her face he would send her away. She hoped he would just send her back to the harem, but a little voice at the back of her mind kept telling her it would not be that easy. It was almost certain that she would face some form of punishment.

It did not matter. Harriet would face whatever they did to her if only Marguerite escaped!

Marguerite was sobbing as she ran through the empty courtyard and into the garden. She had been told that she must not walk here unless invited; although it connected with the harem it was for Katrina's private use. Her fear of discovery made her brave and she entered the garden, looking for the fountain Harriet had described.

Harry! What would happen to her when they discovered what had happened? Marguerite had spent more time in the harem than her cousin and even though her French was not good she had gathered enough to know that the punishment for trying to escape was harsh. Harriet would be blamed for changing places with her.

She ought not to have left her! Marguerite paused as she reached the bed of oleanders, feeling guilty. Should she go back? No, she could not bear it if she were forced to lie in the prince's bed, even though some of the women had envied her.

Breathing deeply, she made her way through the oleanders just as dusk was falling. Harriet had told her this plan was devised by Marguerite's father. Soon she could be with him. She would be safe and free—and they would make a new plan to rescue Harriet.

She saw the gate, her heart pounding as she lifted the latch. It was unlocked. Pushing it open, she stepped through. Although dusk fell swiftly here, she saw the tall figure wrapped in dark clothing and took a step towards him.

'You are alone?'

'My cousin could not come. She told me to come alone.'

There was a muffled curse, then the man moved towards her, giving her a dark wrap that would cover her from head to foot.

'We must go swiftly. The gate must be locked again before the bell or we shall be undone. Come, your cousin has made her choice.'

'But…she thought you would try again.'

'It would be too dangerous. This can only happen once.'

'But…I must go back…'

'Be silent,' the voice said and a hand of iron gripped her wrist. 'You must come with me now, for if we were found together they would kill us both.'

Harriet's heart was beating madly as the eunuchs stopped outside a door that was even more ornately decorated with silver knobs and semi-precious stones than the harem door. She swallowed her saliva with a little gulp as the door opened and she was thrust inside.

A little shock of surprise ran through her as she saw that there were several people in the room. She had expected to be delivered to the prince's sleeping quarters, but found instead that she was in a kind of presence chamber. At one end on a little dais there were three people seated, a young man that she imagined must be the prince, an older man who looked very like him, and Katrina. To either side of the dais men were standing. Harriet's heart pounded as she saw that one of them was Kasim. What was he doing here? He must not see her eyes!

She dipped her head as she was beckoned forwards. The young man rose from his stool, which was ornate and looked like a throne. She remembered that Prince Hassan was his father's heir and reputed to be his favourite son. He came down the three steps towards her and took her hand. He lifted it to his lips and kissed it, then spoke softly to her.

'You are very beautiful, lady. I am happy that this day has come.' He spoke to her in English and she felt a spasm of panic. She would not be able to pretend that she did not understand him.

Harriet could not answer. Her masquerade must not be discovered yet. Had Marguerite had enough time to get away from the palace? As soon as they knew she was not her cousin there would be such an uproar. She kept her head down, her stomach beginning to knot with nerves. What was happening? She had not expected this…it was very different from the tales she had read where women of the harem were ravished. The prince was handsome and he smelled of delicate spices and oils. She thought he must have been prepared in much the same way as Marguerite had and somehow that unsettled her more. Something was wrong, but she could not think what it was.

A man in rich robes had come towards them. He began to speak in a high voice, chanting words that were new to Harriet. Prince Hassan took her hand and clasped it and the man in rich robes, who might have been an important officer of the court, dipped his finger in oil and then anointed her forehead and the prince's.

'We must follow him now, lady,' the prince whispered in her ear. He spoke English well and his voice was pleasant, intelligent. 'I know you have not been taught our ways yet, but I shall teach you. You will become accustomed to things slowly, as my mother did. I have asked for the ceremony to be simple, because I wish to be alone with you.'

Harriet did not dare to look at him. He must have seen Marguerite. If he looked into her eyes she might be exposed. The man she believed to be the Caliph was looking on benevolently and Katrina was smiling. She risked a look at Kasim and saw that he was staring into the corner of the room. He looked grim, remote, as if he had deliberately shut out what was happening. Could it be that he was regretting what he had done when he brought them here?

What was going on here?

'You must incline your head to give your consent,' the prince told her and she realised she was being asked a question by the man in the rich robes. She hurriedly obeyed, anxious not to betray herself. 'Do not be frightened, my love. I shall be kind to you. You are the wife I have waited for and I am so happy that my father gave you to me. I shall never harm or hurt you.'

She was being married to the prince! This ceremony would make her Prince Hassan's bride? Of course. Why hadn't she realised it at once? This must stop. She could not allow it to go on. How long since Marguerite had escaped? Was she safe? It could not be helped. She must stop this now and take the consequences.

Harriet's heart was racing wildly. She put her hand

to her face and pulled the veil away, letting them all see her face.

'This is not the woman I chose,' Prince Hassan cried and a look of disappointment mixed with anger crossed his face.

'No, I am not Marguerite,' Harriet said in a clear proud voice. 'I shall not marry Prince Hassan. I am a free Englishwoman and I have the right to choose. I choose not to marry.'

'Father, what is this? You promised me the beautiful one…'

Kasim was standing close to them. Harriet looked into his eyes, seeing his shock and horror at what had happened. She saw him start, saw the recognition and the dismay followed swiftly by what she thought was anxiety.

'What have you done, woman?' the Caliph said and it was clear he was angry. 'Where is the woman they call Marguerite?'

Harriet lifted her head and looked at him. 'My cousin did not wish to be given to the prince. She declined to come, so I came in her place.'

'Be silent, woman! You have insulted my son. You will be punished. Guards!'

Harriet felt chilled as she looked into his black eyes and saw a cold fury. Kahlid was not like his handsome son; he had a hooked nose, fierce eyes and at the moment his expression was murderous.

She glanced at Kasim and thought he shook his head, his eyes seeming to warn her. She sensed tension in him and realised that she was in serious trouble.

'Am I to return to the harem?'

'Be quiet, woman. You will go where you are taken. I shall consider what should happen to you once the other woman is found.'

'I did not wish to harm you or the prince, but I had to protect my cousin…I would gladly repay the cost of our price if—'

'You make your situation worse, woman. Hold your tongue!'

The guards were each side of her now. They took hold of her arms, their fingers pressing into her skin. Harriet's heart was thumping and she felt sick as she was led away. Where was she being taken? She knew there was a prison somewhere in the palace compound. The other women had spoken of it with fear in their eyes, and she had understood without words that none of them would risk being sent to its stinking cells.

What form would her punishment take? Would she be beaten or would she lose her life?

Harriet closed her eyes against the hot tears. She would not give way to self-pity. If Marguerite were safe, she would face whatever came to her somehow. Had enough time passed for them to get away? Had it all gone as planned? Harriet could only pray and wait.

The eunuch stopped outside a door, took a key from a bunch that hung at his waist and unlocked it, then thrust her inside. She caught her breath, for it was pitch black. She must be in some kind of prison. The door was slammed behind her and she heard the key turn once more. She had been shut here until the Caliph decided what to do with her. His reaction had been so furious that she could not expect mercy.

For a few moments Harriet could not see anything and the darkness was terrifying; then, after her eyes became accustomed to the gloom, she could just make out some sort of a mattress on the floor but nothing more. As she looked upwards at the ceiling, she realised the tiniest glimmer of light came from above her head. There must be some sort of grille in the ceiling, which let in air and from which she could be observed. As in the harem, she could still be watched.

Feeling her way along the rough stone wall towards the mattress, she sat down on the edge. It was much harder than she had been accustomed to and was covered with some coarse cloth. Feeling a knot of misery and hopelessness settle deep inside her, she lay down and closed her eyes. She was not cold for she had the layers of clothes that were supposed to delight her husband as he removed them one by one, but she was trembling.

What would happen to her now? The Caliph was very angry and he might decide to put her to death. He thought she had insulted the prince, though she had not meant to, but she had not understood their ways or the seriousness of what she planned. Kasim had protected them when they were first brought to the palace, but it was unlikely he could save her now—even if he wished to.

'I will not be afraid,' she told herself in the darkness. 'If I die, then I shall be as brave as I can. If only Marguerite is safe, I can bear anything.'

Tears trickled down her cheeks, because she felt so alone. There was no one who could help her, no one who cared whether she lived or died. Yet even as she felt the sting of despair, she remembered the look in Kasim's eyes as he saw her face. Shock and disappointment…and grief. She almost thought she had imagined it and yet somehow she knew that he had felt some deep and painful emotion. He must have known what would happen to her.

'You sent for me, my lord?' Kasim genuflected to the Caliph. He had spent the night searching for Marguerite and trying to think how he could best help Harriet, though he knew Kahlid's anger was just, for she had behaved in a way that implied an insult to the prince.

'Have you news for me concerning the escaped slave?'

'The woman is not in the palace, my lord.'

'And the Janissaries are out looking for her?'

'Yes, my lord. A search party left immediately, according to your orders.'

'Then she will be found.' Kahlid's eyes dwelled on Kasim thoughtfully. 'Had you any idea that the other woman planned this masquerade?'

'You must know I would have warned her against such a foolish trick.'

'You consider it no more than that?'

'I do not believe she intended insult to the prince, my lord.'

'Yet that is what she has done. Hers is a grave offence, Kasim. My son is a noble prince and by taking her cousin's place and then refusing to wed him, she has offered a terrible insult. If a man had insulted my son, he would already be dead. I do not like to take life for no good reason but I believe in this case it may be the only way.'

'I beg you to think again,' Kasim cried. 'For my sake—for your own sake—do not do this thing.'

'Give me a reason not to exact justice for the insult to my son.'

'My lord, please listen to me. She does not understand our customs. She did not know that she was insulting the prince. I ask you to be generous and spare her,' Kasim pleaded. 'I know what she has done, but she meant no insult. She thought only of her cousin, whom she loves. What she did was wrong, but brave, for she knew she would be punished.'

Kahlid glared at him for several moments in silence. 'Is there no sign of the other one?'

'It is as if she disappeared into thin air. However, she must have had help from inside the palace. The culprits will be found and punished.'

'You would punish them, but not her?' Kahlid's eyes held a hint of understanding. He closed them for a moment, then looked at Kasim. 'I shall make a bargain with you, my friend. In return for the woman's life you will make me a promise.'

'What promise? You know you have only to ask. I have always been honoured to serve you.'

'I am dying,' Kahlid said, startling Kasim with the straight look he gave him. 'It is quite certain that I have no more than a few months to live.'

'My lord.' Kasim was stunned, his throat tight with emotion as he struggled to accept. 'How long have you known?'

'I suspected it when I sent you to look for an English wife for my son. I love Hassan dearly, but he is hot-headed. When I am gone he will plunge our people into a permanent state of war—unless you are here to guide him and share my power as Caliph.'

'Hassan would never agree. He is your rightful heir.'

'He will have no choice. It is my decree that you rule together…until such time as you consider he is fit to take my place.'

'Hassan would hate me. It is his right to follow you, my lord.'

'That is your burden to bear.' Kahlid sighed. 'You are the son I need to follow me, Kasim. My head tells me that you should rule alone, but my heart will not allow me to disown him. You must rule together, at least until Hassan can be trusted to do what is right. This is the promise I ask of you.'

Kasim hesitated. He felt as if he were being torn apart. Harriet's life was being given to him, but the price was heavy. He would have no choice but to stay here until Hassan lost some of his wildness and that might be years, a lifetime—but the alternative was unthinkable.

'The woman is mine. I shall have her taken to my harem and make sure she behaves. In the meantime, the search for Hassan's bride continues.'

'I do not think she will be found, and if she were my son would probably refuse to wed her. He is disappointed and angry and it is my fault. I thought an English girl would be good for him, force him to settle down, but I was wrong. I shall approach the Sultan and ask if he has a daughter of a suitable age. Perhaps one of his kadans has a daughter who will please Hassan.'

'I am sure there are many girls in the Sultan's family. It would be an honour for Hassan and may ease the sting of his disappointment.'

'It was what we should have done at the start,' Kahlid said. 'I knew you did not approve of my plan—and it seems you were right.'

'For Harriet's sake I have no regrets. Had I not been there…' Kasim shook his head. 'Thank you for your generosity, my lord. I am grateful for the mercy you have shown her.'

'It would give me no pleasure to see her punished. She reminds me of Anna.' Kahlid looked tired. 'I could not change things, Kasim. Anna begged me to free at least the harem many times. I clung to the old ways. It is the custom of my people and my faith— but it is not always just. Perhaps you can find a better way. I have tried to be just, but there are times when you must do things you find hard. When I am gone you will understand me.'

'When will you tell Hassan that he must share the power with me?'

'Soon. I have already signed the decree. I meant to ask you, but the moment had not come—until now.'

Kasim understood that his friend had feared to ask. He was afraid that once he was dead, Kasim would return to his homeland, as he might have had he not given his word. Although he loved the prince as his brother, he knew there would be trouble as soon as Kahlid was dead, if not before. Hassan would resent being reined back. There was already a keen rivalry between them. Kasim knew that the prince both admired and resented him. He had not yet beaten the man he thought of as an older brother at anything and he could not bear to be second-best. He had accepted that Kasim was older and stronger only because he was the heir and would ultimately hold the power.

When he learned of his father's decision, he would lose his temper. Kasim could only hope that he would come to accept it once he had calmed down.

Leaving the Caliph's presence, he walked thoughtfully towards Harriet's cell. She had spent the night reflecting on her fate. He would see that she had food and clean clothes, but for the moment he would not release her.

There were certain arrangements he needed to make before Harriet was taken to his apartments. She could not live in the harem with the others, but he would not send them all away immediately, because she needed friends.

In time he would offer her a choice. She could either settle to life here or return home to her family. Kasim did not know how he would feel if she chose to return to England. She had got beneath his skin in a way no other woman ever had. Had he been free as before he might have taken her back to England and courted her in the time-honoured manner, but things were altered—he had given Kahlid his word.

In return for her life, he had made himself a prisoner. He wore no chain and he had both position and power, but the promise he had given was binding. Kahlid was his friend. Even had there been no promise, he would find it hard to leave him knowing he was slowly dying of the wasting sickness.

Yet the prospect of trying to rule the Caliph's province with Hassan was a daunting one. He had no doubt that the prince would hate him for usurping his place.

The air in her cell had become stuffy during the night. Waking once, Harriet had not realised where she was and the blackness terrified her. Why could she not see anything? Was she blind?

The memory of what had happened the previous night came rushing back, and once again she could make out the smallest pinprick of light above her head. She felt numb and anxious. What was happening? Had Marguerite managed to get away?

What would happen next? Would she be allowed to return to the Caliph's harem once she had been punished—and what form would the punishment take? She expected at the very least to be beaten with the whips that left no marks, but perhaps her sin was too great and she would be put to death.

The tormented thoughts went round and round in her head as the light gradually strengthened. Now the light above her was daylight. Barely visible at first, as the time went on the small ray of light became warm and she knew it was the sun. Was she outside the palace? Was she in the prison, an underground cell? Now she thought of it, the passage had sloped towards the end.

After some hours had passed, Harriet began to think that they were just going to let her die here alone. It seemed a lifetime since she had eaten or drunk anything. She was beginning to feel thirsty. Was this to be her punishment? A long slow death that would become a torment indeed…

Suddenly the door opened and she blinked in the bright light. Two men were standing there, one of them carrying a basket of food and a jug of water. It took her a moment or two to focus before she realised that one of the men was Kasim.

'Wait here,' he commanded the eunuch. 'I must question the woman.'

Harriet trembled as she heard the harshness in his voice. She stood up and waited for him. He set the basket and water down on the floor and looked at her.

'How did you do it?'

'Do what?' Harriet swallowed nervously. 'If you mean impersonate my cousin, I helped the women prepare Marguerite and used the same oils. I asked if I could have my hands and feet painted and then, when we were alone, I changed clothes with her—that is all.' Harriet raised her eyes to his in an appeal for understanding. He was angry, but he must understand why she had done what she had. 'My cousin was frightened—and there is someone she loves waiting for her at home.'

'You admit that you helped her to escape?'

Harriet realised her slip. 'Has she escaped?' she asked a little too eagerly.

Kasim's tone was measured and careful. 'At the moment we have not been able to discover where she is hiding. The palace and grounds are still being searched, but you must know where she is, lady. If you tell me, your punishment will be less.'

'I do not know where Marguerite is,' Harriet said quite truthfully. 'If I did, I should not tell you. If she has escaped, I am truly happy for her.'

'You let her go knowing that you risked punishment?' Kasim's eyes were icy cold as they rested on her face. 'Have you any idea what could happen to you?'

Harriet did her best to conceal the shudder that went through her at his words. 'I suppose I could be whipped or…I might be killed. I thought I was meant to die of starvation and thirst.'

'Kahlid was inclined to demand the death penalty, but I have managed to persuade him that you did not understand what you were doing.'

'I did not mean it as an insult—but I hope she is not found,' Harriet said and looked him straight in the eyes. 'What I did was for her sake and I am content to take whatever punishment the Caliph decides on.'

'Foolish woman, have you no idea what might have happened? You were almost the prince's wife…' Kasim took a step towards her. He towered over her, reaching out to take hold of her shoulders. His fingers bit into her flesh. His face was set in harsh lines, but in his eyes there was a very different emotion, an emotion that made her wonder. 'No, I shall not speak of this! What is done is done. You will remain here until I fetch you. Try if you can to reach a proper state of contrition. If you continue to defy the rules here even I shall lose patience.' He glanced round the bare room. 'I will have fresh clothes and your combs and perfumes brought to you—also a lamp so that you are not left in the dark.'

'Thank you…' Harriet's throat felt tight. He seemed as if he were in charge of her punishment. What had Kasim had in mind for her and why did she care? 'Please tell the prince that I am sorry he is hurt, but…my cousin…'

'He is in no mood to listen for the moment,' Kasim said. 'We are still searching for your cousin—and the man who helped her leave the harem.'

'What man?' Harriet's eyes widened. Her mouth felt dry. 'Surely he will have left the palace?'

'Do you know who it was?'

'No…I heard a voice, that is all…' She licked her lips. 'What would happen if…?'

'If the eunuch, and it must have been one of the eunuchs, is found, he will be put to death.' Kasim's mouth tightened. 'Did you think he would be reprimanded and allowed to live? No one escapes from the Caliph's harem. Others have tried it and been found and punished. Anyone who helps them is automatically executed; it is the law and one of the most stringently observed.'

Harriet gasped, her face pale. She had asked Marguerite to tell her uncle to send their rescuer back for her, but it was useless—and dangerous. She could not expect it, which meant that she was trapped here for life.

'I knew it was dangerous, but…' She looked at him. 'You cannot know who it was?'

'Believe me, he will be found if he was foolish enough to return. You were seen going towards Katrina's garden—at least it was thought to be you and must have been your cousin. There is a gate the gardeners use under the supervision of a eunuch. He is the only man to have a key; therefore he must have opened it and returned to lock it again.' Kasim frowned as she drew her breath sharply. 'I thought that must be how it was done. Malik cannot be found this morning, but men are searching for him. If he is foolish enough to be taken alive, he will curse your name before he dies.'

'Please…' Harriet's eyes filled with tears. 'Can you not save him? You have influence with the Caliph and the prince.'

'Not enough to save Malik. I may be able to help you, because I once saved Hassan's life. As a child he was in some danger from men who would have abducted or killed him. I prevented his capture and his father rewarded me with my present position at court. You are in my charge, to punish as I see fit, but Malik is a dead man if they find him.'

'No…' Harriet sat down on her mattress. She bent her head, covering her face with her hands as the shock rushed through her. 'I cannot bear the thought.'

'I warned you that escape was impossible. The eunuchs who took you to the prince have already been punished…' Kasim shook his head as her gaze flew to him. 'No, they were not executed, but they have lost privileges. Mellina will also lose privileges.'

'She does not deserve to be punished. She knew nothing.'

'She should not have left you alone together.' Kasim looked at her sternly. 'You should have thought about what you were doing.'

'I thought only of my cousin's fear and distress.'

'She would soon have forgotten it. Hassan is young and generous. In time she would have taken pride in her position as his first wife…it was an honour and by doing what you did, you offered him a grave insult.'

Harriet did not answer. Her throat was tight and she felt like weeping. She could not bear to look at him. Why could he not understand that he expected too much?

'Marguerite loves someone else. She would always have been miserable. I had to help her—you must understand that, surely? I never meant to harm others or to insult the prince.'

'Mellina will be forgiven soon enough. The Caliph still respects her,' he said in a softer tone. 'I shall send some things to make you more comfortable.'

He turned and went out. The door was locked after him.

Harriet had not answered him. She could find no words—there was nothing she could say. If he did not understand why her cousin had been desperate to escape, there was no way of reasoning with him. She felt the dryness in her throat and got up to investigate the contents of the basket. She had been brought fruit and fresh soft rolls, some cold cooked chicken pieces, honey and nougat, also sweetmeats and water. There was enough to keep her from starving for at least two days.

Harriet lifted the jug and drank a few mouthfuls of the cool water. It felt so good on her parched throat. Taking out a fig, she bit into it, the soft fruit tasting delicious on her tongue.

Kasim's visit had lifted her spirits. At least she knew that Marguerite had not been found yet. It seemed that innocent men and women had been punished for her sin by loss of privilege. As yet, her own punishment had been lenient, but Kasim was angry with her. He was deciding what her punishment should be.

It was almost dusk when the door to her cell was opened once more. Harriet looked up, hoping it might be her clothes being delivered or Kasim, but the eunuch standing there was a stranger to her. Her heart pounded with fear as he beckoned to her. Where was she being taken now?

'What is happening? Where are you taking me?'

'You will not speak,' the eunuch said harshly.

Harriet felt the prickle of fear all over her body. He had clearly been warned not to speak to her lest she corrupt him and tempt him into helping her.

She gripped her hands behind her back, trying not to show fear. Whatever happened she would bear it as best she could. They were walking down the long corridor they had taken the previous night— going back to the palace, she thought. Was she being returned to the harem or taken somewhere else? What was going to happen to her now?

They entered a courtyard that led to a part of the palace she knew well. Harriet's heart skipped a beat. She swallowed hard, trying to control her trembling limbs. Harriet was almost certain now she was being taken to the apartments where she had spent some happy times with the Caliph's chief wife—but why?

The eunuch rapped at the door and another opened it. Harriet knew him. His face was expressionless as he bowed and stood back for her to enter. Why was she being treated with respect?

Going into the beautiful room that belonged to Katrina, she saw that her friend was lying on her sleeping couch and that there were several women and one man gathered about her. A man in Katrina's chamber! What was going on?

'Harriet…' Katrina's fretful voice came to her. 'Please help me…they say I may die if my child does not come soon.'

Harriet understood then what was going on and why the elderly man was by the Caliph's wife's bed. She must have been in labour some hours and a doctor had been called to tend her. Quickening her steps, she went to her friend and took the hand she offered.

'How long have you been in labour?' she asked.

'Hours…' Katrina told her. 'It happened this morning when I rose. I had been weeping all night because I was concerned for you—have they hurt you?' Her anxious eyes went over Harriet. She held on tight to her hand as a pain struck. 'It hurts so much…'

'You must not worry about me,' Harriet replied and smiled at her. She had been brought here because Katrina had asked for her. 'All that matters is you and the child you carry. Try not to fight the pain when it comes. You must breathe deeply and push as hard as you can.'

'It is what I have been telling her,' the old man said, looking at her with respect. 'Perhaps now you are here we can be rid of these clacking fools.'

'I am ready to do whatever you ask of me,' Harriet said. 'The others may retire to the other end of the room. My lady needs air and some privacy.'

The old man nodded his agreement and waved the women away. They went reluctantly, watching from a distance. Harriet forgot them as Katrina screamed. She bent over her, smoothing her brow and smiling down at her.

'Hold my hand, my dearest. Pant as if you had been running. I am told it helps. I was with my brother's wife when she gave birth to her daughter and her physician was a clever man. Hold on to me if the pain is bad.'

Katrina responded by squeezing her hand so hard that Harriet almost cried out herself, but she made no sound, continuing to encourage and praise her friend. The doctor was working discreetly on his patient and Harriet did her best to take Katrina's mind from what he was doing. She thought that he might be turning the child, for Katrina was in terrible agony and her screams were pitiful.

'The child comes...'

Katrina screamed, then sobbed, her body sagging as the child was drawn out. In a moment or two the cord was cut and the child handed to one of the other women, who came running. The doctor worked a little longer and then smiled at Harriet.

'The lady Katrina will be best in your hands now, *madame*. I thank you for your help.'

'I did nothing,' Harriet said. 'Lady Katrina did it all herself.'

'You gave her the courage she needed. Excuse me, I must show the Caliph his son—but first the mother should see that she has a beautiful child.'

The babe was brought to Katrina who smiled and kissed the red-faced infant, then returned him to the doctor. 'Show Ahmed to his father,' she said. 'Thank you, doctor. I shall do well with my women now.'

'My lady.' He bowed to her and took the child away.

'Do you not wish to feed and hold him yourself?' Harriet asked and Katrina shook her head.

'His wet-nurses will care for him. Kahlid will allow me to have him for a few hours a day, but it is not fitting that I should have him with me all the time. He must learn to be a man and a prince. When he is old enough to learn with the others we shall teach him, Harriet. He will be special to you as well as me, because you were here when he was born.'

'I am not sure I shall be allowed to teach the children…after what I did…'

Katrina reached for her hand. 'The Caliph can refuse me nothing now that I have given him his son. He has others, but my son will be special, the next in line after Hassan—the other sons are from the women of the harem, not his wives. None of them has given him a son, apart from Hassan's mother.'

'Then your son is special indeed.' Harriet smiled at her. 'I am glad I was permitted to be with you, Katrina.'

'I asked that you be with me during this time. You will not be able to live near me, as I once hoped, for you are to be taken to Kasim's harem, but we shall see each other when I come to the schoolroom. We are to share the teaching, because Kahlid does not want me to tire myself too much. The doctor has told him I must rest.'

Harriet struggled to take in all that she was being told.

'I am to live in Kasim's harem?'

'Kahlid told me he has given you to him. Kasim has been ordered to teach you to behave in a more seemly way.'

'I see…' Harriet bit her lip.

'It will not be so very bad, Harriet. Kasim is very popular with the ladies of his harem. I am sure you will be happy in time, and we shall meet when we teach the children together. My husband, Kahlid, was very angry and he spoke of having you executed, but he seems to have accepted that it was meant to be.'

'Kismet?' Harriet was puzzled. 'Why has he relented?'

'You have been forgiven for my sake,' Katrina said. Her eyes dropped away. 'The eunuch who helped your cousin to escape has been punished.' Harriet gasped and Katrina held her hand tighter.

'Do not look so distressed, Harriet. He rushed at the Janissaries with a sword and died in battle—an honourable death for any man.'

Harriet blinked away the tears. 'He was a brave man. I do not know why he did what he did for us—he must have known the price he would pay if he were caught.'

'I think that perhaps he hated what was done to him,' Katrina offered. 'And he hated those who made him less than a man. Rather than continue his life as he was, he chose a warrior's death.'

'I feel responsible,' Harriet said and brushed a hand over her eyes. 'He died because of us.'

'He died because he wished it,' Katrina said. 'Think what life must have been for him.'

'If you understand him…why…?' Harriet's words died away for she could not ask such a question of her friend.

'Why am I happy as Kahlid's wife?' Katrina smiled sadly. 'I have always known about these things. They are as they are and I have no power to change them. Perhaps one day customs will evolve and change, but I shall play no part in that change. I am spoiled and indulged, and I may sometimes beg a favour, as I did in your case—but I may not demand. I may not ask why a thing must be as it is.' Katrina smiled. 'I am loved and I love. I ask for no more.'

Harriet looked at her, then nodded. 'Yes, I do understand how you feel, Katrina. In my own country it was not so very different. My father loved and indulged me. My brother is lazy and content to leave the estate to my care—but I knew that there was a line over which I must not step. The Queen is powerful enough to make men listen to her, but there are few women with her power—though a few achieve something like. In our house my mother might have been a queen for she ruled my father's heart, and I would have been content with a life such as hers.'

'So you are not so very different from us,' Katrina said. 'Kahlid's first wife would never bend to him and I believe she did much good for the slaves while she lived. Try to be happy, Harriet. I cannot ask for you to be set free. It would only anger Kahlid.' She lay back against the pillows with a sigh. 'Sit with me while I sleep and then someone will come to take you to your new apartments.'

Harriet sat back, holding her hand until she knew Katrina was asleep. Her heart was full and she felt close to tears. She had fought against her imprisonment, but she had no will to resist any longer. Marguerite was free. If they had found the unfortunate eunuch, but not her cousin, then she must be safe. Perhaps she was on a ship bound for England by now. Harriet was happy for her sake.

There would be no rescue for her. Harriet's instincts told her that she was lucky to have escaped worse punishment. However, she would be watched constantly from now on. They knew how Marguerite had managed to leave the harem gardens. That way would be secured. One man would not be trusted with the key. The other eunuchs would know what had happened and would not be tempted unless they too wished for death, and it was unlikely that another martyr would be found. Her uncle had his daughter back. Her brother would be distressed for a while, but he had his wife and his children. After a while Harriet would be forgotten.

A part of her kicked against her fate and longed for freedom, and yet another part of her knew that her life in the palace need not be so very terrible, if she were allowed to teach the children and visit her friends—and she would make new friends if she tried. She might be content if she had what Katrina had. Katrina was loved and she loved. Harriet knew that if she had been told she was to marry Kasim she would be content to live here as his wife, but of course he would not wish to wed her. She was not beautiful like her cousin. Hassan had been horrified when he saw her face. No doubt Kasim had many beautiful women in his harem.

Harriet thought of what was to happen to her now. She would be taken to Kasim's harem, but what would happen then? Did he intend to punish her for what she had done?

'Kasim has come for you. He waits outside.'

The woman's voice broke into her thoughts making her start. She rose and glanced at Katrina. 'Let your mistress sleep for a while. She is very tired.'

'Yes, my lady.' The woman bowed to her respect-fully. Harriet smiled inwardly. It seemed she had become a person of some importance, at least as far as the serving women were concerned.

Kasim was waiting outside the door of Katrina's

apartment. Harriet looked at him, but he would not meet her eyes nor would he smile.

'Have you come to take me to your harem?'

Kasim looked at a point beyond her shoulder, his face unsmiling. 'Who told you? Katrina, I suppose?'

'She said that I had been forgiven for her sake.'

'Then you must be grateful to her.' Kasim's expression was set in grim lines. 'The Caliph may have given you to me, but there will be punishment, Harriet. Or did you imagine that one night in the cells was sufficient for what you have done?'

'No, I expect to be punished.'

'It is my right and my duty. You broke one of the cardinal rules.'

'Are you still angry with me?'

'Whether I feel anger or not does not matter,' Kasim replied without looking at her. 'You did something unforgivable. It is only because I am Kahlid's most trusted adviser that I have been given the task of disciplining you.'

'Yes, I see…' Harriet swallowed hard. 'You can be trusted more than the eunuchs at the moment.'

'Exactly.' A little nerve flicked in his cheek. 'The man has been punished.'

'I hear he chose his death—the death of a man rather than the thing your Caliph made him.'

Kasim turned on her, eyes blazing. 'Watch your tongue, lady. Do not speak so carelessly of things you do not understand. You have escaped punishment thus far, but be careful. You might have died in a way that would be unbearable. Please show a proper modesty and do not force me to treat you harshly.'

She glanced at him and saw a pulse working in his throat. He did care what happened to her! Her heart caught and some of her distress eased. Katrina was right, life in Kasim's harem might not be so bad— except that she thought she might come to like him too much. If she gave her heart to this man, he would surely break it.

'You care what happens to me?'

'Do you think me a cold-hearted monster? Of course I care! I brought you here.' His face worked with some kind of emotion. She could not be sure whether it was guilt, shame or some other deeper emotion. 'I could have sailed away and taken you with me. I bitterly regret I did not listen to your plea.' For a moment as he faced her she saw so many conflicting emotions that she was not truly sure what was in his mind. 'Had I my time again…but it is useless. What is done is done.'

'Kismet?' Harriet smiled sadly. 'Perhaps that is true. I did not believe it once, but that was another time…another world…'

'Harriet…' Kasim stopped and looked at her, then shook his head and indicated the door ahead of them. 'We have arrived.'

Harriet drew her breath in sharply as the door was opened by unseen eunuchs. She entered followed closely by Kasim and saw that the Caliph and his son were seated on silken couches. They watched as Harriet and Kasim approached, but did not stand, as

English gentlemen would have done in the presence of a lady.

'You should kneel to the Caliph,' Kasim's voice said softly behind her. 'You will beg his forgiveness and also the prince. You will apologise for any insult and plead your ignorance.'

Harriet ignored him. Instead she made a reverent curtsy. When she looked up again, she noticed a smile of amusement on the Caliph's face and his son was laughing.

'Is something amusing, my lord?' She broke the cardinal rule and addressed the Caliph without being invited.

'Forgive me, lady,' the Caliph replied. 'You remind us of a lady we both loved. Prince Hassan's mother would never kneel to me. I did my best to make her once, but in the end I was forced to concede. I may be powerful, but I know when I am beaten.'

'Indeed?' Harriet looked from father to son, feeling wary. Were they genuinely amused or was this merely the calm before the storm? 'You asked that I should attend you, lord—Prince Hassan.'

'I wanted you to understand that Kasim is now your master. He asked for you and as a favour to the man I love as another son I gave him his wish. You must be properly grateful to him, and you must give me your word that you will not help more slaves to escape.'

Harriet thought about what they were asking her. If she gave her word, she would be bound by it for she did not take an oath lightly.

'I would give my word—if certain dispensations were granted.'

'Indeed?' The Caliph rose to his feet. He was a large powerful man and his mouth had gone hard, all trace of indulgence gone. Harriet breathed deeply to calm herself. 'You demand where you should thank me for my generosity. You make conditions when you should beg my pardon.'

'You have been generous, my lord,' Harriet replied. Her head lifted as she gave him back his stern look and stood her ground. 'My cousin's escape was my fault and no other—I shall give my promise but no one else is to be punished and Mellina is to be restored to her duties and privileges, and the eunuchs who brought me to you that night should be given back their privileges, for they could not have known who I was. I alone am to blame and I shall accept the punishment my lord Kasim thinks fit.'

The Caliph glared down at her for some moments, then he smiled. 'I think Kasim is luckier than we knew. As for your request, since it was in my mind to do all that you have asked, it shall be done at once...' His eyes narrowed. 'We have your word?'

'I shall not run away or assist others to do so—and I shall endeavour to do whatever is required of me. This is my promise as an English gentlewoman.' Harriet was proud that her voice did not tremble, for she was well aware what her duties might entail. As a member of Kasim's harem he could command her to his bed, if he wished.

'Then I shall accept your word,' the Caliph said

and nodded, a gleam in his eyes. He turned to Kasim and smiled. 'I believe Allah has blessed you, my son. As for you, Hassan, another more suitable bride will be found—and while we wait you may choose any woman from my harem, except Fortunata.'

Hassan looked eager, pleased with his father's promise. 'I wish you joy of your houri, brother,' he said to Kasim. 'She is not as beautiful as her cousin, but I like her spirit.'

'I thank my brother and my father the Caliph,' Kasim said and made them both a deep and reverent bow. 'The Caliph knows that he has my undying gratitude for his mercy. Come, Harriet, it is time for you to see your new home.'

He held out his hand to her and, after hesitating for a moment, Harriet took it. Her hand trembled for an instant as his strong fingers curled around hers in a manner she could only think possessive. She looked at him, and seeing the gleam of satisfaction in his eyes, felt a spasm in her stomach. Since they came to the palace, Kasim had been forced to keep his distance from her, because she was a part of the Caliph's harem, but now she belonged to him. She had a feeling that her life was about to change considerably.

She lifted her head, refusing to be nervous, then glanced at him sideways. 'Are you angry because I disobeyed you?'

'You were fortunate that Kahlid was in an indulgent mood. You reminded him of Anna. He loved his first wife because she was proud and spirited and would never kneel to him, even though she loved him. He threatened that he would have her whipped once and he gave her nothing but bread and water for three days, but in the end he kneeled to her and begged for her forgiveness.'

Harriet turned to look at him, surprise in her eyes. 'The Caliph knelt to a woman? I did not think he would do such a thing. Is he not all-powerful here?'

Kasim laughed. 'Kahlid is a man as other men, Harriet. When a man loves he is vulnerable, because the woman holds his heart within her hand. You may think our rules strange and even harsh, but we guard our women to keep them safe from harm.'

'Yet if a woman loves she would not betray the man she loves. So why does she need to be kept in seclusion away from all other men?'

'Kahlid's wives see other men of the family,' Hassan told her. 'Especially on celebration days. We shall have a celebration tomorrow for the birth of Katrina's son.'

'What happens on a celebration day?'

'We have feasting and sports and contests of strength. My brother Hassan may take part in the wrestling. I prefer other sports.'

'Hassan is your brother?'

'My blood brother.' Kasim turned his head to look at her. 'When he was ten years of age his father was at war with one of the hill tribes. Their leader sent men to try and kill Kahlid but they could not get close to him. They found Hassan watching the Janissaries training in the courtyard and thought to capture him for a ransom or worse, but when he struggled, one of them threatened to kill him. I saw what was happening and fought my way to him, snatched him from the renegade and then killed the assassin. Hassan was bleeding from a wound to his leg. I stopped the bleeding and delivered him to the physician who nursed him. He made a full recovery. Kahlid believed my action saved Hassan's life—and perhaps his too.'

'I see…that is why you are considered family?'

'Kahlid calls me his second son. I have devoted my life to his cause and…must continue to do so.'

'So that is why you would not take me to England.'

'It is a part of the reason. There are others, but I shall not burden you with them now.'

'I should like to understand you better,' Harriet said, watching the little pulse flicking in his throat. 'Could we not try to like each other?'

'You would be my friend?' Kasim smiled oddly. 'Do you hope to avoid your punishment, Harriet?'

'No! I just thought…' She sighed and shook her head. 'I have thought perhaps we might like each other very well if we tried.'

Kasim had stopped walking. 'These are your rooms, Harriet.'

A door was opened and Harriet walked into a spacious covered courtyard, which led into delightful gardens. Everywhere there was water and the perfume of flowers. The marble floors had a hint of turquoise blue in little jewelled insets, and the

walls were pink. The sleeping chamber was large
with silken couches and smaller ones for sitting, and
a white cat had made itself at home on one of them.
There were chests of dark carved wood and a cabi-
net inlaid with ivory and mother of pearl, its shelves
filled with small figurines and delicate carvings.

'How lovely,' Harriet said after she had
glanced round. 'Do they connect with your own
apartments?'

'Yes, through the gardens. In the mornings either I
or one of the eunuchs will conduct you to the schoolroom as usual so that you may continue to teach the
children. Kahlid is pleased with their progress. He
wishes all his children to speak English as well as I
do, because the English are a proud strong nation and
they trade more and more with countries of the east.
He believes that the Sultan must learn to accept these
things and to trade, as the English do. Otherwise, our
country will lag behind in developments.'

'Thank you for explaining these things to me.'
Harriet smiled at him. 'You have told me more today
than at any time before or since I came to the palace. I
am beginning to understand things that were strange
to me.'

Kasim looked at her for a moment. She thought
there was a wistful expression in his eyes, as if he
wished for something more but would not ask.

'I shall leave you to become accustomed to
your new quarters. When I have gone your women
will come to make themselves known. Tell me,

Harriet—is there anything more you wish for that I may give you?'

'I should like some books…fables about your country, herbals for making medicines and cures so that I may help if one of the women is unwell…and a dog, if that is possible. I should also like to ride with you sometimes, if it would be permitted?'

'I shall bring you some of my books this evening, and we shall talk. You should begin your instruction in the faith. If you are to live here, it is right that you understand us and our customs.'

'Are they truly your customs?' Harriet looked at him curiously. 'I thought you might have adopted them simply so that you could live here and prosper.'

'I might once have considered returning to England to live, though there are reasons why I have stayed away this long. However, that time has gone. Make no mistake, Harriet. I am bound to this place whether I wish it or not.'

'I thought you were free to leave whenever you chose?'

'Things are altered. My life is here. I must make of it what I can—as must you, Harriet, since you gave your word not to escape.'

'I shall try to do as you wish.'

'When I go hunting with my hawks I shall take you with me. It may not be so very bad for you here, Harriet.'

'Thank you. If I have books and the opportunity to ride now and then, I shall be content.'

'I hope that you will learn to accept,' Kasim said, his eyes narrowed. 'There is the matter of your punishment. I have decided that you will spend two weeks working in the infirmary. There are several Janissaries unwell and I think it will help both them and you if you tend them. Once you have served your sentence you will be allowed to resume your visits with the children and Katrina.'

'You wish me to help nurse the sick?'

'Yes. You will be allowed to attend the celebration tomorrow. After that you will be taken to the infirmary every day for two weeks. Do you accept the punishment as fair?'

Harriet looked at him and tears stung her eyes. 'You do not wish to have me beaten?'

'I think the experience in the infirmary may humble your pride a little, lady. A beating would only make you more rebellious, I believe.'

'Thank you,' she whispered, feeling humbled already by the nature of his decision. 'I do not think I deserve such forbearance from you. I shall be happy to attend the sick Janissaries.'

A wry smile touched his mouth. 'Be careful, Harriet. This is supposed to be a punishment, not a pleasure. I shall leave you to rest and accustom yourself to your new apartments.'

'When shall I see you again?'

'I shall bring books this evening. I am a busy man, for the celebrations need a great deal of organising. This evening…'

Kasim inclined his head to her and went out. For

a moment Harriet stood perfectly still. She did not know what to think. Somehow she had expected him to show her that he was her master…to demand that she yield to him, but that was not his way. She was beginning to know him a little better at last.

Hearing a whispering sound, Harriet looked up and saw three women standing in the entrance to the garden looking at her. Their expressions were uncertain, as if they were not sure what she would be like. All of them were young and pretty, a little older than the daughters she might have had if she had married when her father first took her to court.

'Hello…' she said and held out her hands in welcome. 'Please come in and introduce yourselves.'

Kasim had spent the day between making sure the celebrations would be suitably splendid for the birth of a new prince and visiting the sick Janissaries, who were his true friends here at the palace and one of his reasons for staying here as long as he had. When he was first captured he had been chained as a galley slave; his back was numbed from the constant beatings. He had been cast ashore when he was ill and unable to work. Thrown overboard near the beach at Algiers to die, he might indeed have done so had a fisherman not found him and taken him home to his wife. Azia had taken him in and nursed him back to health. She was a poor woman, yet she asked for no reward.

Grateful for her care, Kasim had hired himself out to a man recruiting for the Caliph's Janissaries and repaid her for her generosity. When he was first taken to the palace he had not been considered strong enough to fight with the elite army and was put to work in the gardens, but as he grew stronger he began to train with them. After the incident with the hill tribesmen, he became a captain of the Caliph's personal guard and then councillor and controller of the household. Gradually, Kahlid had come to trust him more and more, which was why he had chosen to honour him by making him joint Caliph after his death.

Kasim was anxious that Hassan would lose all sense of balance when he was told of the Caliph's decree. He was already restless and hot-headed and Kasim dreaded his reaction.

Thrusting the problem from his mind, Kasim returned to his own rooms. He liked to bathe after the heat of the day and he was thinking of the books he must select for Harriet. She must have the books that would help her learn about the faith and customs, books he had himself studied when he decided to make his life at the palace. A little smile touched his mouth as he thought of their talk earlier. She had clearly been expecting something very different from the punishment he had given her, but it would serve two purposes. One of his particular friends was very ill and he was concerned that Jason was not getting the treatment he needed. Harriet would see that his wound was properly cleansed as the physician instructed.

He smiled as he recalled her offer to be his friend.

Did she imagine that would be enough for him now that she was his? His mind and body shrieked that it was not near enough. He wanted her in his bed, as his lover. This feeling had come slowly, so slowly and quietly, growing like a small seed in his heart and mind, that Kasim had hardly been aware of it until it was almost too late. If she had not thrown back her veiling when she did and stopped the ceremony, she would have been Hassan's wife and beyond his reach.

Perhaps she was still beyond him. Kasim knew that she longed to return to her home and it was in his power to grant her wish. She had given her word not to run away, but he could send her home to her family.

But he could not go with her. No, he could not let her go. She would learn to enjoy her life here. He would show her how good it could be.

For the first time in years, Kasim thought of his home in England. His father had thrown him out of the house in a rage, accusing him of a crime, so foul that it made him sick to his stomach. He was innocent of the crime but he had been a friend of the man who so wickedly abused a young and lovely woman, and had done nothing to stop the abuse even though he had known that his friend planned to abduct her. Therefore, he was guilty by association, and he had not denied his father's accusations. He had left his home, become a privateer and set out to make his fortune, and in a way he had for he was now a wealthy man, much of it gained through trade. Yet everything he had had come from the Caliph. He could never betray his trust or break the promise he had made.

Harriet must be content to stay here. He would not let her go!

Chapter Seven

Kasim saw that Harriet was sitting in the courtyard in the cool of the evening, with the young girls he had chosen to keep as her companions. She was laughing, stroking the white cat he had bought as a pet for her and the others. At that moment she looked happy and perfectly at home in her surroundings.

He walked towards her. She looked up and a smile of such sweetness lit her face that his stomach tied itself in knots and he knew an urgent desire to sweep her into his arms and carry her to his bed. He thought she might respond to him if he taught her the meaning of love, but it was too soon. If he rushed into a passionate seduction, he would never know if she truly wished to stay. He must control the need she aroused and wait, let her come to him when she was ready.

'I have brought the books I promised,' he said and

motioned to the ladies to stay. 'No, I do not wish to disturb you or your friends, Harriet. If I may, I shall sit here with you for a while. Perhaps Catalina would dance for us?'

'Catalina has been attempting to show me how to dance,' Harriet said and smiled. 'She is so graceful. I told her that I could never dance as she does.'

'I should be honoured to dance for my lady and my lord,' Catalina said shyly. 'If Helene will play for us?'

Helene was the oldest of the three girls. She smiled and picked up her lute, beginning to play soft sensual music that accompanied the beautiful dancing performed by Catalina. Natalina ran to fetch a bowl of fruit and offered it to Kasim. He chose a ripe fig and ate it as he watched the dancing, applauding the girls' performances at the end. When they had finished Kasim nodded and they disappeared into the harem. He turned to Harriet.

'You will study these books when you have time and we shall talk about your feelings when you are ready, Harriet.'

'Yes, my lord. I am sure I shall find them interesting. I have always liked to study.'

'But will you believe, I wonder?'

'I cannot promise that I shall believe all I read, my lord, but I shall learn as much as I can.'

'Then that is all I can ask,' Kasim said. 'In the morning you may visit the children for an hour or so until the celebrations begin. One of the eunuchs will take you, because I have much to do. Afterwards, you

should join Katrina and then someone will take you
to the courtyard when it is time.'

'Thank you…for everything.'

'As yet I have done little. I hope you like the girls
I chose to serve you?'

'Yes. To serve *me*…I thought they were your
harem?'

'I have no harem. I freed my houris when I
decided to bring you here. They have returned to
their homes or chosen husbands from amongst the
Janissaries, as they wished.'

'Oh…' Harriet tingled all over. She waited, expect-
ing him to say more. Was she to be his mistress or…?
A feeling of disappointment swept over her as he
inclined his head and turned away. 'Why? I mean—'
She stopped as he turned and raised his brows at her.
She thought there was laughter in his eyes.

'Perhaps one day I shall tell you. Remember, Harriet, at the moment I am still displeased with you.
You have yet to show me that you have learned your
lessons. When you are suitably repentant we shall talk
of many things.'

Harriet felt her cheeks grow hot. She was not sure
how to take this new Kasim. Was he teasing her?
Why had he sent his houris away—and what exactly
did he have in mind for her?

After lessons, which ended early because it was a
day of celebration, Harriet walked to Katrina's apartments. She knew her way so well that she hardly
needed an escort. The palace no longer had the

power to frighten her and she was able to admire its beauty.

Katrina was sitting up against a pile of silken cushions. She had a bowl of fruit beside her and picked a luscious grape from a large bunch, popping it into her mouth. Wiping away the juice, she offered the bowl to Harriet, who shook her head.

'You are waiting for the feasting I suppose.' Katrina sighed. 'Kahlid will not let me attend, because he says I am not strong enough to sit in the afternoon sun. I love to watch the Janissaries fight, though perhaps the wrestling is the most entertaining.'

'Kasim did not come to fetch me after lessons. I think he must be preparing for the celebrations.'

'Yes, he must. He is the champion and he will be one of those who fight in hand-to-hand combat.'

Harriet frowned. 'Please tell me that it is not a fight to the death!'

'In the time of the Caliph's father it was often so,' Katrina said. 'Now it is until one man disarms the other. Kasim will win the gold spear. He always does—I think because he trains harder than any other man.'

'How do you know?'

'There is a way to see…' Katrina looked mischievous. 'I cannot show you today because I am forbidden to leave my couch—but one day I will take you. There are many places where you can watch the men as they train. It is possible to hear and see many things…things my husband would not be pleased for us to see and hear.'

'You are wicked,' Harriet laughed. 'I thought you always obeyed the Caliph?'

'Oh, yes, I do—but what he does not know…' Katrina smiled naughtily. 'There are always ways to learn what you wish to know, Harriet. We are often watched, in the gardens and all the communal rooms. Why should we not use the spy holes to discover what we wish to know?'

Harriet smiled and shook her head at her. Katrina seemed a submissive wife, but clearly she knew how to turn the tables on her husband. 'I suppose forewarned is forearmed?'

'Yes…'

Harriet suspected there was more to tell, but she was summoned by one of the women and at the door she found a eunuch waiting for her.

'The lord Kasim sent me to tell you that you must get ready for the feasting, lady Harriet. In one hour the contests will begin. You will sit with the ladies from the Caliph's harem, for it is the time when you are allowed to mix and talk.'

Harriet thanked him, but she had made few friends in the Caliph's harem. She had deliberately kept herself apart, because she wished to have no regrets when the time came to leave. Her friends were Katrina and the young girls Kasim had assigned as her companions, to whom she felt almost as a mother.

Making her way back to her own apartments, Harriet bathed and then allowed two of the women to help her dress. The eunuchs came to escort them through the palace. Harriet walked ahead as was her right, the other women a few paces behind, their voices like chattering birds as they laughed and fluttered in their excitement.

In the courtyard some huge awnings had been set up to shade the women from the hot sun. They were escorted to the seats, but allowed to sit where they chose. Seeing that Mellina was there, Harriet sat beside her. Mellina turned her head to look at her and then smiled.

'I must thank you, lady. I believe I owe my privileges to you.'

'You owe me nothing. You were not to blame for what happened that day, and I believe the Caliph understood that—once his anger had cooled.'

Mellina nodded. 'Everyone is saying that you are like the prince's mother. When she died the court was in mourning for weeks. They say the Caliph thinks highly of you.'

'I dare say he thinks I am a nuisance,' Harriet replied and laughed. 'I am glad to see you again.'

Their conversation was interrupted by a fanfare and then several Janissaries rode into the arena. They were dressed in ceremonial style in scarlet and gold and rode magnificent horses, whose coats gleamed from grooming.

A display of daring riding began, with men hanging half out of the saddle to spear a target with their swords. Others rode bareback or stood on their horse's back and balanced as it careered around the arena at speed.

Applause greeted the end of this display, which was followed by other demonstrations of skill. Archery, spear throwing and feats of jumping, dancing and fire eating kept the crowd roaring their approval, and the ladies of the harem were as excited as any of the common folk who had been allowed to gather and watch.

After a pause when fruit and sherbet was offered to the ladies, the contests began in earnest. There was wrestling between evenly matched combatants and this brought more roars of approval from the crowd. Harriet had thought that Kasim might take part in the wrestling, though Hassan won his bout easily. He took his applause and then went to sit with his father. She was a little disappointed that Kasim did not appear, nor as she looked round the courtiers sitting with the Caliph and his son was he anywhere to be seen. It seemed odd and she was beginning to wonder why when a fanfare announced the highlight of the day. The matched fights were about to begin.

The first fight was between two well-matched gladiators, for such they were. Harriet could not help comparing the fight that ensued with the fights, which had taken place in the arena at the Coliseum at Rome, that she had read about in her father's manuscripts. The match was won by a man with dark skin, who had used a net and a trident to defeat his opponent's sword and shield. After them came two more who fought with swords and shields, and then, when Harriet had almost given up expecting it, Kasim entered the arena to roars of approval. He was carrying a golden spear, which he thrust into the ground, it seemed, as a challenge.

Harriet gasped as the winners of the last two bouts walked into the arena. Surely he did not mean to fight both of them at the same time? A shiver ran down her spine and she could barely watch as the men began to circle him. How could he fight two men at the same time?

When she looked again, she saw that Kasim had removed his tunic. His back was tanned to a deep gold and she could see the muscles flexing as he moved against his first opponent. The crowd roared encouragement, but Harriet closed her eyes. She could not bear to watch, because she was sure he would be wounded and perhaps killed. Why was he fighting two opponents?

'Do not be afraid for him, princess.' Mellina's voice was soft and reassuring in her ear. 'The lord Kasim has won against bigger odds before this. He scorns to fight only one man.'

'But...' Harriet's words were drowned as Kasim sent the first man to his knees and the crowd rose to its feet as the second was dispatched soon after. The fight was over quickly, though to Harriet it had seemed an eternity. 'Is it over now?'

'For today,' Mellina told her. 'We shall feast now—and tomorrow there will be other games and other fights to watch. It has been a fine sight, has it not?'

'Yes...I suppose so.' Harriet saw that Kasim was being carried round the arena in triumph. When he was set down before the Caliph, he was invited to join them. She found it difficult to take her eyes from him and wished she might be there to hear what was being said. Kasim turned to look at her and inclined his head. She returned his look, but gave no sign of approval, though other ladies were cheering and throwing scarves into the arena.

She was pleased when the ladies began to move back into the palace for the feasting that would take place inside and attempted to follow them. A eunuch barred her away, bowing to her and directing her towards a smaller group of ladies, who were being segregated from the others. For a moment she felt a flutter of alarm, then realised that the other women looked excited and pleased.

'You are being taken to feast with the Caliph and your lord,' Mellina said. 'The rest of us return to the harem to feast and dance by ourselves.'

Harriet nodded. She followed the small group of ladies into the cool of the palace, shivering a little as they were shepherded towards a large open room where silken couches had been set up on a dais and large cushions set all about the room. She was directed towards the dais with Fortunata and various other ladies of the harem. The Caliph and Hassan came in a moment or two later and then Kasim, who had changed into his usual plain white robes with gold leather slippers and a red belt. His eyes sought and held Harriet's for a moment before he spoke to Hassan and took his place on a couch on the Caliph's right side—she was seated with some of the other ladies to Kasim's left. Hassan had chosen to lounge on some cushions close to the women.

The Caliph was laughing at something Kasim had said to him. Hassan leaned over to Harriet with mischief in his eyes. 'My father says that you do not approve of our contests, lady. He says you had your eyes closed for most of the time Kasim was fighting. Kasim says you do not approve of him at all.'

'Kasim likes to mock me,' she replied.

'Kasim needs a wife to tame him,' Hassan whispered to her.

'Does he?' she asked, her throat tight.

'Of course. I have told him he should take a wife, but he says he does not wish to be nagged.' He chuckled. 'I have heard that he often summons three of his women to his bed at one time.'

Harriet's cheeks flushed, but she said nothing, staring straight ahead as the entertainment began.

A troupe of specially trained dancers, both men and women, moved rhythmically to the music. As the music and dancing continued, a succession of servants offered food and sherbet to the guests: platters of delicious spiced chicken, lamb in rich sauces and wonderful fruit and the rich dark coffee so beloved of the harem.

Was it true that Kasim summoned three women all at once? Were they the three girls that he kept to serve her? Though he'd told her he'd dismissed his harem she knew that he must have enjoyed women's company many times in the past. The thought was painful and humiliating. She tried to dismiss Hassan's careless words, but it was like an unpleasant taste in the mouth and would not go away.

She was not aware that Kasim had moved until he spoke to her and she saw that he had changed places with Hassan.

'Are you not enjoying yourself, Harriet?'

'I have a headache, my lord. I wonder if I may be allowed to retire early?'

'Yes, of course. I shall escort you to your quarters.'

'Please, do not leave the feasting on my account. I am sure I can find my own way.'

'I shall take you, Harriet.' He rose to his feet, offering her his hand. 'I have more to do than watch the dancing and feast.' He turned to Caliph. 'If my lord will excuse us.'

Harriet rose to her feet. She bowed to the Caliph and Hassan, asking them to forgive her, and then followed Kasim from the room. She could still hear the music as they walked together through the palace to Kasim's apartments. At the door of her apartments, Kasim stopped and looked at her in silence for a moment; then he bowed his head and left her without speaking. He was angry with her again! Did he think she was sulking? Harriet had given no sign of her feelings, but once she was inside her own apartments she was aware of the silence. Her serving women came running, anxious to please her, but she smiled and sent them away. She wanted nothing but peace and privacy. As she lay down on her couch the tears trickled down her cheeks, but she brushed them away impatiently.

She should have known that Kasim would be no different from his royal masters! He had embraced their way of life. Kasim had lied to her. He had kept three of his women because he favoured them and he sent for all three to pleasure him at once. Harriet did not know why that upset her so much.

Dismissing the painful thoughts, she sought her couch, but it was a while before she finally slept.

Harriet woke suddenly. She opened her eyes and was startled to see Kasim bending over her. It was still dark so she estimated it must be the early hours of the morning.

'Forgive me,' he said as she sat up and looked at him apprehensively. 'Will you put on your clothes and come with me, please? Jason is worse and I need help to change his dressings.'

'Yes, certainly,' Harriet agreed instantly. 'Please turn your back as I change.'

'As you wish. I did not come here to ravish you, merely to beg for your help.'

'Did you not summon the physician?'

'He is an old man and I did not wish to disturb his rest. Besides, I am not certain his treatments are helping my friend. I should have brought in a younger man, but Kahlid will not offend an old friend.'

'I thought him very efficient when he tended Katrina. It may be that your friend is beyond help.'

'I suppose that is true. Yet I think he can be helped.'

'Perhaps what he needs is proper nursing.' Harriet picked up the long fine scarf she wore draped over her shoulders and sometimes used to cover her head. 'You may turn, my lord. I am dressed.'

'Come with me. Jason was burning up earlier.'

'He may have a fever. Sometimes it helps to bathe a sick person with cool water, as you suggested for Marguerite on the ship. It helped her, and I think it will often ease a patient's rest.'

'You have had some experience of nursing?'

'I was my father's nurse for two years—and when my brother was young he often had fevers. Thankfully, he has grown out of them now.'

'You have a brother?'

'Lord Sefton-Jones,' Harriet replied. 'He must believe me dead—unless Marguerite has told him I am here. Perhaps you would permit me to write to him and set his mind at rest?'

'We shall speak of this another time.'

'Of course. You must be worried for your friend.'

'Yes. I think of Jason as a good friend. I should not wish him to die of neglect.'

Harriet nodded, but said no more as she followed him. He led her out of the palace by the route she had been taken the night she was imprisoned. However, they passed the cells and walked on to the building that housed the infirmary.

Inside it was tiled, cool and clean like the palace.

There was a long room with many mattresses on the floor, but Kasim took her to a small room where his friend lay alone. The first thing she noticed was that the room was very warm.

'Why is he covered with that blanket?' She placed her hand on the man's forehead. 'He is very hot. I think we should bathe him before we change the bandages.'

'You will not object to such a task?'

'Why should I?' Harriet smiled. 'I thought my duty in the infirmary was supposed to be a punishment?'

'For some it would be. I once asked someone else to help me, but she was horrified. She wept and begged to be given some other punishment if she had offended me.'

'And had she?' Harriet asked as she fetched water from a jug, pouring it into a small metal bowl.

'No, I merely needed help with one of the wounded.'

'Do you often concern yourself with the sick?' She had pulled back the covers, a little relieved when she saw that the man's lower half was covered by a white loincloth. 'You will permit me, my lord?'

'Yes, of course. Do what you can for him please.'

'Leave the door open so that the air can circulate. It is very warm in here.'

Harriet smoothed the cool cloth over the man's limbs. Kasim looked on thoughtfully, helping to turn the patient so that she could bathe his back.

'I think the servants here would not have considered bathing Jason to cool him.'

'A physician once advised it for my brother. I often did it for him, because he complained the nurse was too rough.'

'I can see you are gentle.'

Harriet finished her task. She turned her head and saw the speculative expression in his eyes. A little flush came to her cheeks and she dropped her gaze.

'Shall we change the dressing now?'

'Yes, if you can bear it. His wound is not a pleasant sight.'

Harriet waited as he cut the stained bandages away with a knife. The wound to the unconscious Jason's leg was red and angry, but after looking at it carefully and gently prodding the flesh she thought it clean and said as much to Kasim.

'Yes, I think you are right. It has begun to heal at last. If the fever would break, he might begin to recover,' he said as the patient moaned and flung out his arms.

'I think he was not helped by the warm room. Could not a mesh of some kind be fixed over the windows so that the shutters may be left open at night?'

'Some kind of netting might be provided to stop the insects that are attracted to the lamps,' Kasim said. 'I will have the work set in hand as soon as the day begins. I had not fully understood the need to keep the patients cool.' He had brought out salves and clean linen. She helped him by lifting the patient's leg, but saw that he was well able to do whatever was necessary. 'Now I need to give him some of the fever mixture the physician left. I need one part to three parts water.' He mixed a dark liquid in a metal cup. 'Will you see if he will drink if I lift him?'

'Yes, certainly. He may not drink…unless we do this…' She put her forefinger and thumb to Jason's nose and pinched. He opened his mouth and the mixture went down.

Kasim laughed. 'I have not seen that done before. Jason often refuses to take his medicine.'

'My brother was the same.' Harriet smiled. 'I think your friend is not as ill as you feared, my lord. He is settling now and should be better in a little.'

'I thank you for your help, Harriet.'

'It was nothing, my lord. I hope you will rest easier after this?'

'Yes, I shall. We will leave him to rest. You should lie in in the morning. The children will not miss one day's schooling.'

'I shall visit our patient again after I break my fast and then I may spend an hour or so with Katrina—if you permit?'

'Of course. You did not need to ask. There are rules we all must obey here, Harriet. If you follow them, you will be free to move within the palace more or less as you please, though there are certain areas where you should not go without permission.'

'You are gracious, my lord. I shall try to observe all the rules, but you must instruct me.'

'You are too meek, lady.' His gaze was intent as he looked at her. 'What are you planning? I am not sure I believe in this new Harriet.'

'I was merely trying to show you that I have repented—as you instructed, my lord.'

'I did not wish to crush your spirit.'

'You have not, my lord.' Harriet shot him a mischievous glance. 'I thought you wished me to be submissive—was that not your intention? Is it not a woman's place to obey her master?'

'You mock me?'

'I would rather call it teasing, my lord.'

'Indeed?' He smiled wryly. 'I am given my own back, am I not? I believe that your punishment may not be enough. I may have to think of something more suitable.'

'May I enquire the nature of this further punishment?'

'No, Harriet, you may not. Be assured that it will fall when you least expect it.'

She was betrayed into a laugh. 'I do not know if that is meant to frighten me?'

Kasim's smile had vanished. 'Why did you not wish to stay for the feasting last night? I thought you were unhappy…perhaps bored by the dancing?'

'No, of course not. It was beautiful and the food was good…' She shook her head. 'I had something on my mind. It was foolish of me.'

Kasim's eyes narrowed. 'You did not approve of the fighting either. The contests are a part of our culture. You must learn to enjoy these things, Harriet—or I fear your life will be very dull.'

'I did not disapprove of the music or the fighting.'

'But you closed your eyes while I was fighting… why?' Kasim reached out and caught her wrist, forcing her to look at him. 'Something is bothering you, Harriet. You must tell me!'

'Please, let me go. You are hurting me.'

'Nonsense! Don't look at me like that,' Kasim said and his intense look sent shivers down her spine. 'Why could you not watch me? Were you afraid I should lose?'

'I did not care if you lost…' Her voice caught as she felt the pressure of his fingers increase. 'I was afraid you might be hurt.'

Kasim stared at her and then laughed and released her. 'Has no one told you that I have won every year for the past eight years? You had no need to fear for me, lady. Besides, it was not a fight to the death. When we fight the fierce tribes from the north, then you may be concerned for me, but not in a contest amongst my friends.'

'I see…' Harriet turned her face aside, her heart racing as she saw something in his eyes. For a short time as they shared the nursing of Jason, she had felt close to him, but she must not be deceived! He had kept the women he favoured in his bed. 'Yes, you have made friends here. You follow all their customs.'

Kasim's eyes narrowed. He looked at her for a

moment longer and then smiled. 'Do I, Harriet? What have you heard whispered of me I wonder? It is amazing how gossip spreads in the palace. You should not believe all the women tell you. They have nothing to do but spend their days in idle chatter.'

'It was not a woman…' Harriet blushed as he laughed huskily, clearly thinking her jealous and amused. 'You need not explain to me. Besides, it had nothing to do with my headache.'

'The celebrations continue tomorrow. Do you wish me to ask Kahlid if you may be excused?'

'No, of course not. The celebrations are to mark the birth of Katrina's son. Besides, it was quite enjoyable yesterday…some of the time.'

'I am glad that you enjoyed some of the celebrations. Remember, it is unwise to listen to gossip. Anything you should know, I shall tell you.'

Harriet inclined her head. She could never ask if what Hassan had told her was true, and she must learn to forget it. Yet she was aware of a stupid little pain in her heart, though she was ashamed of herself for feeling jealous of the girls who had welcomed her to their hearts so openly. Why should she care who he summoned to his bed?

The trouble was, she was beginning to care too much.

As soon as she had broken her fast later that morning, Harriet went to the infirmary. She had expected that she might encounter some strange looks or be questioned as to her business, but the bare-footed servants greeted her with smiles, seeming to know just who she was and why she had come. Going into the room where the patient she had tended earlier was lying propped up against some soft cushions, she discovered that he was awake and the fever had broken.

He looked at her a little oddly, then apologised in broken English for having troubled her sleep the previous night.

'My lord tell me the lady English come help me…' he said and grinned at her. 'My lord lucky devil…he say I no tell you, but is true.'

'I am glad to see you recovered, sir,' she told him. 'Kasim was concerned for you, but I think your wound is recovering well.'

'I soon better…thank you lady English…'

'I shall come to see you tomorrow. I am glad to see you so much better.'

Harriet toured the other ward, noting one or two changes that she thought could be made for the comfort of the patients. She would say nothing yet, but when she was serving her punishment here she would speak to Kasim about the mattresses, some of which looked as if they were fit only for the bonfire.

After leaving the infirmary, she paid a quick visit to the schoolroom. She knew that one of the Caliph's lesser wives would be with the children, but she wanted to see them for a few moments, because she was growing fond of them. As she entered the schoolroom, she found Lisbet, the pretty daughter of the Caliph's third wife, crying. She clung to Harriet and complained of a stomach ache, but when nursed on Harriet's lap while she read a story of fables to the children, her tears quietened and she was happy again when the bell sounded and the children were fetched by their nurses.

Harriet had stopped only for half an hour, then hurried to Katrina's apartments. When she entered, she discovered that a man she had never seen before was with the Caliph's wife. From the flushed look on Katrina's face, she guessed that something had upset her.

'Excuse me, I should not have come without sending word…'

'Do not go, Harriet. Jamail is my brother—and he is just leaving.'

The man directed a look full of meaning at Katrina and then left the room without glancing at Harriet. She approached Katrina's couch, feeling awkward. Was it within the rules for Katrina's brother to be here with her alone?

'Please do not tell Kasim my brother was here,' Katrina said anxiously, confirming her doubts. 'He should not have come. I did not wish it…he is reckless and he tries to bully me.'

'You should have called the eunuchs, Katrina.'

'It would cause trouble and I did not wish him punished, but I wish he would not say such things to me.'

'What kind of things?'

'He was trying to make me…he says I should

persuade Kahlid that my son should be the heir, because I am of good family and Hassan's mother was an Englishwoman. He says that if Hassan becomes Caliph one day the tribes will not accept him.'

'If the Caliph heard him say such things he would be angry,' Harriet said, anxious for her friend. 'You must not allow him to speak to you like that, Katrina—even if you care for him.'

'I do not. He is a bully and I wish he would not visit me. He has the right to visit sometimes, but I would prefer it to be when Kahlid is with me.'

'Tell the eunuchs he is not to be admitted again— and if I were you, I should tell your husband what he said to you.'

'I dare not.' Katrina turned pale. 'He would have Jamail captured and put to death—and he might punish me too. He loves Hassan and would protect him, though Jamail is right. Hassan will not be a popular ruler, because he is too hot-tempered.'

'Be careful, Katrina. Someone may be listening. For your own sake you should speak to the Caliph.'

'You will not tell Kasim?'

'You know I would do nothing to harm you. I merely say that if it were me I would tell Kahlid. He would honour you for speaking honestly—and he would make sure that your brother could not distress you again.'

'Perhaps...' Katrina sighed. 'I wish I were as brave as you, Harriet. Everyone admires you. Kahlid told me that you are like Anna—the wife he loved and honoured above all others.'

'I am not very brave,' Harriet said. 'But you are my friend and I do not wish you to be in trouble.'

'Let us talk of something else,' Katrina said. 'I have persuaded Kahlid that I am strong enough to watch the celebrations this afternoon. He says that I may as long as I do not tire myself. He says he has a special announcement to make. He would not tell me what, but I think it is important for he is anxious.' Katrina sighed. 'I think he is not well, but he will not admit it. If he should die…I should not want to return to my home. I would rather stay here, even if I must be in purdah.'

'Do not talk of such things. They will only distress you,' Harriet said. 'I am sure there would always be a place for you as Ahmed's mother.'

'Perhaps…' Katrina reached for her fan. 'You should change for the celebrations, Harriet. I shall see you this afternoon.'

Harriet had returned to her own apartments and changed into fresh clothes for the celebrations that afternoon. Summoned to the courtyard, she sat with Katrina under an awning nearer to the Caliph and apart from the other women. Harriet wondered why she had been given such an honour. Glancing at the Caliph, she saw him looking at her. He inclined his head and smiled, seeming to approve of her. Perhaps she had been forgiven for what she had done the night she took Marguerite's place.

The celebrations were much the same as the previous day. Dancing and demonstrations of various feats of skill were played out for the audience, and then the wrestling began. Once again Hassan took part and won easily. Next came the matched pairs of gladiatorial fighters. She was surprised when one of the Janissaries came and bowed to her and Katrina after he had won his bout.

'I dedicate my win to the Lord Kasim's English lady,' he said in a loud voice. Cheers and laughter met his salutation, making her blush. 'May you bear my lord a son with the heart of a lion.'

Harriet felt her cheeks grow hot. She glanced at the Caliph and saw that he was nodding his head in agreement. For a moment she wanted to run from the courtyard, but she conquered her embarrassment and inclined her head, at which point there was wild cheering.

Harriet knew that Katrina was looking at her with a smile of indulgence. Did they all believe that Kasim had taken her to his bed?

'I have no doubt that the sons you bear Kasim will be lions,' Katrina told her. 'He is as brave and bold a warrior as he is a god of love…though do not tell Kahlid I said that, please. I am not supposed to listen to gossip, but the women whisper that he has the stamina of a lion.'

Harriet made no comment. As yet Kasim had left her to sleep alone. She was not even certain that he desired her, though once or twice she had seen something in his eyes that made her heart race.

As if on cue, Kasim walked into the arena. Her heart caught a beat as she saw that this time he was pitted against three opponents. Dear God! How could he possibly win against such odds? Her heart was in her mouth as the men circled him warily, but she forced herself to watch, her hands clenched in her lap, the nails digging into the palms as she willed herself to show no emotion. After a while, she began to realise that it was a display of skill rather than an actual fight. She breathed more easily as one of the opponents was forced to surrender, then the second lost his weapon and retired. Now it was only the last, but he was as skilled as Kasim and they were well matched, their fight seeming to go on interminably. Then, suddenly, Kasim slipped and the other warrior put his sword to his throat. The contest had ended according to the rules and Kasim had lost.

Harriet's heart jerked. Would he be upset or angry because he was no longer the supreme champion? She was surprised to see the two men embrace and then Kasim wrenched his spear from the ground and gave it to the man, who was clearly his friend. His words carried clearly to Harriet.

'I give you best, Rachid. Take the gold spear. I pass on the champion's mantle to you and applaud your skill.'

'You will win it back next time…'

Kasim shook his head. 'There will not be a next time. I have decided to retire from the lists and leave the field to others.'

There was a stunned silence and then cries of disappointment from the crowd.

'No! No! No!'

The slow chant went on until Kasim held up his hand. 'Rachid is a worthy champion. There are others to take up the challenge. Next time I shall enter the wrestling. Your prince and I have a score to settle.'

Hassan leapt to his feet, clearly excited. 'Is that a challenge?'

'If you will have it so.' Kasim grinned at him, then looked at the Caliph. 'Shall we settle it tomorrow, my lord?'

'Yes, yes, yes…' the crowd chanted, clearly intrigued by this new contest. 'Tomorrow, tomorrow, tomorrow.'

The Caliph deliberated and then rose to his feet, holding up a hand for silence. He looked at his son, then, for a long terrifying moment, at Harriet, then at Kasim.

'The wrestling will be later this evening, when Kasim has had time to recover from his display of skill and courage. There will be three bouts—the winner will be crowned the lord of the feast and may command us all for one night. At the end of the wrestling, I shall make an important announcement.'

Cheers of approval greeted his pronouncement, and the following, which was that they should all retire inside to eat and drink before the wrestling began.

Hearing a little gasp, Harriet glanced at Katrina and saw that she looked pale. 'Are you ill, my lady?'

'I feel a little faint…' Katrina moaned and then

swooned against Harriet, who supported her as best she could.

'The lady Katrina is faint,' she cried. 'Please, help…'

She did not need to say more for Kasim was suddenly there. He took the lady Katrina into his arms and gave Harriet a meaningful stare.

'Lead me to the lady's apartments, if you please, my lady.'

'Yes…' Harriet glanced at the Caliph, who nodded his consent. 'This way…'

She walked quickly, Kasim's long strides keeping pace with her. As they entered the palace, doors were flung open before them, but no one hindered Kasim or attempted to take his burden from him. Once they reached Katrina's sleeping quarters, he placed her gently on the bed and then looked at Harriet.

'Forgive me. I shall see you later. Now I must go.'

He was already leaving when the Caliph entered. She heard him murmur an apology for his impulsive action and heard the Caliph's brief dismissal of the need. What Kasim had done was against the rules, for he should never enter the Caliph's harem, but his quick action had been necessary and considerate.

'I could not have supported her. She would have fallen if—'

'My son did what was necessary,' he dismissed her apology and moved past her to the couch, taking Katrina's hand. Harriet backed away, wondering if she should leave. She heard voices murmuring and then the Caliph's voice summoned her.

'Lady. My wife needs you.'

'Yes, my lord.' Harriet glanced at him and saw real concern in his eyes. 'I shall stay with her this evening. You will forgive me if I do not attend the wrestling?'

'It will be best if you stay with her,' he agreed. 'She was foolish to come this afternoon. The physician warned her it was much too soon, but she would come.'

'She wanted to attend the celebrations. It is natural, is it not?'

'You seemed to enjoy them more today. Is your headache better?'

'Yes, my lord. You are kind to enquire.'

'You are Kasim's chosen woman. In the future much that you do may be important to my people. I hope that you can learn to accept our ways and cause the man that is as a son to me no grief.'

Harriet did not know how to answer him. How could she be important to his people?

'Stay with Katrina. I shall come again when the feasting and the wrestling are done.'

'I am sure the lady Katrina will be better by then.'

The Caliph inclined his head and walked away, leaving them together. Harriet bent over her friend and smoothed her hair back from her forehead.

'Shall I bathe your head with perfumed water?

I think it may make you feel better. You were over-
come by the heat.'

'I wanted to get you away,' Katrina said and sat
up against the pillows. 'I did not expect Kasim to act
so swiftly. I pray he has not made things worse.'

Harriet looked at her in surprise. 'What do you
mean? I do not understand—are you not ill?'

'I am perfectly well,' Katrina said. 'When Kasim
issued the challenge I knew that Kahlid would not
approve. He could not refuse but they both knew it
was forbidden.'

'Forbidden?' Harriet stared at her. 'What are you
saying? The Caliph agreed that it should go ahead.'

'Because he had no choice. The challenge was
made and accepted before them all. Kahlid could
not refuse, but he will be angry if Hassan loses. It
is unthinkable that the prince should be beaten in a
wrestling match.'

'But…I thought they had wrestled before? I am
sure someone told me that Kasim is the only man
Hassan has not yet beaten.'

'Many times in private, but never in public. Kasim
will win because he has beaten everyone, as he always
has before in the combat. I do not know why he lost
today, for he was winning until his foot slipped.'

'Perhaps he is no longer the best.'

Katrina looked at her. 'I think it is something
more. Did you not see the way he looked at you? Yesterday you closed your eyes as he fought. I think he
has stepped down as the champion for your sake.'

Harriet shivered. 'Surely he would not?'

'A man will do many things for the woman he wants.'

'I am not sure that he wants me.'

'You must know that he places you above all others, Harriet? Everyone knows. Did you not hear what the Janissaries think of you? As far as they are concerned, you are their beloved Kasim's woman and they will afford you the respect they give him, for this reason alone!'

'I believe they may have good reason,' Harriet said, remembering the way he had cared for his friend the previous night. 'But he has other women.'

'Not like you. You must know that in your heart?'

'I have not been certain…' Harriet faltered as they heard a buzz of excitement and then a serving woman approached them. 'Yes, Ramona, what is it you wished to say?'

'There is fearful news, my lady,' the woman said. 'A messenger has just arrived from the villages in the north. They have been attacked by the hill tribesmen and the lord Kasim is preparing a force to send them on their way.'

'Kasim is going to fight them…' Harriet's heart caught with fear.

'Kasim has fought against the hill tribesmen many times,' Katrina said. 'He will return victorious, as always.' She looked thoughtful. 'It means an end to the celebrations for the moment—there will be no contest.'

'For that I am glad,' Harriet said, but her heart

was heavy as she thought of the danger that Kasim would face. 'I must see him before he leaves. I must tell him—'

'It is too late, my lady,' Ramona told her. 'They were already leaving when I was sent to tell you.'

'Gone? He has gone so soon?' Harriet's heart lurched with fear. She felt a pain so terrible that it threatened to consume her. Kasim had left without saying goodbye to her and it was possible that he could be killed and she would never see him again.

'I love you,' she murmured, but the words were so soft that only she could hear them. 'Please come back to me, my love. If you die…' She choked back a sob, because if he died she did not know how she would bear it.

It no longer mattered if he took one of his women to his bed or three, she loved him so much that it was a physical pain in her breast and she did not know how she would bear it if he did not return.

The next few days passed so slowly. Harriet divided her time between the infirmary, where she showed some of the servants what she thought needed doing to make the patients more comfortable, the schoolroom and Katrina. Her friend told her that she was worrying too much.

'Kasim will return victorious, as always,' she said. 'It has always been so.'

Harriet tried to believe that it would be as her friend told her, but she recalled what Kasim had said the night he took her to the infirmary. He had told her that she did not need to fear when he was fighting with his friends, but if he was called to fight the hill tribes it might be different.

It was as she was sitting with the children on the fifth day that Hassan came to her. She saw that he was anxious by the expression on his face.

'Lady Harriet, I need your help,' he said, looking grave. 'Kasim has been wounded. They brought him back last night and the doctor tended him, but he needs to be nursed. I would have asked Mellina, but she is unwell herself—and none of my women are skilled in the art of tending the sick. Besides, the physician told me you were the only woman in the palace he would trust with such a task. I fear my brother has a fever.'

'I must go to him at once. Is he in the infirmary?'

'No. He asked to be taken to his own apartments. Will you care for him yourself? The physician has tended his wounds, but he says Kasim needs careful nursing.'

'Yes, of course I shall tend him. I must go to him at once.'

Hassan looked relieved. 'I trust you above all the other women, for you are like my mother.'

'Is he very ill?' she asked as they hurried towards Kasim's apartments.

'I fear he will die. He is out of his mind and says things I do not understand.'

Harriet followed him to Kasim's apartments.

She was accustomed to the courtyards and her own rooms, but she had never entered Kasim's sleeping quarters, though she had been tempted more than once. However, she had resisted and was curious to see what it would look like. It was furnished much as her personal apartment, except that it had a more masculine feeling, the colours subdued and the comfort kept to a minimum. The chests that must hold Kasim's possessions were plain oak, sea chests and a hutch of English origin. Instead of a clutter of pretty objects there were only his weapons and boots, and some books piled in one corner.

Kasim was lying on his couch. It had been prepared with linen sheets rather than the silk others preferred and he had tossed them off in his fever, his chest bare save for the bandage around his shoulder. His lower regions were covered with a white loincloth for modesty, but the remainder of his body was naked.

Harriet's heart caught at the sight of his exposed flesh. She could see the evidence of many scars, dark against the pale gold of his skin. As she approached he opened his eyes and looked at her, but she knew that he did not see her.

'No, Father,' he cried out. 'You are unfair to blame me. I am not guilty of the crime of which you accuse me…'

'Hush, my lord,' Harriet said and placed a hand to his brow. She looked at Hassan. 'He is burning up. He must be cooled. There is only one way I know to do that.' She fetched water and a cloth from amongst

his things. Dipping her cloth in the cool water, she
soothed it over his feverish brow, then dipped it in
the water again and smoothed his chest and arms.
One leg was thrown carelessly out of the bed, for he
was clearly too hot. She looked at Hassan. 'Will you
please open the shutters, Highness? It is too warm
in here.'

'Yes, if you think that best.' He went to the window
and opened the shutters sufficiently to let in a draught
of fresh air.

Harriet bathed one leg, then she bathed his other
leg, his arms and his chest. She turned to Hassan.

'If you could help me roll him on to his good
shoulder, Highness?'

Hassan nodded and assisted her to turn him. She
smoothed her cool cloth over Kasim's back and shoulders, and down the backs of his long legs. When she
had patted him dry and he was on his back once
more, he seemed quieter.

'I shall sit and watch him for a while,' Harriet said.
'Did the physician leave any medicines?'

'I believe there is a mixture beside the bed, but
when the physician was here Kasim would not take
it.'

Harriet looked at the small blue bottle beside the
bed. The instructions were written in English, left
by the physician who had attended the lady Katrina's
confinement and, she imagined, meant for her to
read.

She took out the stopper and sniffed, then poured
the required amount into a spoon. Approaching her

patient, she bent over him and pinched his nose between her forefinger and thumb, just as she had done with Jason. Kasim opened his mouth to protest and she poured the contents of her spoon into his mouth. He swallowed, a grimace of disgust on his face.

'How did you learn to do that?' Hassan asked and grinned. 'The physician tried in vain and so did I—he would not part his lips.'

'It is a useful trick when a patient is stubborn and refuses the medicine he needs.'

Hassan laughed. 'I think I almost pity Kasim, Harriet. You will not spare him. Still, you are as wise as you are lovely, Harriet. I think my brother is a fortunate man.'

'Thank you for the compliment, but I am not sure he agrees with you,' Harriet said with a faint smile.

'I shall send a servant to help you, lady.' He inclined his head to her and walked away.

Harriet found a stool and sat down near the bed. Kasim seemed to have settled now. He was less feverish than he had been. When she touched him a little later, he seemed cooler.

The servant had arrived and Harriet told her that they needed clean sheets—those already on the bed were damp where he had sweated so much. The girl went away to fetch them, and Harriet stood over her patient. She bathed his forehead, her heart catching with pain as she heard him cry out once more.

'Father! I am not guilty of rape or murder. I beg

you to believe me. I would never have been party to such a foul crime.'

'I believe you, my dearest,' Harriet said softly and stroked his damp hair back from his face. 'Rest easy now. You are safe. There is nothing to fear.'

Kasim's eyes opened and for a moment he seemed to know her. There was alarm in his eyes. 'You should not be here. If you are found they will punish you…'

'Hush, Kasim. It is all right. Do you not remember? The Caliph released me to you.'

Kasim muttered something and closed his eyes. The servant had returned with clean sheets. Between them they rolled their patient to his side and pulled out the damp linen, replacing it with fresh, then very carefully rolled him on to his injured shoulder to do the same. He gave a muttered cry of pain, but once he was returned to his back he seemed easier. Harriet threw off the damp sheets, covering him with a clean dry one.

'It is time for your medicine,' she said and repeated the action she had earlier. Once again he swallowed, grimaced and settled.

After an hour or so, the physician came in and nodded at Harriet approvingly as she sat reading one of Kasim's books. He placed a hand on Kasim's fore-head and smiled.

'He is very much better. I understand that he has taken his medicine?'

'Twice. This time it has settled him. He has been sleeping since he swallowed it.'

'That is good. I knew that you would be the one to nurse him, my lady.'

'I am glad to be of help, sir, but I fear I have very little knowledge.'

'Allah has given you wisdom beyond your years, lady. If Allah wills it, our patient will recover.'

'I pray that he will.' Harriet held back the sob that hovered on her lips. She had not wept though the tears were very near.

'I shall leave him to your nursing, lady. You must not tire yourself. If he continues like this, the crisis will pass in a few hours and then the servants may see to him. I shall return to change the dressing this evening.'

'Thank you for coming.'

The physician bowed to her and went out.

'May I fetch something for you, my lady?' Harriet turned to the woman who had spoken. She was older, a strong woman, used to serving in the palace. 'You have not eaten for many hours. You should rest and eat, or you will tire yourself.'

'I am well enough, but I would like some fruit and sherbet—if it is no trouble for you to fetch it?'

'It is a privilege to serve you, my lady.'

Harriet smiled as the woman left. She went over to the bed, putting a hand to Kasim's brow. He felt cool. She experienced an overwhelming desire to press her lips to his, but knew she must not do it. Even here there might be eyes watching her.

'Harriet?' Kasim opened his eyes and looked up at her. 'Why are you here?'

'Hassan sent for me. I came to nurse you, my lord. I have been nursing others in the infirmary—should I do less for you? You had a fever and frightened the prince because you were rambling.'

'What did I say?'

'You said something about not being guilty and asked your father to forgive you. Hassan did not understand.'

'It was to my birth father I spoke.' Kasim's mouth hardened. 'He disowned me for a crime that was not mine. Because he cast me out I left England and… came here.'

'He should have trusted your word. If you told him you were not guilty, he should have believed you. I know that you do not break your word nor do you lie or betray those who trust you.'

'To my cost,' Kasim said. 'Have you forgiven me, Harriet? I know that in bringing you and Marguerite here I wronged you.'

'I believe my cousin is safe with her family…for the rest, it does not matter. My life may be of more use here than it was in England. At least I am of some use in the infirmary—and the children seem to love me.'

'You sound as if the prospect pleases you?'

'Yes, it does. I am learning to be content. I should like the freedom to ride out when I choose but I know that is too much to ask.'

'It would be too dangerous. This is not England,

Harriet. On your father's land you were safe, but here you would be in danger. Yet when I am well I shall take you riding with me. Will that content you?'

'Yes, I believe it will,' she said. 'Do not try to talk too much, my lord. I will have the servant bring you a cooling drink—and perhaps something light to eat. I could make you a milk posset if you wish or a tisane?'

'Just some coffee.'

'The coffee you drink is too strong. You should drink water and eat something—perhaps some soup if there is any to be had.'

'I am not an invalid. I shall eat some couscous made with lamb and drink coffee.'

'Indeed, you are an invalid and I am your nurse. You will have some broth and water until I am certain the fever has gone.'

Kasim stared at her with a rebellious light in his eyes for a moment then he nodded. 'You nag like a wife,' he muttered and lay back against his pillows. 'I must be mad, but I think I might grow to like it.'

Chapter Eight

'I hear that Kasim is well again,' Hassan said. They met as she was leaving the children three days later. 'My father sends his thanks to you, Harriet. I also thank you for his life.'

'I did very little,' she replied. 'You should thank the physician.'

'I should not like it if my brother died,' Hassan replied, looking thoughtful. 'If it were not for Kasim I might have died long ago. Besides, he has promised a wrestling match the next time we have a day of celebration. I shall not fight him yet for it would be to take an unfair advantage.'

'I wish you would tell him that he is not ready to fight. Already he has begun to train with the Janissaries. I have told him that it is too soon and so has Doctor Ali, but he will not listen to us. He should take things easily for at least another week, but he is restless.'

'Kasim never listens to the physician,' Hassan told her and grinned, looking like the boy he was at heart. 'He must be well soon for I am to be married—and Rosalinda will not run away from me. She is the Sultan's cousin and she thinks it an honour.'

'As it must be for any woman who knows you, Highness. My cousin was young and she feared what she did not understand.'

'I have forgiven her and you. Rosalinda is very beautiful and I cannot wait for my wedding.'

'I wish you happiness, Highness.'

'If she is as good a wife to me as you will be to Kasim, I shall be satisfied.'

Harriet watched as he walked away. Did he think Kasim was going to wed her? Kasim had certainly given no indication of it to her. Indeed, he had hardly spoken to her since the day he left his bed and went to train with the Janissaries. She thought he was annoyed with her for nagging him when he was ill, but she had not had the chance to ask.

'Good morning, Harriet. I have decided to take you riding. Hassan wants to go on a hunting trip and he suggested I bring you too.'

Harriet was sitting by the fountain in her court-yard. She searched Kasim's face, looking for some sign of his illness, but he seemed to have recovered his strength.

'Do you mean it?' Harriet asked, her heart racing. 'When will this happen?' She was suddenly eager.

'We shall go tomorrow early in the morning. You will be given the right clothes to wear. You must wear the veil until we are away from the palace and prying eyes, but after that you may remove it so that you can enjoy the day.'

'Will it be just the three of us?'

'Hassan must be protected at all times. Five of my handpicked men will accompany us.'

Harriet's heart beat with excitement. She had begun to think that he was avoiding her and she had missed him, more than she dared admit, even to herself.

'I shall look forward to it, my lord. Now, if you will excuse me, I must go to Katrina. She is waiting for me.'

'Of course, Harriet. I shall be working this evening, but tomorrow will be a day of leisure for us all.' He inclined his head. 'Until then.'

Harriet walked away, her heart racing. Tomorrow they would ride together outside the palace. For the first time since she left England she would be able to ride, to watch the hawks fly. She would have the illusion of freedom even if in truth she were still a prisoner.

'You are fortunate,' Katrina said when Harriet told her. 'I have never been taken hawking with the Caliph.'

'Would you wish to go?'

Katrina hesitated, then smiled and shook her head. 'If I am truthful I should not enjoy such an outing. I like to visit the bazaar and buy trinkets from the merchants. Perhaps Kahlid will allow us another visit soon.'

'Yes, perhaps he will,' Harriet said. 'Kasim has been generous to me. I should like to purchase materials so that I could make a gift for him, something special that he could not buy.'

'If I tell Kahlid that he will certainly allow it,' Katrina said and looked happy. 'He will give you money to purchase what you need, for you must know that he is pleased with you. He says that you have helped the wounded and will be of great use to Kasim in the future.'

Harriet smiled at her. 'Did you see your son this morning?'

'Yes…' Katrina sighed. 'I am not sure that he thrives as he ought. He cried a great deal and looked pale.'

'You must ask the physician to look at him,' Harriet said. 'I dare say he has a colic of some kind…'

The early morning was cool and Harriet felt glad of the *casacche* that covered her from head to toe, shielding her from the wind. She was given a white palfrey to ride, and Kasim helped her to mount. She saw that both he and Hassan were riding thoroughbreds. Kasim's was black and had eyes that looked a little wild. Hassan's mount was white like hers, but strong and wilful. It snorted and tossed its head when the prince mounted, but she noted that he was an excellent horseman and soon had the horse under control.

The men formed a guard around her and the prince, Kasim out front at the start. Hassan spurred his horse to catch him and ride by his side, and she sensed a kind of rivalry between them. Hassan clearly admired the man he called his brother, but there was a look in his eyes that told her he was determined to outride and outshine him today.

Was he trying to impress her or Kasim? She was surprised when he went galloping off alone, weaving his horse from side to side, and lying to one side and then the other in the saddle as the Janissaries had at the celebration day. Kasim beckoned to one of the other guards and the man spurred his horse to catch him. Kasim dropped back to ride at her side.

'We must protect the prince, for even here there may be enemies,' he told her. 'Hassan resents it and feels that he is being treated as a child, but he is his father's heir.'

'Yes, I understand. Yet you can understand his frustration, can you not? He is a man, not a child, and he should be allowed to prove it.'

'I see that you understand. Excuse me, Harriet. I shall challenge him to a race.'

'Is that wise?' Harriet asked, but Kasim ignored her. He spurred his horse to catch up to the prince and she saw them exchange words. Then, all at once they started to gallop, clearly determined to race each other. The other Janissaries looked at each other in alarm, but instead of setting out after Kasim and the prince, they closed ranks about her. Clearly they felt it their duty to protect her in the face of their leaders' madness.

Kasim and the prince had gone out of sight. Several minutes passed before she saw that they had turned at some point and were racing back to her. Kasim was in the lead at that moment, but as the distance between them lessened, she saw that the prince was gaining on him, and in the last seconds Hassan passed him and rode triumphantly up to her.

'I won!' he crowed, his face alight with pleasure. 'It is the first time I have managed to beat Kasim at anything.'

'You have improved your skills,' Kasim said as he rode to join them. 'I do not think any of the Janissaries could best you now, Hassan.'

'I do not care about the others,' Hassan said. 'It was you I wanted to beat.' He grinned, highly pleased with himself. 'I shall ask my father for a day of celebrations and then I shall best you in a wrestling match.'

'Perhaps you will win,' Kasim told him, a gleam in his eyes. 'Perhaps you will not...'

Hassan stared at him, then he threw back his head and laughed. 'We shall see, my brother. Now we shall fly the hawks.'

Harriet glanced at Kasim. There was such an odd expression in his eyes. She wondered why he had allowed Hassan to win, for she was almost certain that he had.

* * *

Kasim watched Harriet as she rode just ahead of him; her face was intent as she listened to Hassan describe his hawks. His emotions veered between satisfaction at witnessing her pleasure and the pain that never quite left him, a pain that burned him most when he lay on his couch at night.

It was obvious that Harriet was an excellent horse-woman. He knew that she must have ridden often at home and understood the frustration that must chafe her at not being free to ride out whenever she wished. Her laughter was testament to the joy she felt in the outing and it struck him to the heart, making him fully aware of all that he had stolen from her when he took her to the harem. He and he alone was to blame for the situation in which she found herself.

Pain and regret coursed through him as he accepted that he *had* had a choice. His conscience would not let him rest and it was just that he should suffer the torments of hell, because he had brought about his own purgatory. He had allowed his loyalty to a man he respected and cared for cloud his judge-ment. Even as he refused to listen to Harriet's pleas to be ransomed, he had known that he was wrong. Useless to tell himself that she was better off in her present position than what might have been a fate worse than death.

She must miss her home and family, but more than that she must yearn for the freedom she could never have if she stayed here as his wife. He had put off the moment of telling her that he could never leave the palace, because in his heart he was certain that she would choose to leave him. Night after night he had longed to go to her and make her his own. He wanted her in his bed, but more than that he wanted her to love him.

Hassan turned and called something to him. He answered and smiled. His brother was in a good humour because he had won their race—a race Kasim had allowed him to win, because he knew that very soon now Kahlid would tell him of his decree. Kasim knew that the prince would be furious and rightly so. He was being denied his heritage and no young man worth his salt could stomach that easily. They had always been friends and rivals, but would their friendship disintegrate once Hassan knew the truth?

It would cause him pain to lose the prince's trust and friendship, but if Harriet chose to leave him it would tear the heart from his body. Yet how could he ask her to stay, knowing that her life here must be restricted?

Watching her as her gaze followed the hawk's flight, Kasim felt the desire and longing burn deep inside him. His loins ached and his arms felt empty without her. She was both joy and pain to him, and his suffering was well deserved. For too long he had turned his head when he saw something he did not like; he had accepted what he felt to be wrong and done little enough to change things. One day soon he would be in a position of power, but could he rule with Hassan—or would he be forced to take charge and force his brother to comply? The years ahead were fraught with difficulty and he was not sure he could face them alone.

A wry smile touched his lips—he was caught in a bramble bush and the more he struggled, the more the sharp thorns tore his heart.

'I am summoned to attend the Caliph,' Kasim said the next morning when he met Harriet in the courtyard. 'I fear the time has come for his announcement.'

'What announcement?' Harriet asked, puzzled. 'Why do you fear it? Is he angry with you?'

'No, the opposite.' Kasim sighed. 'I have been trying to find a way of telling you this, Harriet— Kahlid intends to make me joint ruler with Hassan when he dies.'

'When…is he ill?' She saw how disturbed he was and touched his arm. 'This worries you, does it not? Why do you not simply refuse the offer? You could leave and—'

'No, I could not leave. I made Kahlid a promise and I must keep it even though it may ruin my hopes.' Harriet's brows arched. 'I shall explain this evening. I have waited too long already. I should have told you before, but…' He shook his head. 'This evening. I shall send for you and we shall talk in private in my rooms. I do not wish to be overheard.'

Harriet's heart raced. He was going to send for her at last. She had waited for the summons so many nights, but it had not happened. Now at last she might become his woman in truth. Her heart told her that it was what she wanted, though if she could choose she would have liked to return to England and wed him in a church with her family about her.

'You do not need to send. I shall come when the sun begins to set.'

Kasim smiled. 'Very well, Harriet. I shall not send. You will come to me of your own free will. Be careful that I do not take that as a sign of your submissiveness.'

'It pleases my lord to mock me.'

'No,' he said, suddenly serious. 'It does not, Harriet. I do not have time now. Kahlid is waiting. I shall expect you this evening.'

'I shall…look forward to it.'

Harriet sighed as he walked away from her. She knew that he would not break his promise to the Caliph, which meant that her dreams of returning home and being married to him must be forgotten.

'You cannot do this,' Hassan burst out when his father had finished speaking. 'I am your eldest son. The throne is mine by right.' His face darkened with anger. 'I refuse to accept your decree.'

'Hassan, your father is ill,' Kasim said. 'He is concerned that you are too young to be burdened with the affairs of state—'

'It is you who has turned him against me,' Hassan cried, his fists balling at his sides. 'How dare you scheme against me to gain what is mine by right? I should kill you.'

'I shall not allow it,' Kahlid said, giving his son a cold stare. 'It is my right to nominate my successor. There is no given right for you or any other of my sons, Hassan. You will rule alone in time. Allah knows that Kasim does not want this burden. I forced him to accept it.'

'I do not believe you.' Hassan glared at them both.

'He gave me his promise in return for Harriet's life,' Kahlid said. 'You should not blame your brother, Hassan. He would rather sail away and leave you once I am dead.'

'He is not my brother. I have no brother.'

'You had a brother once,' his father reminded him. 'He was stolen from us as a baby and it broke your mother's heart and mine—but we still had you. I have loved you too well and indulged you too much. Now you must do something for me.'

'No, I shall never agree.' Hassan looked from his father to Kasim. 'When you are dead I shall kill him and then I shall rule alone, as is my right.'

He stormed from the room, leaving a silence behind him. Kahlid pressed a trembling hand to his face, but in a moment he had recovered.

'He will return and apologise. He is hot-headed, but once he has calmed down, he will see that it must be this way. My son is my son, but he is not yet fit to rule—and I fear the time is coming soon.'

'Are you feeling ill, my lord? Should I call the physician?'

'No, there is nothing he can do. I foolishly allowed

Hassan to take his future for granted and I must bear
his displeasure. I am certain he will return and beg
my pardon.'

'And if he does not?'

'Then I shall make you the Caliph immediately
and you will rule in my stead. If Hassan will not
accept it, he must face the consequences. You may
banish him or…' Kahlid could not continue. 'No, you
would not do that because you love him.'

'I do love him as a brother,' Kasim said. 'I fear
that he must hate me and I cannot blame him if he
does.'

Kahlid sat down heavily. 'Leave me now, Kasim.
I wish to meditate and pray. I can only ask Allah to
guide my foolish son and hope that he sees fit to grant
my prayer.'

Harriet had spent the afternoon studying. She
thought that Kasim might wish to test her on what she
had learned…unless he had other reasons for saying
that he would send for her. Her heart was thudding
wildly as she bathed and dressed, choosing a simple
white tunic over white pants and a red scarf to drape
over her shoulders.

The young girls who helped her were giggling
and giving her sly looks and she thought they had
guessed that she was going to Kasim that night. She
had acquitted them of being the women Kasim had
taken to his bed, because they were too young and
innocent and one of them had confessed that she was
a virgin. If the story were true, it must have been the

houris Kasim had sent home. Harriet no longer felt racked with jealousy, though she was uncertain that he loved her in the way she loved him.

There were moments when she saw a look in his eyes that made her heart leap. Yet at other times he was withdrawn, distant, as though deliberately keeping a barrier in place between them.

The sun had begun to sink on the horizon as Harriet crossed the courtyard that connected her apartments to Kasim's. The first room she came to was small and open to the gardens, the one beyond it was his sleeping quarters and where she would find him. Her heart was beating like a marching drum as she walked in and saw to her surprise and consternation that it was empty. Where was he? Surely he had told her to come at this hour…the breath left her throat as he entered from a door she had not noticed before at the far corner of the room, a towel over his head as he dried his hair. He was naked apart from a white cloth wrapped loosely over his hips, his chest, arms and long legs still damp from his bath. She had time to drink in the strength and beauty of his body before he came out from under the towel and saw her. A spasm of raw desire spiralled in her stomach as their eyes met. For a moment he stared as if he did not believe his eyes, and then she saw the recollection in his eyes.

'Is it that late?' he said. 'Forgive me, Harriet. I have had much to do and our appointment had slipped my mind for the moment.'

'Perhaps I should go?'

'No, I would rather you stayed. It is important that we talk. I should have spoken to you before this, but—'

'You were wounded and I know you have been working hard to recover your fitness. You are a busy man, my lord.'

'And likely to be more so,' Kasim said. He glanced at the white kaftan lying on a couch. 'If you will turn your back, my lady, I shall make myself decent.'

Harriet smiled and turned her back. 'You forget that I nursed you when you had the fever, my lord.'

'I forget nothing,' he replied. 'You may turn now if you wish.'

She did so and saw that he was tying a red sash around his waist. White and red were his colours and she had chosen to wear them this evening. Harriet wondered if she had done so to show him that she was his to do with as he would—but surely he knew that?

'Why will you have more duties?'

'Kahlid told Hassan this morning that we are to rule together. Hassan left the palace in a temper. Kahlid was angry. He called the ministers together and told them he is too ill to continue to hold council meetings. He informed them that I would stand in his place—and that he would advise me while he could.'

'Yes, I understand. You will have a great burden to carry, my lord.'

'I shall carry it with pride, but it does mean that

I shall be tied to the palace for some years to come. I must try to make my peace with Hassan and to help him to an understanding of what his position as Caliph means. I am not free to go where I choose—and that means the woman I marry must be prepared to stay here and live according to the rules we all follow…'

Harriet's heart was thudding wildly. What was he saying to her? Her chest felt tight and she could scarcely breathe.

'Perhaps she would feel proud and happy to be your wife, my lord.'

'Yet if she had been used to freedom—if she resented being unable to ride out as she chose…if she must always be guarded lest someone make an attempt to abduct or kill her…' Kasim's eyes carried so much meaning that Harriet's mouth ran dry. 'Could any woman be happy to live that way, Harriet? An English woman of spirit? Would she not come to hate her life and long for her home? Would she not hate the man who had made her a prisoner here?'

'It might depend upon how she felt about the man. If she loved him, she might be prepared to make the necessary changes…to live as he did, devoting his life to duty and to change.'

'Change?'

'You will have great power. There are things that might be changed for the better…nursing for the sick might be improved and the lives of the harem and the slaves could be eased.'

'Yes, that is possible, though I could do nothing

about Hassan's harem—and other men have several wives. It is the custom and cannot be changed. I have no power in the Sultan's palace or in the homes of others.'

'No man can do everything,' Harriet said and smiled. 'But a small act of kindness may sometimes set new thought in motion and an acorn will grow to a mighty oak in years to come.'

'A butterfly's wings' flutter may cause a storm across the ocean,' Kasim said, his gaze intent on her face. 'You speak as a philosopher, Harriet. Have you eaten?'

'No, I was not certain…I was not hungry.'

'Then you will sit and eat with me,' Kasim said and clapped his hands. A male servant came running and he asked for food to be brought to them. The man looked surprised, but schooled his features swiftly before disappearing to carry out his order. 'My servants will be certain their lord has run mad—a man does not send for his woman only to eat with her.'

'You did not send for me. I came to you, my lord.'

'Yes, you did, Harriet.' He indicated that she should sit on one of the couches near the open arch that led into the gardens. 'Had you not done so I should have sent for you. It was in my mind that we must talk.'

The servant returned with a tray, which he set on a low table. Cheese, cold chicken, bread, butter and fruit were set out on platters; there was also a jug of fruit juice and sherbet in tall Venetian glasses.

'Thank you, Roald,' he said to the servant. 'You may leave us… Stay a moment, I have a question for you.'

'Yes, my lord.' The servant glanced at the food. 'Have I forgotten something?'

'No, my friend, everything is as it should be. Please tell my lady—are you my slave?'

'No, my lord. You gave me my freedom when you bought me from the slave master.'

'Why do you serve me? Why do you not leave and find your fortune elsewhere?'

'Because you are a good master and the money you pay me goes to feed my family.'

'Thank you, Roald. I shall not need you again this evening.'

The man nodded, glanced at Harriet once and then left as silently as he had come on bare feet.

Kasim's gaze was intent on Harriet. 'All my servants are free to leave if they wish, yet still they must follow the rules, as I must—and as you must if you stay.'

'If I stay?' Harriet's heart jerked to a sudden stop and then raced on. 'I do not understand…are you offering to ransom me to my family?'

'You would never be for sale,' Kasim said, his eyes unfathomable. 'Yet if you wish it I shall have you returned to your family.'

'Why have you decided this?' Harriet raised her eyes to his.

'It has been in my mind, from the first moment the Caliph placed you in my care. Is that not what you want, Harriet? You asked me so many times and it might have been better had I listened.'

Harriet had taken a ripe fig from the dish. She held it, but made no attempt to eat. 'I am not sure I understand you, my lord. Do you wish me to leave you? You told me that I must learn to accept and to show a proper respect…now you offer me freedom.'

'Is it such a mystery, Harriet?' Kasim rose to his feet. He offered her his hand, pulling her to her feet so that they stood close together, looking into each other's eyes. 'Surely you know that I care for you? You must know that I want you?'

Harriet could not speak. She shook her head wordlessly, her lips slightly parted, her eyes wide and wondering as he reached out and drew her closer. Her heart slammed against her chest as he bent his head, taking possession of her mouth. His kiss was sweet, gentle at first as he explored the softness of her lips, becoming more demanding as she opened to him and their tongues met and danced. Heat pooled low in her abdomen and she longed for something she had never known, the sweetness of being one with a man—this man. Only he had ever raised this need in her, a sweet hunger that made her part her lips and sigh. When he let her go and stood back, looking down at her, she was breathing fast, her senses spinning.

'If you want me, why have you not—?'

'Sent for you before?' He smiled oddly. 'I have spent many restless nights burning for you. I wanted you in my bed, but the time was not right. When you came here you hated me and you had good cause. You fought for your cousin like a lioness for her young—risking terrible punishment and even death. I thought that Kahlid might demand your death, but he spared you.'

'Yes…' Harriet gazed up into his face. 'Katrina thought it was for her sake…but you made him a promise. You bound yourself to him for me…to save my life.' She felt a spasm in her stomach and for a moment the world span about her. 'Why did you do that, my lord?'

'Because I could not let you die,' he said and ran his fingers down her cheek. 'I knew that I had made a terrible mistake the moment you disappeared inside the harem. I wanted you for myself, but it would have been cruel to separate you from your cousin. You would have hated me even more.'

'Yes, perhaps I should. Marguerite was so terrified. From the moment we were captured she wept and clung to me. When you bought us I sensed that you were not like the others, but my cousin was so afraid. I had to help her escape.'

'You were not afraid of what could happen to you?'

'At that time I thought only of Marguerite—and yet there was a moment when I knew that I should lose something I might never find again if I left you.'

'Did you, Harriet?' Kasim smiled and lifted her chin, kissing her lightly. 'Are you sure you can bear to tie yourself for ever to a barbarian and a savage? A man without honour?'

'I should not have said that to you…' She blushed as she saw the teasing light in his eyes. 'Those pirates…how could I know then that you were so different?'

'How could I know that I bought a treasure beyond price that day?' Kasim whispered. 'I could so easily have forced them to sell me only your cousin. Yuri said you were a hellcat and it was in my mind that you would cause trouble in the harem.'

'You threatened to leave me in Algiers.'

'Yes, I did.' Kasim laughed softly. 'Even then I sensed that you were the best buy. Hassan saw only your cousin's beauty, but his father recognised true quality. He told me that I should make you my chief wife, for you would give me wise advice in the years to come.'

'Your wife…' Harriet gazed up into his eyes. 'You will make me your chief wife?'

'If you choose to stay you will be my only wife,' Kasim said. 'There are many things about this life and the faith I chose to adopt that I find comfortable, but others I prefer not to follow. I do not keep slaves, neither shall I take more than one wife.'

'Yet you had a harem…'

'Yes, but I purchased none of the women. They were given to me as gifts and I allowed them to stay. I am a man and there were times when I amused myself, as men will—but when I knew I could have you I sent them away.'

'Yet you offered me freedom?'

'I give you the choice. Either you stay or you

leave—but if you choose to stay then you will belong to me. You will be the woman I love, my wife and I shall never let you go—but you will not be a slave. You will be as free as I am able to make you.' He looked rueful. 'That is not as free as I would wish—but the choice is yours.'

'Surely you know my answer?'

'I have thought…hoped that you might have ceased to hate me.'

'I never hated you, only what you had done—all the time accepting the unfairness of a culture that allows a man to buy another human.'

'I cannot wave a magic wand and make that go away, Harriet. I may make small changes but that is all.'

'A butterfly flutters its wings and a storm rages somewhere across the ocean.' She reached up to touch her lips to his. 'I love you, Kasim. I belong with you. I think I should be forever wretched if I left you.'

'Then you are mine and I shall never let you go.' Kasim's arms tightened around her possessively, his eyes dark with passion. 'We shall be wed, my—' A sound behind them made him turn to look. The servant had returned. 'Yes, Roald—I need nothing more this night.'

'Forgive me, lord—the Caliph sends for you. News has reached him that a large force of hill tribesmen is moving towards the palace. They mean to attack us. The Janissaries are preparing to muster and you are needed.'

Kasim muttered something rude beneath his

breath. He glanced down at her face. 'The plans for our wedding must wait until I return.' He saw her expression and shook his head. 'Lightning does not strike twice, my beloved. I swear I shall return to you.' The servant had lingered. 'Yes?'

'The prince returned this evening with his bride, my lord. He insists that he will ride with you and no one can dissuade him. The Caliph says that he must learn to use his head instead of his heart, but he has not denied him.'

Kasim's face clouded with anger, as the servant left them. 'Hassan is a young hot-head and will be more trouble than he is worth, but if Kahlid has given his permission there is nothing I can do.'

'I shall return to my apartments, my lord,' Harriet said, lifting her face to gaze up at him anxiously. 'Please promise you will come back to me.'

'It will be as Allah wills,' Kasim said and bent to kiss her. She clung to him, feeling the desire and sweet regret swirl inside her. She longed for him to claim her, but she knew that she must lose him to his duty, and that was the way it would often be in the future. 'But nothing will keep me from you now, my love. I shall return as soon as the battle is won.'

Chapter Nine

'Kahlid remains with a sufficient force to defend the palace should it be attacked,' Katrina told her the next morning when Harriet came from the children. 'The patrols have gone out to see if there is any sign of the enemy and the elite of the Janissaries have ridden out to intercept and challenge the tribesmen.'

'Even the children are talking,' Harriet said. 'They had heard that the men were leaving to fight a big battle with the hill tribesmen. Some of the boys are excited, but Lisbet was crying. Her mother had been crying all night and she was frightened.'

'Poor Angeline. I must ask her to spend some time with me. I know she is a little jealous of me, but she loves Kahlid and fears his reaction if anything should happen to Hassan. The Caliph loves his son dearly.'

'Yes, of course he must,' Harriet said. 'I know he

loves the prince—but Hassan was determined to go and the Caliph could not deny him.'

'What did Kasim say?'

'That he must protect the prince...' Harriet decided it was best to say no more for there were always people listening in the palace.

'Kasim is a clever captain. He will lead his men against the enemy. We shall be safe here—he will defeat these men and bring us victory.'

'Kasim was wounded in the last skirmish.' Harriet had spent the night praying for the safe return of the man she loved.

'Wounded, but not defeated. These attacks happen every few years. There was some trouble just before you came, but that was a minor thing, though there have been attacks on the villages. The leader escaped last time, but this time he will be brought back to face his punishment.'

Harriet shivered as something dark and cold seemed to hover over her. 'I wish it had not happened.' She did not know why, but she had a feeling that something bad would come from this.

'We should attack through the pass,' Hassan said. 'The enemy are camped in the vale at the other side of the hills. If we go round by the easier route, they will know we are coming and we shall lose the element of surprise.'

'They may surprise us if we go that way,' Kasim said. 'These mountain passes are treacherous. In some places the way is so narrow that the men must go in single file. The enemy could lie in wait and pick us off one by one with a bolt from a crossbow or rocks. They could start an avalanche and send a rockslide down on us, cutting us off and then attack from the rear. It is much better to take the longer route, even if they know we are coming. We shall be in a better position to defend ourselves.'

Hassan's eyes glittered with annoyance. 'I have studied warfare since I was a boy of no more than five and I know that surprise is the best way to win battles. I intend to take my detachment through the pass. Go the other way if you wish, but I shall be there before you.'

'Hassan—' Kasim stopped as he saw the flash of temper in the younger man's eyes. 'Highness, please listen to me. Your father will never forgive me if anything happens to you. Your men should stay in the rear—'

'Damn you! I am not a child, Kasim. Rosalinda will be proud of me when she learns what I did. I refuse to be treated as a child any longer. My father must see that I am a man.' He walked away, calling to his men and leaping up into the saddle. His heels kicked against the horse's flanks and he sped towards the pass, signalling to his men to follow.

'The young fool!' Captain Suleiman looked at Kasim. 'What do we do now? Your plan was sound. He may bring us to ruin.'

'What will be will be,' Kasim replied tight-lipped. 'We must follow or leave him to his death. Perhaps fortune will favour the brave...' Kasim mounted his horse and gave the signal to follow the prince into the narrow pass. 'Death to the enemy!' He spurred his horse to catch up with Hassan. The prince looked back at him, determined to be the first into the pass. 'Let me go first, Highness,' Kasim cried but Hassan would not listen, pushing his horse faster in an effort to go ahead.

Kasim galloped after him. The plan was a mad one, but perhaps the tribesmen had not reckoned on them being foolish enough to try for there was no sign of an ambush as they rushed headlong over the rocky path. It was not until they had almost reached the end of the pass that the sound Kasim had dreaded reached his ears. He called a warning to Hassan, but he was too far ahead or perhaps he refused to heed the shout. As the rocks began to tumble down the hill with a roaring sound, Hassan eventually became alert to the danger. He looked up, pulling frantically at his horse's reins as he attempted to stop its mad flight, but it was too late. The boulders were huge and there was a flood of them, catching man and horse in the tide of rubble, mud and rock.

Kasim jumped down from his horse and rushed towards the scene of carnage. He saw at once that the horse was dead, but by some miracle Hassan was still alive. His eyes were closed and blood covered his face and hands. One leg was broken, the bones protruding through the flesh, but he was still breathing. As Kasim bent over him, he opened his eyes and smiled.

'Forgive me. Your advice was wise, as always, my brother...' he whispered and fainted.

'The stupid, stupid fool,' Kasim said, his cheeks wet with tears. 'Why could he not listen?'

'You were his elder brother. Everyone speaks of your bravery, your leadership. Hassan had to be better...'

Kasim looked at the man who had spoken, his expression grim. He bent down and gathered Hassan's broken body into his arms.

'We must bind his wounds and send him back to his father. You will lead his bodyguard. The rest of the men come with me.'

'You will go after them?'

'This ends with their deaths or mine. I shall not rest until he is avenged.'

Captain Suleiman saluted him. 'I shall tell the Caliph that the prince refused your advice, my lord.'

Kasim nodded. 'Tell him that his son will be avenged and I shall pray that Allah is merciful.'

Kasim handed the prince to others and then mounted his horse. He lifted his right arm in the air.

'Death to the enemy. Any man who dies this day in glory will live in Paradise.'

The cheer that welcomed his call to arms echoed through the mountain pass. Kasim's face was grim as he led the Janissaries the long way round. There would be no surprise for the enemy, but the men had seen their prince cut down and their righteous anger would carry the day. Hassan was loved and respected and there was anger in every man's face.

Kasim had no way of knowing whether his prince would live or die, but he would not return to the palace until the tribesmen had been crushed. He would show no mercy this day.

Harriet was with the children when the summons came. Angeline came to take her place and she was told to go quickly to Katrina's apartments. No more was said, but, from the expression on the woman's face, Harriet knew that something was seriously wrong. As she hurried past servants and eunuchs the same look was on everyone's face. Her heart was beating rapidly and she felt sick as she entered Katrina's apartments. Something was wrong. She knew it instinctively. A cluster of servants and the elderly doctor were by the bed. The servants parted as she approached, letting her through.

Katrina came to her. 'The prince has been wounded. When they told me, I asked them to bring him here so that you could tend him. It would not have been fitting for you to go to his apartments.'

Hassan was lying with his eyes closed. She could see the cuts and bruises on his face, and one leg was lying at an odd angle, as if it had broken. He had bandages around his head and another about his chest; the bandage about his chest was stained with blood.

'He is still alive,' Doctor Ali told her. 'His breathing is shallow, but he managed to speak—and he asked for you, my lady.'

Harriet bent over the young prince. She reached out to touch his forehead. He felt cold. She knew that he must be in such terrible pain for his injuries were many and severe. He opened his eyes and smiled at her.

'I led the charge, but they sent rocks down on us to block the pass…' He made a little choking sound and there was blood on his lips. 'Tell my father it was not Kasim's fault. He warned me against the pass. He told me to go the long way…I would not heed him.'

'Oh, Hassan…' Tears fell from her eyes and wetted his face. 'Yes, I shall tell him.'

'I wanted my father to see that I was as strong and brave as Kasim…' A little moan of pain left his lips.

Harriet smoothed his forehead, looking at the doctor. 'He is in so much pain…' The doctor shook his head. 'Is there nothing?'

'I can ease the pain, but he will not let me. He wants to talk to his father.'

'Has the Caliph been sent for?'

'Yes, but he was at prayer and none dare disturb him.'

'He must be told at once.' Harriet looked at Katrina. 'You must go. He must come at once.'

'Kahlid does not like to be disturbed when he meditates.'

'Tell me where to find him and I shall go.'

'You are needed here. I shall go.'

Harriet turned back to the young prince. He was shaking, having some kind of fit, and she saw from the doctor's expression that it was serious. She bent over Hassan, soothing his fevered brow. He gave a little cry and clutched at her hand. Harriet held him tightly as she stroked his brow.

'You will feel better soon,' she comforted. 'Your father will come and Doctor Ali will give you something for the pain.'

'Tell my father I died well…'

'No, Hassan,' Harriet said and swallowed hard. 'You will not die. You must get better for your wife's sake—and your father's. You are much loved. Kasim loves you.'

'Kasim loves you.' Hassan smiled at her. 'You are like my mother. Kasim is fortunate…'

He made a choking sound and a trickle of blood ran from the corner of his mouth.

'No…' Harriet gave a little sob, because she was saddened by his death. 'No…'

'He died bravely. He died a man's death. He will be in Paradise.'

Glancing up, Harriet saw the Caliph watching her. How long had he been there? How much had he heard? She had not been aware of him nor had she realised he had entered the room. She moved away and let him take her place. Katrina beckoned to her and they went out into the chamber that led onto the gardens.

'Kahlid will want to mourn alone.'

'Yes, we must leave them together. It is a terrible tragedy.'

'Kahlid loved Hassan. He will blame himself for allowing him to fight.'

'Yes, I expect he will.'

It was Kahlid's insistence that Kasim should rule jointly with Kasim that had made the young prince so determined to fight. The father would feel his guilt and it would increase the burden of his grief a hundred times.

Harriet returned to her rooms alone. There was nothing more she could do. A dreadful hush had fallen over the palace. Everyone was aware that the prince was dead and the Caliph was in mourning for his son.

Harriet had known that Kasim was not one of the party who had escorted the prince back to the palace, so she had spent the night in his apartments, praying that he would return safely, but he did not come. In the morning she went to see Katrina to ask if there were any news.

'Have you spoken to the Caliph since last night?'

Katrina shook her head. 'He had Hassan taken to his rooms and keeps a vigil over his body. He will not speak to anyone. He is waiting for Kasim to return.'

'Kasim has not yet returned?' Harriet asked. She had thought perhaps he was with the Caliph and too busy to send for her. 'Have you heard anything since the men brought Hassan home?'

'Kasim led the men into battle against the tribesmen who set the avalanche,' she said. 'He told them that they must avenge the prince or die in the attempt. They say his fury was dreadful to see.'

'He loved Hassan dearly,' Harriet said and her throat caught. She could not imagine what Kasim was feeling at this moment. He had called the prince a young hot-head, but he loved him as a brother, and he would take the blame on himself for what had happened.

'He will take revenge on those who did this evil thing,' Katrina said and there was a look in her eyes that made Harriet wonder.

'You are worried about something,' she said. 'Do you wish to tell me?'

'I think…' She shook her head. 'No, I am not sure. Yet Jamail told me that if I did nothing…'

'You think your brother might have been amongst the tribesmen who caused the avalanche?' Harriet saw the fear in her eyes. 'Surely not? I know he thought your son should be the heir instead of Hassan, but…' Harriet held back the words that trembled on her tongue. It was obvious that Katrina did not know what Kahlid had decided.

'My father was a good ruler of our tribe, but when he died and my brother became the leader he made war on other tribes. I believe he has been behind the recent uprisings. He is jealous of Kahlid's power. My husband is not well, Harriet. If he were to die and my

son were the heir…Jamail would take over here, for
he could command me, and who would deny him?'

'I should.' The women turned as they heard
Kasim's voice. Harriet gave a glad cry and started
towards him, but the look on his face stopped her.
He looked angry, his eyes cold and bleak. Her heart
caught. 'How long have you known that your brother
plotted treason against the Caliph's son, lady?'

Katrina's face turned pale. Her eyes widened in
fear and her hands clenched at her sides.

'I did not know anything. He said… I told Harriet
that he wished me to persuade Kahlid to make my
son his heir, but I refused. I—I was afraid of him,
but when Harriet came he left me and he has not
returned.'

'You knew of this plot and did not see fit to tell
me?'

Kasim looked at Harriet and his eyes were so cold
that she shivered. 'There was nothing to tell you,' she
said and yet even as she spoke she was remembering that she had sensed something menacing about
Jamail.

'Had either of you seen fit to tell me, this tragedy
might have been avoided.' He looked from one to the
other. 'We fought the tribesmen and defeated them,
but their leader escaped. We did not know who to
look for, but now I believe we know where to find
the man who murdered Prince Hassan. He will be
caught and punished.' Kasim looked at Katrina scorn-
fully. 'You have betrayed your husband, lady… As
for you, Harriet, I shall deal with you later. You are

both confined to your apartments. Neither of you will visit the other. Until this business has finished there will be no privileges for either of you.'

'Kasim. Katrina is my friend. She meant no harm.'

Kasim's eyes flashed with anger. 'Do as you are told, Harriet. Go to your apartments and stay there until I send for you.'

Harriet raised her head. She moved towards Katrina and embraced her. 'Do not be afraid, my friend. I know that you are innocent.' Then, giving Kasim a look of reproof, she turned and walked from the room unhurriedly.

Kasim was clearly in torment, but he should not blame Katrina for what had happened. She had no control over her brother—and Hassan had brought his fate on himself, for if he had listened to Kasim he would not have been caught in the trap.

Harriet held back the tears. She would not weep. The man she loved seemed to have gone and in his place was a hard-eyed stranger.

'You are a great warrior and I owe you much,' Kahlid said as he invited Kasim to sit with him in his private rooms. 'I know that Hassan ignored your advice not to attack through the pass and I absolve you of any blame. I should have forbidden him to ride with you, but it would have dishonoured him. He was determined to prove himself and I could not keep him here against his will for ever.'

'His death hurts me as much as it hurts you,

my lord,' Kasim replied. 'I know that your loss is terrible.'

Kahlid waved a hand in dismissal, but a little pulse flicked at his temple. 'I have other sons, though none I love as I loved Hassan. None of my other wives have given me a son, though I have many by women of the harem. I do not wish any of them to be my heir, though Abdulla is a good devout son. He is but sixteen, but I think he will take the path of religion.' Kahlid sighed. 'Hassan was my chosen heir.'

'He was the son of your first wife, Anna.' Kasim looked thoughtful. 'There was another child…a son who was stolen from you as a baby? Hassan told me once and I know it grieves you.'

'It was my fault. I insisted on taking the child to visit my cousin and the abduction happened there. Anna never forgave me for his loss and I blamed myself.'

'Have you searched for him?'

'I sent men to look for him; month after month they came back and told me there was no trace of him.' Kahlid's gaze narrowed. 'Why do you ask?'

'I have not spoken because I was not certain, but one of the prisoners we took tried to save his own life by telling me that he could reveal the whereabouts of your lost son. He swore that he had been sold to a slaver.'

Kahlid sat forwards, his hooded eyes alert and eager. 'If he has such information I would spare him.'

'There is a boy. I found him at the slave auction

when I purchased Harriet and her cousin. At first I was not sure, though I saw the likeness at once, but I hesitated to speak.'

'You thought Hassan might resent another rival?'

'I cannot be sure that the boy is your son, but you may judge for yourself.'

'Bring him to me. I would see him.'

Kasim inclined his head, walked to the door and gave an order to the eunuch who waited outside. He returned to the Caliph.

'There is a matter I need to discuss with you, concerning the leader of the rebels.'

'I thought you said he escaped?'

'He did—but I may know where he can be found.'

'Find him and kill him.'

'Whoever he may be?' Kasim questioned.

'Even if he is one of my sons or my cousin. I want him dead.' Kahlid's hands shook with emotion.

'I shall obey your wish, my lord.'

'I intend to announce that your rule is now absolute,' Kahlid said. 'Tomorrow we shall hold a day of mourning for the prince. After that I shall retire from state affairs. The province will be in your hands. If you need advice…' His voice died away as the door opened and a young boy walked in.

'You sent for me, my lord?' Yuri asked, looking nervously at the man he knew was the Caliph, but had seen only from a distance. 'Have I displeased you?'

'No, Yuri, you have not displeased me,' Kasim

said. 'Please come closer so that the Caliph can see you.'

Yuri approached, looking apprehensive. Kahlid held out his hand, beckoning him closer. 'Let me look at you, boy.'

Yuri went closer. The Caliph leaned forwards, taking hold of his arm and staring into his face. For some minutes he stared at him, then he looked at Kasim and the tears began to trickle down his cheeks.

'He is Anna's son,' he said in a voice hoarse with emotion. 'He is Hassan's brother.'

Yuri stared at Kasim. 'I do not understand, my lord. I am the son of a slave.'

'No, she was not your mother,' Kasim told him. 'Men of a certain hill tribe stole you from your father when you were a baby. They intended to kill you, but one of the slave women hid you and took you as her own. She was later sold to a new master and taken to Algiers where you were both sold again. When your mother was sold at the auction the owner did not want you and the slave master's wife took you. I suspected the truth as soon as I saw you, but I could not be certain until recently. You are the Caliph's son—and he will tell you of your future.'

'Come and sit by me,' Kahlid said and his eyes were warm with love. 'You will visit me every day, but you will also have tutors who will instruct you in the things you should know. One day you will be Caliph, but until then Kasim is your ruler and you must swear to obey him and be loyal to him. When he believes you are old and wise enough to rule he will pass the mantle to you. Will you so swear?'

Yuri looked at Kasim and then nodded. 'Kasim has been like a father to me. No one but my lord has ever treated me with kindness. I shall always honour and obey him. I swear it on my life.'

'Then I shall acknowledge you as my lost son returned to me,' Kahlid said. 'When we have mourned Prince Hassan for two weeks we shall hold a celebration. Kasim will receive the robes of office from my hand and you will be my son and his ward.' He pressed a hand to his chest, closing his eyes for a moment. 'Yuri may stay with me for a little if it pleases him. My good friend, I know you have much to do. Hassan must be honoured in the way of his forefathers—and there is the matter of the punishments.'

'Yes, my lord. I shall see to it at once.' Kasim genuflected and smiled at Yuri. 'Take care of your father. He is not well and needs to rest.'

'Yes, my lord.'

Kasim left the apartment. He was frowning as he walked towards the guardhouse. He had not told Kahlid that Katrina's brother was concerned in the murder of the prince, but once Jamail bin Rachid was brought back as a prisoner, he would learn the truth.

Harriet was angry because he had spoken so coldly to Katrina, but she did not understand that there were often plots against the life of the Caliph and his sons. Katrina's duty was to her husband. If she suspected her brother of plotting against Kahlid she should have told him. Had she done so he would not have blamed her, but now… Jamail was already condemned to death once he was captured, but what would the Caliph decree for his wife?

Katrina was his favourite. Kasim hoped that was enough to save her from punishment. For the moment at least he would say nothing, but once Kahlid knew that it was her brother who had set off the avalanche his anger would know no bounds.

Kasim had been furious when he heard Katrina and Harriet speaking of the plot that had led to the prince's cruel death. He had blamed Harriet for not telling him what she had seen that day, but she had not understood how important it was to crush the tiniest spark of rebellion before it could flare into an unstoppable fire.

Harriet was unable to settle. She could not read or embroider and she had been forbidden to teach the children or visit her friend. Kasim had been so angry with both her and Katrina. It was unfair of him to blame the Caliph's wife because her brother had been involved in the rebellion. She wished that she had mentioned her unease at once, but so much had happened that she had dismissed it as unimportant. Katrina disliked her brother, even feared him. It would be wrong if she were to be punished for something Jamail had done without her knowledge or consent.

Harriet felt chilled as she remembered the bleak

look she had seen in Kasim's eyes when he heard them talking. He seemed like a stranger—a man she did not know and would not care for if she did. What had happened to make him change so much? Or was it that she did not truly know him?

She had fallen in love with him slowly, believing that despite his stern looks and determination to keep his word to the Caliph, he was a just man. He had told her that he did not like everything about the life he had chosen here and he had offered her freedom—yet when he sent her to her room he had behaved as if she were his slave. He had ordered her to remain in his rooms until he sent for her, rescinding both her privileges and Katrina's.

He had no right to treat them so harshly. Neither she nor Katrina was responsible for what had happened to Hassan. Had Hassan not been so determined to have his own way, he might have returned to the palace as part of the triumphant force that Kasim had once again led to victory.

Why should she stop here? She was not a slave and she would not behave like one. Carried on a surge of rebellion, she walked to the door that led into the palace and opened it. No one was guarding the entrance. Kasim had obviously believed that she would tamely obey his orders. Well, she would not. He had told her that he cared for her and that as his wife she would be free to move wherever she wished within the palace. He could not then turn round and confine her to her apartments.

Her anger carried her to Katrina's rooms in a

spirit of defiance. However, when the eunuch opened the door for her, she discovered that her friend was nowhere to be found. Had her husband sent for her?

Harriet wondered if Kasim had told the Caliph what he suspected. Was Katrina being punished?

Restless, and determined to discover the truth, Harriet went out into the gardens that led to the Caliph's harem. She intended to ask Mellina if she knew what was happening, but she halted as she saw that the gate through which Marguerite had escaped had been left wide open. Her curiosity aroused, she went to investigate. She saw that some gardening tools were lying near the gate, but there was no sign of the eunuch assigned to duties here.

Her heart beating fast, she approached the gate and looked out. No one was to be seen and no one called to her. Harriet hesitated and then went out. She pulled her scarf over her head, draping it across her face. Walking hesitantly through a narrow walkway, she came to a courtyard. Thinking that at any moment she would be challenged, Harriet looked about her, but there was no one. She walked on through several more courtyards and gardens and then came to the compound where the celebrations had been held. She could see the gates through which she and Marguerite had been brought the night they arrived at the palace under Prince Hassan's escort. Normally they were closed and guarded, but for some reason they too were open.

Glancing round, she saw that an altercation was

going on. It looked as if some prisoners had been brought out into the compound. She shivered as she realised that they were going to be punished. Two of them had been tied to wooden stakes and a large eunuch with a whip was standing in front of them. As her horrified eyes took in the scene, she realised that the man in charge of the punishment was Kasim. Her throat caught with horror as he gave the order and without realising what she was doing, she started forwards as the eunuch lashed out with his cruel whip.

'No! That is barbaric…'

Kasim turned and saw her. His shock turned swiftly to anger, his expression cold and forbidding as he strode towards her. His hand curled around her wrist as he grabbed her and began to propel her towards the palace. Behind her the punishment continued. She put her free hand to her mouth as the tears started to her eyes.

Kasim's grip on her arm did not relent as he strode through the palace without speaking. Not until he reached their personal apartments did he look at her.

'How dare you?' he thundered. 'You will never do such a thing again. Do you hear me?'

Harriet raised her head, looking at him defiantly. 'I thought you were different. I thought you cared about others…but you are as cruel as the Caliph.'

'Be quiet, Harriet. Another word and I shall have to punish you.'

'What will you do to me? Leave me in the cells

without food or water or beat me—as those poor men were being beaten?'

'Those poor men as you describe them were some of the rebellious tribesmen. They were being punished as they deserved.' Kasim glared at her. 'What were you doing in the compound?'

'I looked for Katrina, but she was not in her rooms. The gate in the harem gardens was open. I found my way to the compound.'

'Were you trying to escape?'

'What if I were?' Harriet's eyes flashed with temper. 'What will you do with me? Beat me? Put me to death? Sell me to another master?'

'Do not be ridiculous. You know that I would never be so cruel to you.'

'Why not? I am just a slave like all the others in the palace. You forbade me to see Katrina and you threatened us.'

'You should have told me what you saw and heard, Harriet. If Jamail is responsible, and I am certain he is—he will be caught and punished.'

'Beaten like those men—' Harriet saw the look in his eyes. 'No, you will have him executed. How could you do it, Kasim? I thought you meant things to be different when you were Caliph.'

'I am to be confirmed very soon. Kahlid no longer wishes to bear the burdens of state. It falls to me to administer justice. The men you saw being beaten were lucky. I could have ordered them put to death. I was merciful.'

'Merciful?' Harriet threw him a look of scorn.

'You are not the man I believed you to be. I thought I loved you, but I did not know you.'

'Then it is as well you discovered it in time,' Kasim said. 'You will stay here—and this time I mean it. When I have time we shall discuss what will happen to you.'

'I am not a slave. I will not be treated as one.'

'At the moment you are behaving like a spoiled child,' Kasim told her. 'Since you refuse to oblige me by remaining here where I know you are safe, I shall set a guard at the door. Until I say, you will not be allowed to leave these apartments. It is for your own good, Harriet. Had you obeyed me you would not have had to witness that beating.'

'I could have run away,' she said staring at him angrily. 'You are just like all the others—and I hate you.'

Kasim stared at her for a moment, then inclined his head. 'So be it. I shall leave you to reflect, Harriet. You have made your decision.' He turned and left her. Harriet shivered as the chill slid down her spine.

What did he mean by that?

Chapter Ten

'**Y**ou are sent for, Lady Harriet.'

Harriet looked up from the sewing she had been concentrating on. For the past two weeks she had seen no one but her women and they had been subdued. The palace was in mourning for its prince and an atmosphere of gloom and apprehension had spread everywhere.

'My lord sends for me? Am I to go to his rooms?'

'No, my lady. You are to join the lady Katrina for a celebration of the victory. The period of mourning is over and the Caliph has an announcement to make.'

'Oh, I see.' Harriet sighed. 'I do not think I wish to attend. I have a headache.'

'The lord Kasim said that you must come. I am to have you dressed and taken to the courtyard whether you wish it or no. I would rather not to have to force you, my lady, but I must do as the lord commands.'

Harriet stared at her. Mellina was quite capable of carrying out her orders if forced. Kasim had forestalled her. She put down her needlework and stood up reluctantly.

'Very well, I shall bathe and dress. You need not stand over me, Mellina. I know when I am beaten.'

'The lord Kasim has had much to do, my lady. The burdens of state are many. Everyone is saying he will be a great and merciful Caliph and we are fortunate that he is to take Kahlid's place.'

'Yes, I know it must be a heavy burden,' Harriet said and inclined her head. As usual everyone knew exactly what was happening, even though the Caliph had not yet made his announcement. 'I know Kasim has been busy. I have not seen him for two weeks.'

'You should not have tried to interfere, my lady. Any other man would have had you beaten for disobeying him. Your lord was lenient. You should be grateful.'

Harriet did not answer her. She was well aware that she ought not to have been in the compound that day, and she should not have protested at what she saw. It had seemed such a barbaric punishment, yet she knew that had the Caliph still been in charge the men might well have been put to death.

'Has the leader of the rebellion been taken?'

'That I may not tell you, my lady. I know better than to speak of things that are not my concern.'

'Very well.' Harriet left her. She was thoughtful as she bathed and dressed. A part of her acknowledged that Kasim had been merciful in his way. He had

punished the men, as he must if he wished to control
the wild hill tribesmen for had he allowed them to
leave unpunished they would laugh and think him
weak. That would have led to yet another rebellion.
Yet she could not accustom herself to the need for
this constant fighting and all the pain and death that
resulted from it. She did not know what the answer
might be, and suspected there was none. The tribesmen were fierce proud people and once a feud was
begun it continued, handed on from father to son.
Kahlid had hoped to end it when he took Katrina
as his wife, but her brother saw her as a means to
an end—he wanted to take the Caliph's place. If he
was allowed to live he would no doubt continue to
plot and scheme against Kasim and anyone else who
stood in his way.

Mellina had brought her a beautiful robe of white
silk embroidered with gold and tied with a red sash.
Harriet stared at it thoughtfully. Kasim always
favoured white and red. If she wore his colours he
would think she had repented. She hesitated, then
chose a robe of pale turquoise blue with a gold sash
and hem. She chose a white and gold scarf to wear
over her head.

Mellina looked at her as she emerged fully clothed,
but though her mouth set in lines of disapproval she
said nothing. Instead, she walked a little ahead of
Harriet as they left the apartments. The eunuch who
had been guarding the door since Harriet's disgrace

was no longer there so it seemed that her time of punishment was over.

'Where are we going?' she asked after a few moments. 'This is not the way to Lady Katrina's apartments.'

'She is waiting with some of the other ladies in the courtyard. She is no longer the Caliph's favourite wife. She has been sent back to the harem.'

'Katrina is in disgrace, too?'

'Not exactly.' Mellina shook her head. 'It is not for me to tell you, my lady. Everything will become clear soon.'

'It is unfair of Kahlid. She has done nothing wrong.'

'You speak hastily, lady. You do not know of what you speak.'

Harriet felt anger stir inside her once more. She had had time to regret her quarrel with Kasim, for it was true that she should not have been in the compound and in her heart she knew that there must be discipline.

She saw the small group of ladies waiting. Instead of the usual laughter and anticipation, they looked subdued and nervous, as if they feared what would happen to them.

'Katrina, are you all right?' Harriet asked as she joined her friend. 'Why have you been sent back to the harem?'

'Kahlid was angry because my brother was taken. He confessed his guilt and would not ask for mercy.'

'Oh…what happened?'

'Kahlid said he should be put to death, but I begged for mercy and—the lord Kasim ordered that he be sent to the galleys for a period of five years. Kahlid said that because he had favoured me above others my brother had thought he could rule through my son. Angeline has taken my place and he is considering what to do with me.'

'Oh, Katrina,' Harriet said. 'He must know that you had nothing to do with your brother's plotting.'

'Kasim asked me to tell him everything and I did. Kahlid said that I would not be punished, but he would not favour my son above others. Yuri is Anna's son. Today he will accept him in front of everyone—and Kasim is to assume the robes of the Caliph. Kahlid will retire, perhaps to another palace nearer the capital. He wishes to be left in peace to die…' Katrina gave a little sob. 'I do not care that I am no longer the favourite but I wish he would take me with him. I love him and would be with him to the last.'

'Perhaps he will relent. He must know that you did not plot against him.'

'He says that my brother would have used Ahmed and me to claim power,' Katrina gave a little sob. 'I wish that I had not born a son. If my child had been a daughter, Jamail would not have plotted to seize power through him.'

'Hush, do not blame yourself,' Harriet said and squeezed her hand. 'Perhaps once today is over the

Caliph will relent and take you with him when he retires to his seclusion.'

Katrina forced a smile. The women were being beckoned to the courtyard, where awnings had been set out so that they could be sheltered from the hot sun. Glancing to where the Caliph sat, Harriet saw the young boy she had first met at the slave auction. It was such a strange story. He had been stolen from the Caliph as a babe in arms and was restored to his father more than ten years later. She saw that Kasim was sitting on the Caliph's right hand and her heart caught. When he glanced at her she tried to smile, but her lips felt frozen. His eyes went over her and he frowned as he saw she had chosen to wear turquoise rather than the beautiful robes he had sent her.

Harriet felt a pang of regret, because she had disobeyed him. It was churlish and she wished that she had worn his colours, but it was too late for regrets.

The women took their seats. The display of dancing, music and various acts of skill and daring were performed, as she had seen before. Then came the parade of the Janissaries. They put on a show of daring, riding bareback, leaning from side to side with no hands on the reins, and standing on the horse's back. After the cheering died down, the Caliph rose to his feet and a silence fell over the courtyard. It seemed that today there were to be no matched pairs and no wrestling. Watching the Caliph, Harriet noticed that he seemed a little frail and she understood why the celebrations were so much shorter than usual. He raised his hand and everyone held their breath.

'My people and friends,' Kahlid said. 'We have mourned our prince and he has gone to the arms of his ancestors and God. He will live in Paradise. I had hoped to see him rule after me with the lord Kasim to guide and counsel him as his brother and joint Caliph, but he was taken from me.' He paused, his face grey with grief. 'I have lost a son—but a son that was lost to me many years ago has been returned to me. My friend and adopted son Kasim found him and brought him back to me. One day he will be your Caliph, but until the day when he is old and wise enough to rule over you, the lord Kasim will be Caliph. He is my chosen heir and he will take command completely from today. Tomorrow I shall leave you and retire to pray during my last days. I ask you to give your loyalty to the lord Kasim.'

For a moment there was silence, then a burst of cheering from the Janissaries, which was gradually taken up by others around the courtyard. The Caliph smiled and sat down, Harriet thought a little shakily, as though his strength was almost done. She thought that the past two weeks and his grief had aged him and he was noticeably ill.

Kasim stood up as the chanting began. The Janissaries were clearly delighted that one of their number was to be their Caliph, and Harriet realised how popular he was. He held up his hand and silence fell. They respected as well as liked him.

'My friends, I am honoured by the Caliph's trust

and I shall do my best to lead you wisely and with justice. The lord Kahlid has been my true friend and I—'

What Kasim was about to say was lost as a man broke from amongst the people and started towards the dais. A gasp of horror went up as the long knife in his hands was seen and his intention became clear.

'No, Jamail!' Katrina cried, jumped to her feet and started running towards him. 'You must not. This is evil and wrong…'

'Katrina!' Harriet saw that she meant to throw herself at the would-be assassin and prevent him from his murderous intent. It was like a slow agonising nightmare. Harriet saw Jamail's arm go back and the cruel blade slash at his sister's breast. Immediately, she was on her feet and running towards Katrina.

'No, Harriet!'

She heard Kasim's anguished cry, but she had reached Katrina, who had fallen to her knees and was clutching her shoulder. Her brother's blade had slid off the heavy jewellery she wore, cutting into her shoulder, and blood was pouring from the wound.

'Katrina,' Harriet said, kneeling beside her. She tore off her head covering and pressed it to the wound. 'You will be all right. It is but a flesh wound…'

Feeling a rough hand on her arm, she was hauled to her feet and held by a fist of iron. Staring into the maddened eyes of the escaped prisoner, Harriet held her breath and prayed. She must be calm for Jamail had lost all reason. Yet she must try.

'If you kill me, you are dead,' she said sounding

much calmer than she felt. 'The Caliph has been merciful, but—'

'Be quiet woman of Satan,' Jamail spat the words at her. 'You may have bewitched the lord Kasim, but you will not cast your spell on me.'

'Let her go.' Kasim's voice rang out strongly. 'Let her go, Jamail, and face me like a man.'

'Why should I? You will kill me—but first you will see your woman dead.'

'I will make you a promise,' Kasim said. 'Face me in combat and win and you will gain your heart's desire. If you kill me, you will be Caliph in my stead.'

'No…' Harriet moaned, but she was thrust away with such violence that she fell to her knees. Mellina came and dragged her away. Two other ladies were supporting Katrina, hurrying her inside the palace. 'I must stay here,' Harriet insisted. 'I must see my lord fight. I must be here if he needs me.'

One of the Janissaries had thrown Kasim a shield and sword. Kasim gave the order and another sword and shield was cast into the arena for Jamail to pick up. Kasim had pulled off his long tunic, his muscles rippling beneath the golden skin as he stood prepared for battle. Stripped to the waist and wearing only his leggings and boots, he held his shield in his left hand, the long curved sword he favoured in his right.

Jamail had swooped on his weapons and turned to face Kasim, his eyes glittering. He rushed at Kasim violently, clearly hoping to take him by surprise, but Kasim was ready and thrust him back with his shield.

They broke, circled and eyed each other warily, then Jamail rushed again. Once again Kasim met his wild swings with his shield and thrust him so hard that he staggered back and almost fell. Kasim could have rushed on him, but he waited, letting Jamail right himself. This time he approached more cautiously and they circled each other, then Jamail lunged forwards. Kasim met his thrust, but brought his left arm up sharply so that Jamail's shield spun out of his hand and went skittering away. One of the watchers picked it up, but did not return it to him. He growled and placed two hands about his sword hilt, rushing at Kasim once more. Kasim threw down his own shield and battle was joined.

Harriet's heart was in her mouth as she watched, listening to the ring of steel against steel. She had hardly dared to watch Kasim fight in gladiatorial combat, but now she saw the difference. The bouts Kasim had won had been between friends, fighting for the love of skill and testing each other's strength. This was a fight to the death.

Jamail was strong, but she had begun to see that Kasim's cool head and his skill was giving him the upper hand. He was wearing his opponent down gradually. Jamail was sweating, his thrusts becoming wilder and wilder as he tried to inflict a deadly wound on the whirling fighting machine that was Kasim. As the minutes ticked away he matched Jamail's every attempt to pass his guard, feinting, parrying and avoiding the wild thrusts that were now becoming noticeably less and less effective. Now

Kasim's superior skill was showing. He was like an avenging god as he struck blow after blow, forcing Jamail back step by step until his back was against the wall.

'Kill him…kill him…' the chant started as the crowd scented victory.

Harriet held her breath as Jamail's sword suddenly went skittering from his hand and then he fell to his knees in the red dust of the compound. He raised his head, looking up at Kasim defiantly, as if daring him to kill him. Kasim's sword hovered, then he lowered his arm.

'You are not worth staining my sword with your blood. You will go to the galleys until you die,' he said and turned away.

Harriet felt the tears spring to her eyes. 'Kasim,' she whispered and began to walk to meet him. 'Kasim, my love…' Then, seeing that Jamail had a blade in his hand, she screamed, 'Behind you! Murder…'

Kasim turned, but before he could act one of the Janissaries had thrown a spear. It pierced the traitor through the heart and he fell forwards, the blood oozing from the fatal wound. Kasim glanced at Jamail's prone body for a moment, then turned back to Harriet as she rushed towards him.

'Now do you understand why it is not always wise to show mercy?'

'You should have killed him,' she said and tears began to trickle down her cheeks. 'Forgive me, my love. I didn't know. I didn't understand…'

Kasim's long stride closed the short distance between them. He crushed her to his chest and kissed her to an accompaniment of loud cheering. Laughing, he turned to face the Janissaries as he swept her up in his arms, carrying her towards the dais, where he set her on her feet before turning to the watching crowd.

'This is my lady Harriet,' he announced. 'She will be my wife. Together we shall care for our people and try to bring peace and prosperity to you all.'

The Janissaries stamped their feet and cheered. Jamail's body had been taken away and a troupe of dancers and entertainers swarmed back into the arena to entertain them.

Mellina came up to her, whispering in her ear. Harriet turned to Kasim. 'The lady Katrina asks for me and the C…Lord Kahlid begs me to come to her.'

'Then you must go. I shall follow soon,' Kasim said, his eyes dark with passion as he looked at her. 'Tonight you will come to me—or would you have me come to you?'

'We shall meet in the courtyard,' she said. 'Excuse me, my lord. I must go.'

Katrina's wound was slight and soon tended, but the Caliph was very frail. He had not felt strong enough to stay and watch the fight, instead following his still much-loved wife to her old apartments where she was treated. Now he was lying on his couch and his doctors and friends had gathered about him.

Harriet had comforted Katrina, but she had dismissed her own wound. She had begged to be allowed to sit with Kahlid in what everyone knew were probably his last hours. Harriet was not asked to share the vigil, though she knew that Kasim would probably wish to spend some time sitting with his friend.

Alone in her apartments, she ate a light supper of peaches and dates and then went into the gardens to sit and wait for Kasim.

It was late when he came at last and she had begun to think he might sit with his friend all night, but just as it was growing dark she saw his commanding figure walking towards her. She was wearing the robes he had sent her earlier that day and she rose from the bench on which she had been sitting and went to meet him.

'You came. I was not sure you would.'

'Kahlid is sleeping. The end must be near but Katrina and Angeline are with him, and Yuri. We spoke briefly, but all that needed to be said has been said. He knows that I shall keep my promise to him, Harriet.'

'He chose well, Kasim. Everyone loves you. You will be a wise and just ruler.'

'This from the woman who called me a cruel barbarian and told me she hated me?' He looked down at her, a question in his eyes. 'Have you thought long and clear about this, Harriet? If you give yourself to me I shall not let you go. You must choose now because there is no going back.'

'Surely you know?' she said softly. 'When I thought I might lose you... I should not want to live if you were dead.'

'I must be sure that you understand, Harriet. When Kahlid dies I shall set his harem free. Those who wish may return home; others may choose to marry amongst the Janissaries or to remain here as your friends—but I cannot free every slave in the province. If I made a decree to free them, it would cause terrible unrest. All I can do is lead by example. Every servant in the palace will be free and no more slaves will be brought here. I will create no more eunuchs. If a man or woman chooses to work for me, he or she will be paid a fair wage. It is the most I can do and it will not be universally approved. I can do nothing about the custom of a man taking more than one wife or keeping a harem. It is a matter of religion and culture, and each man must live according to his beliefs. Prisoners must be punished and some may be executed or sent to the galleys.'

'Yes, I understand,' she said. 'I have studied the books you gave me and I am ready to accept that much of what you believe in is just and good. If there are some things I do not like I shall learn to accept—as you have.'

Kasim took her hand, leading her into his apartments. 'The time is right to tell you the truth about myself, Harriet. I am the son of Lord Albert Hadley and rightful heir to the title, though I dare say he has long given me up and handed his estate to his nephew. When I was very young I made friends at court—wild friends who drank and consorted with whores and behaved in a licentious manner. I shall admit that for a time I did much as they did, gambling and drinking…but they went too far and I began to sicken of their pranks.'

'Did something happen to make you leave England?'

'One of my friends abducted and raped a young woman of good family. She escaped when he got drunk and she drowned herself in the River Thames. When I saw her body dragged from the water I vowed I would have no more of them—but my father was told I was the one who planned the whole thing, though I swear to you I played no part in the sordid affair. In his rage, my father disowned me and cut me off without a penny. I had a small inheritance from my mother and I purchased a ship. I sailed with the intention of being a privateer, but I was naïve and fell victim to a corsair vessel. My crew and I were taken prisoner and set to work in the galleys, as I have told you before.'

'I saw the scars on your back and shoulders,' Harriet said and reached out to touch his hand. 'I begin to understand why you care for Kahlid so deeply.'

'He was more of a father to me than Lord Hadley. My father was never a loving parent and he closed his mind to my pleas for understanding. Kahlid trusted me and honoured me. I repaid him by showing loyalty.'

'But he demanded a promise of you in return for my life?'

'Yes, because he was afraid that my love for you would be too strong. He would not have put you to death, Harriet. From the start he saw that you would be the right wife for me, and he knew that I loved you. He made me promise because he thought you would draw me back to England and it was the only way he could keep me here.'

'What will you do if I choose to return to England?'

'It would tear me apart,' Kasim said. 'Yet if you wish to go I shall arrange it. I have already written to your brother and invited him to visit. I told him that you were to be my wife. Do you think he will come?'

'I cannot tell. Richard lives in London and will seldom visit his estate in the country. I do not think he will travel all this way to see me.' Harriet frowned. 'He may think me lost…beyond the pale.'

'And will you mind if you never see your family again?'

'Yes, a little,' she admitted. 'If you were free to return to England, I might have preferred to live there, but you cannot leave and I shall not go without you.'

'I should send you away,' Kasim said, his voice heavy with emotion. 'It is unfair of me to keep you here, where you can never be as free as you are in England—but I love you too much to let you go. Without you, my world would be an empty sham. Nothing means anything to me without you, Harriet.'

'Promise me you will not send me away,' she said

and pressed herself against him in a burst of passion. 'I want to spend my life with you, Kasim. You must believe me.'

'Then you belong to me and I shall keep you with me always.'

Kasim bent down and swept her up in his arms, carrying her into his bedroom. He laid her down amongst the silken covers and then sat beside her, bending down to touch his lips to hers.

'I have pictured you here so many times. Wanted you here with me so many lonely nights. Are you ready to be mine, Harriet?'

'You know I am. I burn for you.' She smiled up at him, her lips parting invitingly. 'Take me, Kasim. Make me your woman. I want to be yours always.'

'My beloved Harriet,' he murmured and kissed her. 'I adore you. I love your spirit, your courage, your honour—and your lovely body.' He reached out and pulled at the knot in her sash. 'Why did you not wear my colours today? Was it just to spite me?'

'It was my foolish pride,' she said and laughed huskily as she helped him dispense with her clothes. 'Had you not sent them I should have worn a white robe I had selected and a red scarf.'

Kasim raised his brows. 'I must remember that…' he murmured and stroked her cheek with his fingertips. 'You are so beautiful, Harriet. How could I have thought your cousin the better prize?'

'I am not beautiful,' she said and smiled. 'It is just that you have become accustomed to my plainness.' She watched as he disrobed. His body was so honed and strong, the golden tan of his skin broken only by thin white scars, proof of the beatings he had endured and the wounds he had taken in battle. 'You are beautiful...like a Greek god...'

'And where have you seen pictures of a Greek god?' he questioned as he bent over to touch his lips to hers. 'Must I remind you that you are the Caliph's wife and must have no eyes for other men?'

'It was long ago in my father's library,' she whispered. 'I see no other man but you, Kasim. I have never loved any other man or wished to lie with them...and I am not yet your wife.'

'Oh, yes, you are,' he said. 'We may not have had the ceremony yet, but when you promised to love me in the courtyard you handfasted yourself to me in the way our ancestors saw fit—and that means you are mine. You will always be mine. I shall never let you go...'

Harriet opened her lips as he kissed her, their tongues touching lightly, tasting and inflaming. Her heart thundered as he stroked her thigh and his mouth sought her nipples, licking and caressing them with his tongue until they peaked, aroused and sensitised. His kisses moved lower and lower, making her arch her back and cry out as she trembled with need and longing, rising to meet his caressing hand as he slid between her thighs and found her moist centre. She thrilled as he stroked and caressed, his kisses moving lower, and then he pressed his face against her damp mound, his tongue licking delicately until she whimpered and her nails scored his shoulder.

'Kasim…' she shrieked his name as he sent her spiralling out of control. 'Kasim, I love you…'

Then she felt his weight pressing on her and the hard length of his manhood pressed against her thigh, seeking entrance. He thrust up inside her and she stilled as she felt sudden pain. Feeling her tension, he eased back a little, not moving for a moment, but she ground her hips against his, wanting the glory that his earlier caresses had foreshadowed.

'Come deep into me,' she whispered. 'I want to feel you inside me. I want to be a part of you.'

'Cry out if I hurt you too much.'

She pressed her mouth against his shoulder, tasting the salt of his sweat as he thrust deeper. Yes, there was some pain for he was big and she a virgin. But she clung to him, letting her body dissolve in the tide of love and need that engulfed them both, and when he came in her she cried out with pleasure and clutched him to her, feeling the tears run down her cheeks.

'I did hurt you. It was too much for your first time.'

'No,' she said and buried her face against his chest. 'It was what I wanted. The pain will go.'

'It will not be so bad next time,' he murmured and stroked her hair, holding her clamped against him with his leg. 'I wanted you too much, but next time it will be better.'

Harriet woke to discover that the bed felt cold beside her. Kasim had risen earlier, leaving her to

sleep in. She stretched, feeling blissful and almost
too lazy to get up. Then she laughed and threw the
thin sheet back. Life was too good to waste in bed
unless Kasim was sharing it with her. She knew that
he must have a hundred and one duties as Caliph
for he was also the commander-in-chief of the Janissaries. She would visit the infirmary before she went
to the schoolroom, because she intended to show that
she was as industrious as her husband.

Returning to her own apartments, she bathed and
dressed in a white tunic and pants with a red scarf
over her shoulders. She left and walked through the
palace to the infirmary, where she pulled the scarf
over her hair, though she did not hide her face, as
some of the women did here.

She made a tour of the wards, inspecting water
jugs, bedding and floors, and she ordered three bandages changed. Everyone hurried to obey her, their
smiling faces testimony to the pleasure that was felt
throughout at the palace at Kasim's appointment.

The nurses were a mixture of men and women,
but she thought that she might begin a school for
young men and women, where they could be taught
the ideas she herself followed. Although her knowledge of medicine was slight, Harriet believed that
keeping the surroundings clean as well as the patients
and the dressings was as important as the doctor's
pills. Now that Kasim was Caliph he could set up
schools for medicine and nursing. Harriet found a
lot of pleasure in thinking of the good that could be

done here. Kasim could not change all the old ways, but he could make improvements.

After leaving the infirmary, she went to the schoolroom and spent an hour or two with the children. While she was there one of the eunuchs came to ask her if she would visit the lady Katrina in her apartments.

'Is she back in her old rooms?' Harriet asked and was told that it was so.

When she joined Katrina it was to find her with her arm in a sling, but looking happier.

'How is the lord Kahlid this morning?' Harriet asked.

'Much better. We all thought that he might die last night, but he rallied at dawn and this morning he says he feels rested.' Katrina smiled. 'I am to join him at his place of retreat. He is no longer angry with me. Indeed, he wishes to make recompense for his unkindness and he has arranged a trip to the bazaar for us this afternoon, Harriet. He has given me a purse of gold so that we may buy all the trinkets we need—do say you will come with me, please. It may be the last afternoon we spend together for I am to go to my cousin's home when Kahlid dies.'

'Yes, of course I shall come with you,' Harriet said. 'I must put on a *casacche* and leave a message for Kasim, but then I shall return.'

Katrina's face lit up. 'I want to buy you a lovely present,' she said. 'Had you not run to me yesterday I think Jamail would have killed me. You have been a good friend to me and I thought this a way of repaying some of your kindness.'

'We have shared many troubles and sorrows,' Harriet said and embraced her. 'There were times when I did not know how to bear my life here, but I had you to help me.'

'You are happy now?'

'Yes, of course. I love Kasim very much.'

'And he loves you.' Katrina smiled at her. 'I see you wear his colours. You should buy something for him at the bazaar…perhaps a fine leather belt or a gold ring.'

'Yes, I shall buy a token, perhaps a leather belt. I saw some lovely tooled-leather items the last time we were there.'

Harriet hurried away to her rooms. She put on the dark blue *casacche* she had worn to the bazaar before. It enabled her to see through the veiling, but covered her face and hair so that no one could see her face. She left a message with her women and, seeing Mellina as she left her apartments, she told her that she was accompanying Katrina to the bazaar.

'If my lord should ask for me, be sure to tell him where I have gone,' she said. 'I would not have my lord wonder where I was.'

Chapter Eleven

〜〜〜〜

'Look at these rings,' Katrina said as they stood gazing at the display set out on the merchants stall. She glanced at the merchant, an old man with a wizened face and dark eyes that had sunk into his face. 'May I try this one, please?'

'Your highness may try anything you wish,' the man said and his eyes gleamed. 'Would the Caliph's lady like to try?'

'No, thank you,' Harriet said. She had noticed a stall selling leather goods just two stalls away and, after admiring the ring Katrina displayed on her right hand, told her that she would move on. 'I wish to look at the leather stall, Katrina. You should buy the ring if you like it.'

'I am not certain,' Katrina said and took it off, indicating another she would like to try.

Harriet smiled and moved on. Katrina had already

purchased shoes, scarves and a fine gold chain. As yet she had bought nothing. They had brought two servants with them to carry their purchases and three armed Janissaries. As she moved to the next stall one of the guards followed her and the other two remained with Katrina.

The stallholder came out to her at once and invited her to see his goods. 'I have more inside if her highness would like to see?'

Harriet looked through the belts on sale. There were several made of fine soft leather and tooled with gold, but she could see none that appealed to her. Kasim preferred plainer things, but she wanted something of good quality.

'Do you have anything like this in red leather?' she asked, indicating a very fine belt of tan leather. 'I would like it tooled, but without the gold.'

Her guard interpreted and the stallholder smiled and bowed. 'If her highness would step inside I can show her many examples of fine leather. A belt can be made to her exact requirements.'

'Yes, I should like to pick the leather and the design,' Harriet agreed. 'Is it all right if I go inside, Rachid?'

'Yes, highness. I shall come with you.'

Harriet glanced at Katrina and then went into the shop. It was dark inside and smelled strongly of new leather and dyes. She saw piles of leather all over the place, but none in red. The stallholder beckoned her and she followed him to the rear of the shop. A pile of leathers in different shades of red caught her eye and she moved towards them with a cry of pleasure. She felt various skins and picked three she liked, turning to the stallholder to ask if they would make a pair of boots as well as a belt, just as she saw a dark shadow move towards her guard. She cried a warning as the blow fell, but it was too late. Rachid had been knocked unconscious.

'What have you done?' she cried, but the stall-holder was being restrained and she suddenly became aware that two men had come from a back room.

'You will be quite safe, Lady Harriet,' an English voice told her. 'We have come to rescue you.'

'No, I do not wish—' Harriet cried, but the next moment a hand was placed over her mouth. She inhaled something strong that made her feel sick and faint. Her senses swam as someone put a blanket over her and then everything went black.

'Please ask my lady to come to me,' Kasim told the body servant who had brought him clean clothes. 'I wish to speak with her before I return to the lord Kahlid's apartments. He is worse again and I may need to be with him for some hours.'

'The lady Harriet has not returned from her trip to the bazaar, my lord,' the servant told him.

Kasim frowned. 'When did she leave the palace? Why was I not told? Did she go alone? How many guards went with her?'

'I believe she went with the lady Katrina,' the servant replied. 'Does your highness wish me to ask—' He was interrupted by the sound of voices and then the door opened and one of Kahlid's eunuchs entered.

'Yes—is Lord Kahlid worse?' Kasim demanded. 'What is it, Ninon?'

The eunuch looked scared. He fell to his knees before Kasim. 'Forgive me for bearing such news, my lord—but the lady Katrina has just returned to the palace. One of the Janissaries has been injured and the lady Harriet has been stolen.'

Kasim felt the chill slide down his spine. 'My lady has been abducted? How—tell me exactly what happened immediately. You will not be punished.'

'The lady Katrina was buying a ring. The lady Harriet went to the leather merchant a few steps further on and entered the shop in search of red leather—and Rachid was struck from behind. He knows nothing more of what happened. The merchant swears he knew nothing until the men appeared, threatened him with a knife and then carried off your lady.'

'Has the leather merchant been brought to the palace?'

'Yes, my lord. He is in the cells. He took the lady into his shop and swears the abductors must have come through the back. It would seem true for nothing was seen at the front and it was some minutes before the discovery was made. The lady Katrina insisted that a search was carried out at once, but no trace of your lady was found.'

Kasim's hands balled at his side. 'I shall come at once. Tell the men that I want the village searched house to house, and a patrol must be sent to search every road leading to the hills and the capital. She must be found.'

'The men are already out looking for her, my lord. As soon as Rachid was discovered, messengers were immediately sent to the Janissaries and they are searching the village now.'

'I shall question the merchant myself,' Kasim said. 'I shall also want to speak with the lady Katrina. If Harriet has been taken in reprisal for Jamail...'

He left the rest unspoken as he strode away. A terrible feeling of loss and despair was crushing his chest, because he knew that if Harriet were a prisoner of the hill tribesmen he would never see her alive again.

Why had she gone to the bazaar with only a small escort? Surely she must have known that it was too dangerous after the last uprising? Was this just another instance of her rebellious spirit—or had she walked into a trap?

Harriet moaned as she opened her eyes. She was immediately conscious of feeling sick and she turned on her side and vomited on the floor. Her head was thumping and her mouth tasted vile. It was a moment or two before she realised that she was on a ship. The rocking motion she could feel must mean that the ship was moving. They were at sea!

Sitting up in alarm, she forced her eyes to focus through the drugged haze that still cloaked her vision and looked about her. The cabin was spacious, clearly the kind reserved for the captain or his officers. Her head was spinning, but she swung her legs over the side and stood up. Immediately, the floor came up to meet her and she gave a little moan and fell back against the bed.

As she struggled to regain her balance, the cabin door opened and someone entered.

'Harriet! What are you doing?' a man's voice asked. 'You should not try to stand. The fools drugged you and you have been unconscious for hours.'

'Richard...?' Harriet gave a cry of relief as she realised it was her brother. 'What is happening? Why have I been brought here?'

'We have been searching for you for months,' Richard Sefton-Jones told her. 'We knew where you were after Marguerite escaped, but it was impossible to discover which part of the palace you were being held captive in—and too difficult to attempt a rescue. We have been trying to negotiate your ransom with the Sultan, but thus far he has refused to see me.'

'Richard...' Harriet sat back against her pillows. 'You must put back to Istanbul at once. Kasim will be so worried—and angry with me for being careless.'

'Kasim...that is the damned fellow that bought you and Marguerite,' her brother said and his expression hardened. 'I wish that I could call him out. I would kill the devil for what he has done to you.'

'Kasim did what he considered his duty,' Harriet said. 'You do not understand Richard. He loves me and I love him. We are to be married soon. We should have been married before this had the Caliph not been so ill.'

'Married! According to Muslim law, I suppose? That is no marriage and not fitting for my sister.' He looked at her oddly, a mixture of compassion, anger and shame in his eyes. 'I do not know if we can keep this a secret, Harriet. Your chance of making a decent marriage would be finished if it were known that you were a prisoner of the harem.'

'I have no wish to marry anyone but Kasim,' she told him. 'I never had, Richard. You must know what my life was like after Father died. I was doomed to a lonely old age. With Kasim my life has a purpose and meaning. I help care for the sick and I teach the children—and I love Kasim. He makes me happy.'

Richard was silent for a moment, then, 'Your mind has been corrupted by their evil drugs and forced to accept their ways. I was warned that you might not thank me and might need to be abducted. In time you will realise what was done to you and thank me for what I have done.'

Harriet's head was clearing. She put her feet to the floor and discovered that she could stand.

'I do not wish to return to England with you,' she said. 'Please, Richard. Take me back to my husband. I am his in every way and I can never be happy without him.'

'You are still suffering from the effects of your captivity,' Richard replied. 'Lady Sefton-Jones insists that you live with us. She says that we can cover up the scandal and that I must find you a kind husband who will care for you.'

'No! I shall marry no one but Kasim.' Harriet's

face was proud as she looked at him. 'I may be carrying Kasim's child.'

'God forbid you have that heathen's seed in you!'

'He is not a heathen, even though he chooses to follow a different religion. He was born in England and is the son of Lord Hadley.'

'Then he is a rogue and should know better than to enslave two English ladies of good birth.'

'Had he not bought us, we should probably both be dead,' Harriet said and then gasped as she saw the look in her brother's eyes. 'Perhaps you think death preferable to the shame of having lain with a man of another faith?'

'I said nothing of the kind, Harriet. You are my sister and I care for you deeply. Why else would I come all this way to search for you?'

'If you love me, Richard, let me go back to him. I beg you. I will beg you on my knees if you wish— please take me back to the man I love. I belong to him. I shall never know happiness without him.'

'The village has been searched, the merchants questioned, but no one knows what has happened to her. Patrols are on all roads to the hills and to the capital.' Rachid raised his head, looking into his Caliph's eyes. 'Take my life, my lord. It is forfeit, for I have betrayed you by allowing them to take her. I thought she was safe in the shop, for Ali bin Masood has served you many times in the past.'

'Neither you or the merchant are to blame,' Kasim

said, but his eyes were dark with grief and suppressed anger. 'Harriet should have known better than to leave the palace with no more than three men to guard her. She knew how dangerous things still were for I had told her.'

'She is but a woman, my lord, and as such should be protected. I have failed in my duty. You would be within your rights to have me punished and the others too—though they guarded the lady Katrina.'

'I have no wish to punish a loyal friend. You obeyed the lady Katrina and she was thoughtless. She should have known that her brother's death might bring reprisals, though I believe her innocent of complicity—' Kasim broke off as he heard voices and then one of the Janissaries entered. He genuflected and hesitated, waiting for permission to speak. 'You have some news?'

'We have learned that the men who took the lady Harriet were not of our people, my lord—they were English. It seems that they have been seeking an interview with the Sultan for more than two weeks, but his magnificence would not grant it. They were in touch with the men who helped the lady's cousin escape. We have learned that they are a secret group working to free slaves when they can find and rescue them.'

'Who told you this?'

'I did, my lord.' Mellina entered the room and looked at him. 'My brother Malik was executed for his part in the affair of the escaped harem slave, but I was the one who told him that the two English women were here in the first place. He was paid to help them escape, but only one went with him. Recently, I was asked to help with the lady Harriet's escape, but she told me she was happy here and I refused to tell them anything. I do not know if others knew of the trip to the bazaar, but I did not send word, even though I helped Malik the first time.' She raised her eyes to his. 'My brother hated his life here. He gave the money he was paid to me so that I might one day purchase my freedom.'

Kasim's hands clenched at his sides. He was tempted to strike her or send her to the cells for punishment, but he knew that it had taken great courage to confess her part in the earlier escape.

'You are certain that these men were English?' He looked at the Janissary captain who had brought the news.

'Yes, my lord. We are making enquiries. There was a ship in the harbour. We shall send to see if it has sailed.'

'It would have sailed at once if the wind were in the right quarter,' Kasim said and frowned. 'If this information is correct, it means that Harriet is being taken back to England.'

'Your own ship is in harbour,' Rachid said. 'Will you go after her, my lord?'

'How can I leave while Kahlid is so ill?' Kasim felt a surge of frustration. 'Who will guard Prince Yuri if I am gone some weeks?'

'I will.' Kasim was surprised as he heard the soft voice. Unnoticed amongst all the commotion, the young man had come into the presence chamber. Dressed in white and with a book of prayer in his hand, he was studious and gentle, so quiet that he was seldom noticed. 'I have no wish to take your place, my lord—but I will be happy to hold the palace and the province for you until you return.'

'Prince Abdulla...' Kasim frowned as he looked at the young man he had hardly ever seen with his nose out of a book. 'You are sixteen—younger even than Hassan. You have no experience of war or of controlling the men who would try to wrest the power from you while I was gone.'

'Alone I might be vulnerable,' the young man said, 'but if I have the loyalty of your men I believe I should manage.'

'I would guarantee the loyalty of the men,' Rachid told him. 'You will never know true happiness again unless you go after her, my lord.'

'That is true,' Kasim said. 'She told me that her brother is known as Lord Sefton-Jones and that he likes to live in London—and that is where I must go to find her.'

'You will return? I have your word?' Kahlid looked up from his couch, where he lay close to death. 'I know how much she means to you, my son—but I cannot go easily to my death unless I have your promise that even if she will not come, you will return.'

Kasim saw the plea in his eyes and could not refuse. 'I gave you my promise when you spared her life. I do not lightly break my word, my lord—as you well know.'

'I should never have held such a threat over your head. I should be well served if you decided the promise was invalid.'

'Abdulla is honest and will do his best while I am gone,' Kasim said, 'but you have my word.'

'Then may Allah guide and bless you.' Kahlid held out his wasted hand. 'You have my blessing to leave for I know that you could not rest unless you had her answer from her own lips.'

Kasim inclined his head, turned and left. He knew that he had little hope of catching the ship before it reached England—too much time had passed. He could only pray that Harriet was safe and that he would find her when he reached England.

Kasim left the palace soon after his interview with the lord Kahlid and rode swiftly towards the capital, where his ship was in harbour. The captain had been told to prepare to leave as soon Kasim arrived and he could only pray that the winds would be with them. If Harriet reached England, there was no telling what might happen to her. He knew that her family might consider that she had disgraced their name. She might be forced into marriage against her will or…under Muslim law some brothers would put to death a sister who had shamed them. Surely Harriet's brother would not stoop to such measures?

His thoughts were confused and angry. Had Harriet been abducted, as Katrina believed—or had she gone with the rescue party willingly? She had given herself to him so sweetly the previous night, declaring her love, but had the temptation to return to England been too much?

If she were harmed he would never cease to blame himself. He should have left orders that she was not to leave the palace without a sufficient guard. He had been concerned with the necessity to placate ministers who were jostling for position now that Kahlid had stepped down, worried about his friend and satisfied that Harriet seemed content to stay in the palace. Once again Kahlid had forced a promise from him, but Kasim had already considered himself bound. He did not know what he would do if Harriet refused to return with him...if he could find her.

For a few hours life had seemed sweet, but now the future loomed dark and lonely, filled with the burdens of state. He could do much good for the people of Kahlid's province as Caliph, but without Harriet by his side it would be joyless and much harder to bear.

'Harriet, my dearest sister,' Lady Sefton-Jones said and held out her arms as Harriet and Lord Sefton-Jones walked into their London house one afternoon soon after their arrival in England. It had been an uneventful journey and they had made good time. 'How well you look. I am so glad to see you here. I made Richard go himself to look for you and it seems that he has been fortunate.'

'I am glad to see you, Lucy,' Harriet said and

kissed her. 'I thank you for your concern for me, but I wish that Richard had asked me what I wished rather than abducting me. I have been begging him to let me return to my husband, but he refuses to listen.'

'To your husband?' Lady Sefton-Jones looked concerned. 'Were you forced to marry one of those heathens? My poor Harriet! Do not look so sad. We shall find you a kind and loving husband and you will soon forget all that has happened—as poor Marguerite has with Captain Richardson.'

'I look sad because I love Kasim,' Harriet told her. 'Why will no one listen to me? Marguerite was in love with Captain Richardson and that was why I took her place when she was to have married the prince. I was not forced to marry him, but what I did was considered an insult and I was lucky to escape severe punishment. Kasim saved my life at some cost to himself, and I love him. He was to have been my husband and is already in my heart. I know you mean well, Lucy, but I do not wish to find a husband. I met no one I wished to marry before I left England and I would prefer to live as a spinster than marry someone I do not love.'

'You have been taught to accept your fate,' Lucy said, looking at her sadly. 'We were told that it might be so—but no one need know what happened, Harriet. We shall take you to court and introduce you to our friends and you will learn to be happy again.'

'I should prefer to go home to the country,' Harriet

said. 'As soon as I can manage it, I shall find a ship and return to Istanbul and my husband.'

'Give yourself a little time,' Lucy said. 'Come and see my children, Catherine and William, and tell me that you would not miss all the pleasures of family life.'

'I love you and my brother, also my nephew and niece,' Harriet said. 'Yet my life is with Kasim and nothing will change my mind.'

She saw the stubborn look in her sister-in-law's face and realised that nothing would convince her that she was not doing what was best for Harriet. Neither she nor her husband understood that Harriet's heart was breaking. All she could think about was Kasim. Would he be thinking of her, wondering if she were alive or dead? He would probably be thinking the hill tribesmen had taken her and imagining the worst.

'I would rather not accompany you to the court,' Harriet said one evening a week after her return. 'Since you are determined, I shall come, but—if I do as you ask, will you then allow me to go home to the country?'

'I was at court last week and her Majesty questioned me about you for half an hour. I wrote as Richard bid me to inform her that you had returned to England, and you have been bidden to court this evening. You cannot refuse, Harriet, for it would insult her Majesty. There is a grand reception and I think we should attend for many people will have heard of your return by now and they will wish to give you their good wishes.'

'I am not sure that everyone will accept me, Lucy.'

'Do not be foolish, my love. Everyone knows that you were sold and enslaved against your will. I think you will be admired for your bravery. That is why you should make your entrance at court as soon as possible. If the Queen accepts you, you will be courted and fêted by everyone.'

Harriet smiled at her sister-in-law's enthusiasm. 'What if she decides she cannot acknowledge me for fear that my shame might reflect on her?'

'You are speaking of Queen Elizabeth,' Lucy said with a laugh. 'She will do exactly as she wishes.'

'Lady Harriet...' Queen Elizabeth said her eyes narrowed and intent as Harriet sank into a deep curtsy before her. 'You look very well. I trust you have taken no harm from your...adventure?'

'No harm, ma'am,' Harriet replied, lifting her head proudly. 'I have learned much about the customs and culture of the Ottoman Empire.'

'Indeed? You sound as though you approve.' The Queen's gaze intensified. 'I understood you were taken captive against your will?'

'Yes, I was. However, I came to admire the man I was to marry—the Caliph of the Northern Territories. He is of the Muslim faith, Your Majesty, but he was born an English lord and he keeps no personal slaves. He would have given me my freedom, but I chose to stay and wed him. I intend to return when I am able.'

'Indeed?' Elizabeth looked thoughtful. 'I should like to hear more of your…adventures another day. You will be sent for so that we may talk privately, Lady Harriet.'

'Your Majesty is very gracious.'

The Queen inclined her head and Harriet moved on to join her brother and his wife. Lucy looked at her, her blue eyes bright with excitement.

'What did her Majesty say to you, dearest?'

'She was interested in hearing of my adventures and intends to send for me another day so that we may talk privately.'

'What did I tell you?' Lucy's laughter was warm and loving. 'I told Richard it would be all right and so it is. No one will turn their nose up at you now. I think you will be the most sought-after lady at court this evening. Everyone will be mad to hear what it is really like in a harem. You must know that it is the secret fantasy of many women.'

'I do not think they would like the reality as much as their own fantasy,' Harriet said and laughed softly. 'It is one thing to be free and quite another to be a slave, even if a pampered one.'

'Then why do you wish to return?'

'I was not a slave. Kasim would have sent me home without a ransom, but I chose to stay. I would have been his wife—his only wife.'

Harriet became aware that everyone was looking at her. Several of the courtiers inclined their heads to

her and it was not long before two gentlemen saun-
tered over to engage in conversation.

'Lady Harriet, I believe,' one gentleman dressed
in puce with a silver lace ruff said and flicked the
little fan he carried. 'I dare say you might recall me?
We met when your father brought you to court some
years ago. You do not look a day older—indeed, you
look more beautiful than I remember.'

'Thank you, Sir Philip. I do remember you. I seem
to recall that you married Miss Jane Featherstone.'

'My poor Jane.' The gentleman sighed. 'She died
in childbed a year past. My son survives and needs
a mother—as much as I need a wife.'

'Oh, I am sorry,' Harriet said, wishing that the
ground would open and swallow her up. She had not
cared for the gentleman the first time and she certainly did not enjoy the speculation in his eyes now.
She could almost hear him wondering what clever
tricks she had been taught in the harem. 'It must have
been a sad time for you. Death is always so final.'

Harriet was relieved to see that some ladies were
drifting their way, though several more gentlemen
had joined the group around them. Her sister-in-law
had judged correctly. Since the Queen had seen fit to
single her out for some conversation and obviously
approved, Harriet had become not just an object of
curiosity, but the centre of attention.

'Did you truly escape from the Caliph's harem?' a
lady asked curiously. 'You must be very brave. I have
heard that there are terrible whips that inflict pain
without breaking the skin…and awful things happen

to men. Well, they aren't really men afterwards, are they?'

'Sadly, they are very much men, but terribly mutilated. I was never subjected to the punishment you describe, though the eunuchs were always there to guard us,' Harriet replied, hiding her smile as she saw the woman's eyes gleam. 'I might have been had I tried to escape. However, I had no reason for I was happy there—and I did not wish to leave.'

'I still think you are terribly brave—and to come here this evening, knowing what people may say—' The woman broke off and blushed. 'Not that I mean to criticize.'

'You would be within your right to do so,' Harriet said graciously. 'I know what you must think, madam, but in my case it was not so. I was not treated ill nor forced to the Caliph's bed.'

'Oh…' The woman laughed nervously and moved away, looking a little disappointed. Harriet guessed that she had been hoping for some titillating secrets that she could impart to others.

She was not the only one to ask similar questions, some from the gentlemen, even bolder. Harriet bore it all with patience, giving the inquisitive courtiers quiet sensible answers. Their curiosity was natural for they had never experienced an adventure like hers, and had only heard vague things of savage and cruel customs. Some of the men asked questions about the palace, what it looked like inside and what kind of clothes the men wore, as well as what she found to do with herself all day.

Harriet grew bored with their questions and looked about her. She had not particularly cared for life at court when her father brought her, disliking the petty jealousy and rivalry amongst the courtiers. How soon could she ask Lucy and her brother if she might leave? Her sister-in-law had obliged her to attend this evening, but she would rather be at home making plans for her return to Istanbul.

Suddenly, she became aware that a man was staring at her intently. As she met his gaze, a shock of recognition went through her. She knew him immediately, despite the fact that he was wearing the clothes of an English gentleman.

'Kasim…' she said, her throat tight with emotion and then with a glad cry. 'Kasim…'

She began to move towards him, but he had turned away and was leaving the room. Harriet walked swiftly, running the last few steps though she knew people were watching her. As she left the great hall and entered the narrow corridor she saw him just ahead of her.

'Kasim…wait for me, please…' He stopped and then turned slowly to face her, a look in his eyes that sent the chills running down her spine. 'What is wrong? Why are you angry with me?'

For a moment he stared at her in silence, then, 'I am not angry, Harriet. I was leaving because I had seen all I needed to see.'

'What do you mean?'

'You were clearly enjoying yourself as the centre of attention. I feared you might have been punished by your family, sent into exile in the country or forced into marriage. I even feared that you might have been killed, but I see my fears were foolish. You are happy and I am glad it is so. It would have been better had you not seen me.'

'No, Kasim, no,' she said and moved towards him, her hand reaching out. 'Please do not be angry. I came here this evening to please my brother's wife. She said I must not refuse the Queen's invitation and she thinks that I shall learn to be happy here—but I shall not. I begged my brother to turn his ship back and return me to you, but he would not. I planned to go home to the country as soon as I could and then find a ship that would bring me back to you. You know that I love you. You must know that I want to be your wife. You must!'

'Harriet…' Kasim looked at her in silence for a moment. 'You looked so right amongst all those people. This is your rightful place in society. I should never have taken you to the palace. I wish that I could stay in England, become Lord Hadley and wed you— but it is impossible. My father is dead and the estate is mine, but I am not free to take it, Harriet. I have told the lawyers that my cousin should inherit the title. It may be years before I could leave the province and bring you home.'

'I have no wish to stay here without you,' Harriet replied, moving closer. She gazed up into his eyes. 'Yes, there are things that I love about my father's home in the country. I know that in the palace I can never be as free as I would be here, but without you

I should be alone and without hope. At the palace I have work to do, people who need me—and I shall be your wife. Life holds nothing for me without you.'

'Harriet, my love.' Kasim moved towards her, drawing her closer as he gazed down into her face. 'You know that I love you? I want you for my wife—but you must be certain that you wish to return, because you know the dangers. There may be more rebellions and you will always need an escort. You should have been more closely guarded. When they told me you had been stolen, I thought I might never see you again…and I blamed myself. I wished that I had been with you. I would have died rather than let them take you.'

'Hush…' Harriet reached up to touch her lips to his. 'You are here now and I shall come with—'

'Harriet!' She stiffened as she heard her brother's angry tones. 'Unhand my sister, sir. How dare you take foul advantage of her?'

'Richard, you mistake the situation,' Harriet said. 'This is…' She faltered and Kasim smiled.

'The son of Lord Robert Hadley,' Kasim said. 'I left England more than ten years ago. We should not have met for you are younger, sir. These days, I am known as the lord Kasim, Caliph of the Northern Territories—and Harriet is my promised wife.'

'You damned rogue!' Richard cried, his hand moving to his sword hilt. 'I have heard what you did and you shall pay for your insult to my sister and cousin. You will meet me, sir. One of us will be dead before the night is out.'

'No! Richard, please,' Harriet cried. 'You must not do this. I love Kasim and I want to be his wife. If either of you were killed, I could not bear it. Please, please do not fight.' Her anguished eyes sought Kasim's. 'Please make him understand. He could not win against you.'

'Hush, my love.' Kasim touched her hand. 'My lord Sefton-Jones. I must beg your pardon for what was done. I made a promise to my Caliph and as a man of honour I kept it. Had I not paid the price I did for your sister and cousin, they would have been bought by a man who would have used them and then given them to his men for sport. Your cousin was meant to marry a prince, a great honour in my adopted country. I would ask you to grant me your sister's hand in marriage. Harriet has made her choice. If you deny us, she will defy you and come with me and you will never see her again. Will you not give consent to our wedding and perhaps we can arrange for Harriet to visit sometimes—and you may come to us. I would grant you safe passage through my country.'

'Please, Richard. It is what I want…' Harriet's eyes filled with tears. 'Do not condemn me to a life alone.'

'You will marry her in a church?'

'Yes, if you wish it,' Kasim said and squeezed Harriet's hand as she would have protested. 'I must return to Istanbul, but Harriet will be free to return to England for a visit whenever she chooses.'

'You give your word as an English gentleman?'

'I give my word as an English gentleman and as

Caliph of the Northern Territories. Harriet is loved as much as any woman ever could be. I shall do everything within my power to protect her and make her happy.'

'I am happy when I am with you.' Harriet raised her eyes to meet her brother's. 'Please, Richard…'

'Very well,' he said. 'I suppose you are of an age to please yourself, Harriet. I have never tried to stop you doing anything you wished—and I dare say you know your own mind. I shall arrange the wedding at our home in the country and in the meantime I shall expect you to behave with the proper dignity and restraint, Harriet.'

'Thank you, Richard,' she said and flew to embrace him. 'Thank you so much. You are very good to me.'

'I shall expect you to call on me,' Richard said and looked hard at Kasim. 'I shall require a proper settlement for my sister so that if she should wish to live in England she would have the means to do so.'

'Yes, of course,' Kasim said and smiled at Harriet. 'It was in my mind to arrange it. I think you will be satisfied with my arrangements, Lord Sefton-Jones. Harriet will have land and property here in England that she may pass on to her children if she wishes.'

'Then I suppose I have nothing to object to,' Richard said. 'For goodness sake, Harriet. Go and find somewhere private to say your farewells for the moment. I shall take Lucy home soon and you must be ready to come with me.'

Afterword

Turning in her husband's arms, Harriet pressed her face to his chest, inhaling the musky smell of his body, tasting the salt on her tongue as she licked delicately. A shudder went through him and he held her closer, his hand caressing the small of her back. She looked up and saw he was smiling.

'Did I please you, my lord?' she asked softly. 'Shall I dance for you?'

'You pleased me more than you can imagine,' he said, hoarse with desire. 'And, no, you will not dance for me. You are my wife, not my houri. We have been married in the Christian way to please your brother, and when we return to the palace we shall be married again to please the people—but for me you have been my wife since the night you first looked at me with love in your eyes.'

'We shall be twice married,' Harriet said and

stroked his cheek. 'When we are home again you will not be too busy to spend time with me? When I did not see you for weeks at a time I thought you had forgotten me.'

'I could never forget you, even when I had to show you that you could not behave so recklessly, Harriet. I suffered as much as you by our parting.' His expression became serious. 'I never meant to hurt you, my love. Can you ever truly forgive me?'

'I have forgiven you,' she whispered and lifted her face for his kiss. Tangling her fingers in his hair, she drew him down to her. His kiss lit a fire that had her begging for more, her hips arching against his, her thighs opening for his seeking hand. 'I love you, want you, need you, my own darling Kasim.'

'I want you to be as free as you can, my love, but you know there are things you will not be able to do there that you can here.'

'If I can ride with you when you have time it will be enough. Perhaps as Yuri grows up we shall have time to visit England and my family.'

'I believe that Abdulla may become a great councillor and an adviser to the prince, and it may be in years to come that we can travel to England and other countries. I truly believe that he has no desire to rule because he prefers his studies. I think he will lean towards teaching the faith for I know him to be devout, but he can advise his half-brother as he learns himself.'

'That is for the future. I believe you can do many good things for your people, Kasim. I am prepared to accept the restrictions of the palace if you will let me help you where I can.'

'Your work in the infirmary has not gone unnoticed and I have given the order that the schools you suggested be set up. Together we shall find a way to help and serve our people, Harriet.'

'Then I am content to love and be loved.'

'My beloved wife,' he murmured and bent his head to kiss her. She felt the heat of his desire against her inner thigh as he sought and found entrance, thrusting deep inside her. 'Allah truly blessed us the day he led me to that slave market, for without you my life would have been as empty as the desert sands.'

She sighed, surrendering herself to him body and soul as he took her with him to a far, far place. Their bodies moved together of perfect accord, seeking, reaching…seeking again and again, and finding… the exquisite pleasure that suddenly broke over them in waves.

Afterwards they lay in silence holding each other, content, at peace, because there was no need for words.

* * * * *

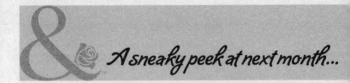

HISTORICAL

IGNITE YOUR IMAGINATION, STEP INTO THE PAST...

My wish list for next month's titles...

In stores from 2nd September 2011:

❏ Seduced by the Scoundrel — Louise Allen

❏ Unmasking the Duke's Mistress — Margaret McPhee

❏ To Catch a Husband... — Sarah Mallory

❏ The Highlander's Redemption — Marguerite Kaye

❏ His Enemy's Daughter — Terri Brisbin

❏ His Dakota Captive — Jenna Kernan

Available at WHSmith, Tesco, Asda, Eason, Amazon and Apple

Just can't wait?

MILLS & BOON® Book Club

2 Free Books!

Get your free books now at

www.millsandboon.co.uk/freebookoffer

Or fill in the form below and post it back to us

THE MILLS & BOON® BOOK CLUB™—HERE'S HOW IT WORKS: Accepting your free books places you under no obligation to buy anything. You may keep the books and return the despatch note marked 'Cancel'. If we do not hear from you, about a month later we'll send you 4 brand-new stories from the Historical series priced at £3.99* each. There is no extra charge for post and packaging. You may cancel at any time, otherwise we will send you 4 stories a month which you may purchase or return to us—the choice is yours. *Terms and prices subject to change without notice. Offer valid in UK only. Applicants must be 18 or over. Offer expires 28th February 2012. **For full terms and conditions, please go to www.millsandboon.co.uk/termsandconditions**

Mrs/Miss/Ms/Mr (please circle) _____

First Name _____

Surname _____

Address _____

_____

_____ Postcode _____

E-mail _____

Send this completed page to: Mills & Boon Book Club, Free Book Offer, FREEPOST NAT 10298, Richmond, Surrey, TW9 1BR

Find out more at
www.millsandboon.co.uk/freebookoffer

Visit us Online

0611/M1ZEE